THE FRENCH
CORRECTION

Truman Cottrell

THE FRENCH
CORRECTION

Erser & Pond

Cover design by Benjamin Beaumont
Cover photography: ©iStockphoto/Brasil2

Printed in the U.S.A. by Erser & Pond Publishers, Ltd.
1096 Queen St., Suite 225, Halifax, N.S., Canada B3H 2R9

Library and Archives Canada Cataloguing in Publication

Cottrell, Truman
    The French correction / Truman Cottrell.

ISBN 978-0-9810470-7-2

I. Title.

PS8605.O885F74 2010   C813'.6
    C2010-903424-4

10 9 8 7 6 5 4 3 2 1

First Edition

*This book is dedicated
with love and gratitude
to my wife,
who has helped
and supported me
in everything I have done.*

CAST OF CHARACTERS

Kate Evans, American
M.A. candidate in French

René Martin, Inspector of
National Police, Marseilles

Pierre Mondragon,
Corsican hit man

Tiffany Chance, American
student at the Sorbonne

©iStockphoto/peepo

Leslie Jolicoeur, Professor of French at the Sorbonne

©iStockphoto/SensorSpot

Henri Casanova, Corsican Mafia boss

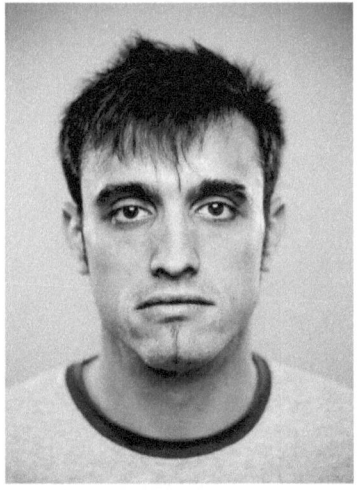

©iStockphoto/SensorSpot

Didier Albertini, young Corsican Mafioso

©iStockphoto/SensorSpot

Shlomo Litwak, Israeli diamond merchant

SECONDARY CHARACTERS :

Marlene Jolicoeur	Professor Jolicoeur's wife
Maurice Benamou	Assistant Inspector of police
Carlo Santori	Bodyguard to the Mafia boss
Giovanni Rossi	White collar Mafia criminal and computer technician
Guido Mattei	Mafia telecommunications expert
Marius	Limo driver for the Mafia
André	Fisherman
Luciani	Corpse

CHAPTER ONE

It has always been a question whether the old black-and-white French films starring actors like Jean Gabin and Jean Paul Belmondo were modeled on the underworld of actual Marseilles racketeers, or whether the "film noir" genre of that time created a totally imaginary picture of a certain stratum of Gallic tough guys. On the grimy docks of the real Marseilles, however, there is no question about the existence of an organized crime ring. It is a matter of fact.

The management of the illegal operations in the south of France trace all the way back to Caesar's occupation of Gaul. Wherever there is brutal foreign government control, there is usually an equally brutal illegal resistance in the oppressed population. By providing opposition, even one that is not much kinder than that of the oppressive official authorities, the local populace takes heart and finds self-esteem in having its own personal tyrant. Nepotism is as flagrant among the oppressed as it is among the reigning authorities.

Over the decades the hierarchy of the French internal crime organizations took on an unspoken resemblance to the Cosa Nostra in southern Italy. French criminals, however, hated the comparison with the Italian Mafia. They felt that they were a much smoother, more professional group than the hoodlums portrayed by the American gangster films. In actuality there was no moral difference between the French and Italian mobs. The difference was great, however, in the manner in which the American filmmakers portrayed the Italian crime organizations that sprang to life along with the immigration of Neapolitans, Calabrians, and Sicilians. With the advent of Technicolor films and the fantastic strides in special effects, the Americans brought the presentation of violent gangsters to a popular fine art.

Kate Evans knew nothing about the French Mafia, nor was she conversant with the early ventures of the French into cinematic criminality. She was, after all, just twenty-four years old. She had been a French major as an undergraduate at Middlebury and had taken her Junior year at the Sorbonne, where she had studied twentieth-century French literature. She wasn't quite sure how she'd become a Francophile in the first place, but her time in Paris had sealed the deal. She guessed that her attraction to French as an area of study had come about because she'd always done her best work as a student in her language courses. She had won plaudits from her professors, but none from her father.

After graduation, and following numerous discussions with her parents about the practical aspects of pursuing a career as a specialist in French language and literature, she resolutely accepted a scholarship from the Alliance Française to do a Masters degree in a university of her choice. Forever interested in bolstering the French language as a competitor to English in the world of affairs, the Alliance Française sponsored a number of outstanding students from prestigious American and British Universities to do advanced studies in their field. The Alliance Française hoped that if a few elite American and British students could be persuaded to use French as the language of diplomacy, then perhaps these turncoats could rescue the French language from the defeat it was currently suffering as English replaced French all over the world. In the field of language studies this would be the equivalent of reversing the results of the Battle of Waterloo.

Kate's sponsors wanted to use her as a weapon in the Alliance Française's struggle to keep French in its proper place as the lingua franca of the civilized world. Conscious of her sponsors' motives, Kate went along with their efforts. She tried very hard to keep an open mind, for she needed the scholarship in order to continue her education. Her initial reaction had been that English was the superior route to the promised land of world communication. She was not sure, however, that French should even be a backup for English, especially now that Spanish had recently been making such a noteworthy appearance on the world scene. The Alliance Française was determined to oppose those who felt that the language claiming the most speakers should have the most prestige.

The part that Mlle Evans was to play in putting forth the case for French hegemony was based on qualitative issues, not on quantitative ones. The Alliance Française hoped that Kate would build on the generally held belief that French was a subtler tongue and more suitable for diplomatic efforts than the coarser English language. The hope was that Kate, being a native speaker of English, could provide an example and demonstrate that it was easy to master French, and that once mastered, French was more useful for the businessmen and diplomats of the world. Traditionally French had always been the language of love, art, cuisine, diplomacy and the finer things of life. The goal of the Alliance Française was to keep it that way. Exactly how Kate could demonstrate this was being left up to her, but she understood very well that her thesis topic was supposed to lend scientific credence to her sponsors' theory of French linguistic superiority.

Kate had completed her course work for the Masters degree, which had included mostly formal academic courses. Her professors in Paris were well aware of the position of the Alliance Française on the matter of the French language, and they were totally sympathetic. The teachers of French were bound to be supportive, as their very livelihood depended on having as many students of French as possible. So Kate had been let loose on France to discover a thesis topic that would earn her a degree and justify the expense to her sponsors for having helped educate her. Her initial ideas had to do with exploring the ability of the French language to absorb the intrusions of modern slang, the absorption of foreign words into the basic vocabulary, and the addition of technological terms to everyday speech. If she could demonstrate that for non-native speakers French proved to be a language that was easier to master than English, then she might have a useful hypothesis for her thesis. She was currently traveling around France in an effort to discover some thread that she could weave into an intellectual tapestry that would satisfy her professors as well as the Alliance Française.

That was how Kate Evans ended up wandering around the seaport of Marseilles. She listened to the peculiar French spoken by the fishmongers and their customers. When she'd had enough of the noisy quayside commerce, she decided to walk up the hill to visit the Neo-Byzantine Basilica of Notre Dame de la Garde. The famous wind known in Provence as the mistral was refreshing her as she began the forty-five minute ascent. Kate's pulse was elevated from the climb, but whatever breath remained in her was taken away by the awe-inspiring view of the city, sea and mountains.

When Kate went into the basilica she was immediately overwhelmed by the strange sight of model boats suspended by wires from the ceiling in the entryway. They appeared to be sailing through space as the mistral moved invisible air currents within the basilica, keeping the models in perpetual motion. Models of all the vessels that had ever plied the waters of the Mediterranean during the past 2,600 years were represented in the church. She was fascinated by the ghostly vision of the boats bobbing together simultaneously in the same space. The basilica itself was an anachronism, having been built in the 19th century to look like its older and more famous sisters. It was the last of the Catholic cathedrals, and took over forty years to complete.

A tour had moved closer to the place where Kate was standing, so that to an observer it appeared as if she might be part of the group. The guide was speaking to her audience in English, telling them about the arcane construction details in the basilica. A male figure who was not a tourist regarded the group intently from a distance. He quickly noticed that the single woman was not part of the group that trooped around after the guide. He made it his business to circle around so that he would come upon Kate from behind. The man was about thirty, and had a thick head of dark hair and an olive complexion. He was wearing a sports jacket, open-necked white shirt, dark trousers, and Italian loafers. Pierre Mondragon was dressed in his best hunting outfit, but he was not hunting for game.

Mondragon was an experienced hunter. He had learned that the most interesting and most susceptible quarries were to be found in the cathedrals, museums, and the old historic parts of the port. His appraising eye had focused on Kate as he studied her movements and assessed his chances with her. Pierre was surreptitious and remained out of sight. He hadn't gone to the cathedral that day to meet a woman, but the habit was hard to break. He deduced that her native tongue was English, probably American English, but he guessed that she was also fluent in French, or nearly so. He had come to these conclusions because she clearly understood the tour guide's English, and although she seemed to be alone, she wasn't intimidated by being in a foreign situation.

He had learned from experience that foreign women represented his best prospects because they were out of their normal element and were, therefore, interested in adventure. Foreign women also had to return home, which saved Pierre the problems of getting rid of them after he was through with them. Of course in these days women of many nationalities knew English, and some knew French as well. Although he had completed his other business in the cathedral and could have left the church building, he decided to try his luck with the Yankee woman.

Something about Kate gave her away as an American. She didn't flaunt the self-assurance of the typically cynical European women who imagined that they knew everything about men. Pierre had found that American women usually possessed a more open view to possibilities, which European men regarded as naïve. He decided to speak to her in French. His decision was based on the supposition that if she had come to France to learn about the culture she would prefer to be thought of as a local person rather than merely a tourist.

Speaking to strange women was always an interesting challenge for Pierre Mondragon, and he felt it would help if he began on a flattering note. He had found that praising a woman's linguistic ability was one of the best ways to start up a conversation. Mondragon used the basilica as one of his favorite hunting grounds, and had made many conquests under the auspices of the church, as it were. He was aware that he had the home court advantage in these situations. He knew his way around Marseilles, and he had listened to the spiels of the tourist guides in all the venues favored by visitors. After listening to their explanations, he had become as knowledgeable as any of them, but he had interests other than those of educating tourists.

"Excusez-moi, Mademoiselle, s'il vous plaît. Est-ce que vous faîtes partie de cette groupe de touristes?"

"Non, je suis seule. Pourquoi est-ce que vous me le demandez?"

Her French was fluent but she had a slight American accent, so Pierre continued speaking to her in English.

"I couldn't help noticing that you have a greater interest in this cathedral than the others. Perhaps I can offer you a private exposition on a superior level?"

As he hoped, she asked him to speak to her in French. From this point on they spoke only French together.

"I'm a student, and I'd like to practice my language skills," she explained. "Do I take it that you're an off-duty guide or docent?"

"That's correct Mademoiselle, or is it Madame?"

"It's Mademoiselle."

His accent belied his pretension of being a professional guide, or for that matter, a well-educated person. Kate wasn't taken in by him at all, but because his accent in his native French was so decidedly street Marseillaise, she continued the conversation out of linguistic interest. He was for her a subject to study, and possibly a connection to his stratum of society with its peculiar accent and contemporary idioms.

In typical male fashion, Pierre thought he was being charming. He assumed that Kate hadn't dismissed him out of hand because she was attracted to him. For her part Kate's thoughts related to how she could use his speech patterns to form a portion of her thesis. In fact, Kate had already made up her mind that the more she got to know him the less she would like him. To a linguist Pierre's speech was the interesting thing. To her ear it resembled poetry – one one level it was an attempt at refinement, and on another it was raw with centuries of passion and violence. As wine to a connoisseur contains hints about its origin, his speech had many different highlights recognizable to a linguist. There was a North African Berber cadence, a husky Arabic tone, and the careless use of vowel endings typical of the ordinary residents of the Midi. Kate detected all these subtleties of speech before he had uttered another sentence.

Pierre attempted to interest her by telling her that the basilica was a hoax.

"What do you mean, a hoax?"

"Well, it was built in the latter part of the nineteenth century to look as though it was an old cathedral like Notre Dame in Paris. It's an attempt by the church to fool tourists into thinking it's a venerable old building. Foreigners flock to it because of its size and location, but in reality it's a fraudulent architectural structure."

"It's still an impressive building," Kate said, wanting to listen to him continue speaking his version of French.

"Yes, but aesthetically it's similar to what we'd get if we constructed the Vatican out of today's modern building materials. Know I mean?" He bowed slightly and extended his hand. "By the way, I'd like to properly introduce myself. I'm Pierre Mondragon, at your service."

"How do you do, Mr. Mondragon, I'm pleased to meet you, but I must tell you that I'm only a poor student and I'm unable to pay you for a personalized tour, so you may not wish to waste any more time on me."

Pierre acted somewhat offended.

"No, no Mademoiselle, you're mistaken, I don't want you to pay me. I'm pleased that an obviously well-educated person such as yourself is interested in the culture of my country. My intention was only that you not think this church more worthy of your esteem than it is."

"I see, Mr. Mondragon. And what sights in Marseilles do you regard as worthy of my esteem?" Kate replied.

"Well, if you'd permit me to show them to you I'd be pleased to take you to see them, at no cost to you, of course."

Kate was not surprised by his pick-up tactic. She had already encountered many brash young Frenchmen in the course of her time in France, and her experience made her unafraid to deal with them in a public place. She would not, however, go with him to any private place. She realized that he was on his best behavior, and also that he was attempting to speak with an upper-class French accent in order to impress her with his erudition. Kate wasn't taken in by it, but he couldn't know that. She wanted to continue to study his speech, but she wanted him to relax and use his standard vernacular. She thought about whether she should let him squire her around to the sights, and decided that it was worth the effort, particularly if he let his guard down and spoke normally. It would also be helpful if she could meet other people through him who might have interesting speech patterns.

"That's very kind of you, Mr. Mondragon. Do you think I've seen enough of the basilica?"

"I do, except for the views of the city. Let's go outside so I can point out the impressive figure of Our Lady that dominates the landscape of Marseilles. Then perhaps we can have a spot of lunch at a place nearby."

As they walked along one of the long aisles that led to the entry doors, they passed several wooden confessional booths that lined the basilica's walls. Kate noticed that the door of one of them was ajar. She could see nothing of the person that was inside in the semi-darkness, except that a male foot protruded at a peculiar angle, and it was that foot that was keeping the door from closing. Kate followed Pierre out into the plaza that surrounded the basilica. Perhaps it was only a mistaken impression, but she thought her guide was anxious to get her away from the church.

Mondragon walked briskly to the furthest point in the plaza, which presented the best view of the golden statue of the Virgin Mary that was mounted atop the church spire.

"She's ten meters tall," he said, looking up. "That's the equivalent of thirty of your feet."

"Are you saying that I have big feet, Mr. Mondragon?" Kate asked coyly.

"No, certainly not," he replied. "I'm sure you have well proportioned feet, although you won't be needing them to walk to lunch because I have my car here."

He led her to a black BMW convertible, and opened the door for her in gentlemanly fashion.

"You have a lovely car," Kate said, but she thought the car was very expensive for a seasonal itinerant tour guide.

"My car is my one luxury in life," Pierre lied. Actually Pierre's life was made up of one luxury after another, for he was not a tour guide by profession. Indeed, if his career had a name, it would be *gangster*.

"Where are we going?"

"I know a café near the marina where they serve the most amazing lobster bisque. I think we should go there so you can try it. In spite of all the cathedrals and museums, the number one tourist attraction in France is the food."

"I think I've heard that, Mr. Mondragon."

"You'll soon see that it's true. Won't you please call me Pierre? *Mr. Mondragon* sounds so formal. When I hear you say it I'm expecting my father to be standing right behind me."

"All right, Pierre. What kind of name is Mondragon, anyway? I don't believe I've ever heard it before."

"It's unusual, and I suspect I'm related to everyone with that name. As far as I know it originated in Corsica just like Napoleon, but whether it was originally Italian or French, I don't know. When I feel exotic I explain that it originated with the ancient Phoenicians, when they were in control of the Mediterranean Sea."

"Have you any idea what it means? Does it have anything to do with dragons?"

"Yes, I don't doubt that in the days of the Phoenicians it referred to the sea dragons that they had to avoid or slay when they sent their ships out to trade."

They arrived at the little bistro by the marina and Pierre jumped out, ran around, and opened the passenger car door for Kate in a chivalrous way which she found incongruous coming from a man who looked like a tough guy and spoke like one, too. She couldn't shake the feeling that he wasn't behaving in his normal fashion, nor was he speaking in his ordinary mode of speech. She attributed the deep timbre of his voice to a smoking habit, although she had yet to see him smoke.

Once inside the restaurant, Pierre took control. Kate ascribed his authoritarian behavior to some form of Gallic display of masculinity, but whatever it was, it worked. A very subservient hostess fluttered around to find him the best seat in the restaurant while she called him "Mr. Mondragon" in every sentence.

"Obviously they know you here," Kate said. "Do you come here often?"

"Oh yes, quite often," he replied. "Will you allow me to order for you? I know the menu very well. And now you must permit me to call you by your name. Which is...?"

"My full name is Kate Evans. I'm twenty-four, single, American, and studying for a Master's degree in French."

"And what kind of a name is Evans?"

"Evans is a Welsh name, and it means son of Evan. It's quite a common name, really."

"I see," Pierre said, after thinking for a moment. "But you are not a son."

"That's right. I'm a female," Kate said, smiling.

"And a very beautiful one, if I may say so," Pierre replied, giving her an appraising look.

It was obvious to Pierre that Kate was a woman from a class several notches above his own. This fact didn't deter him a bit. He knew from experience that women away from home often went for men who were socially beneath them. He didn't care what their motivation was, just as long as he ended up bedding the woman.

"Do you wish to order, Monsieur Mondragon?" said the waiter, approaching the table. "Or would you like a bit more time to discuss the menu with the young lady?"

"Will you permit me to order for you, Miss Evans?" Pierre inquired. "I know all the best dishes."

"Sure, go ahead," said Kate affably. "You know best."

"We'll have the moules marinières with a fresh baguette and a bottle of Château Lafitte."

"Yes, Monsieur Mondragon," said the waiter, bowing slightly as he turned away.

Mondragon sat back and looked at Kate, hoping she had been impressed with the panache and decisiveness with which he had ordered the meal. His forté was boldness, not subtlety. The best intellectual ground that he felt he could occupy with Kate was the one he had memorized from the information he had learned from tour guides. If he could keep her mind on the charms of Marseilles, perhaps in time she would transfer her affection for his city to him.

Kate felt that her first impressions of Pierre Mondragon were essentially correct, and she had little if anything in common with him. The things about him that attracted her were his knowledge of the area and the life going on inside it, and of course his "gangsta" French speech. As the lunch proceeded she had to add to his scanty list of attractions the fact that he knew how to pick the best seafood restaurant in the city. The unprepossessing décor of the waterfront bistro didn't detract at all from the seafood. The mussels were delicious, and very appropriate for a place in a port city that had probably sold fish since long before Roman times.

As Kate studied his face, she came to the conclusion that his nose was too large, his brown eyes too cold, his arms and chest too hirsute, and his general demeanor too confident for her to be romantically interested in him. She was just trying to work out in her mind how she would get rid of him after lunch, when his cell phone rang. He excused himself and answered it. Kate watched him as he turned away from her to speak to the caller.

"Did you complete your assignment?" a male voice said to him.

"I did sir," Pierre replied, in a respectful tone.

"Good, come and see me as soon as you can. I've got another job for you."

"I'll be there soon, Boss," he said, and rang off.

"I've got to go," he said abruptly to Kate. "My boss needs me now. I can drop you at your hotel on the way."

Kate was relieved to be rid of him so easily, but she felt it was unusual for a customer to walk out of a restaurant like that without paying. She decided that he must have a tab at the bistro, since he seemed to be so well known there.

CHAPTER TWO

He had an interesting mind – at least that's what Kate thought about her French professor at the Sorbonne. His reputation as a lady's man, however, kept her from becoming too friendly with him. Leslie Jolicoeur was the only son of an American mother and a French father. He settled the question of his preferred nationality early on during his high school years in the U.S. His father was in the French diplomatic corps and spent several years as envoy and consul in New York. Leslie didn't like the mauling he had to absorb from his male classmates because he was not interested in athletics, but the mauling he received from his female classmates was another matter altogether. The girls loved his French accent, and they thought that his European mannerisms were fascinatingly exotic. His success with the female component of his classes became legendary. Now in his late forties, Jolicoeur was still mining the same lode.

Leslie's teaching assignments were given in the popular portion of the Sorbonne curriculum that was targeted to foreign students, particularly Americans, who had come to France to soak up French culture. He had both undergraduate and graduate students, and with each new academic year he was presented with a host of young mistress candidates to replace the ones who graduated. Having split his education between France and the U.S., Jolicoeur was in a perfect position to both understand and take advantage of his young students. Aside from his academic interest in language, his main occupation was the sexual pursuit of the young women students who had been thrown into his sphere by ambitious but naïve American parents. The university administrators tacitly approved of Jolicoeur's Franco-American version of international relations, and avariciously welcomed the influx of tuition money to their coffers.

When the phone rang in Kate's hotel room in Marseilles she presumed it was her parents calling to check on her welfare, but she was wrong. It was Professor Leslie Jolicoeur.

"Kate, is that you?" he asked.

Kate had left her contact number with her roommate, who had obviously given it to the professor. Although she knew who was calling, Kate decided to play it cool.

"This is Kate Evans. Who's calling, please?"

"It's Professor Jolicoeur. I'm just calling to see how you're getting along with your work."

"It's going well, I think. It's very nice of you to be so concerned," Kate replied, though she didn't believe for an instant that he was calling for that reason.

"That's good to hear. So you're not having any trouble getting the research information you need?"

"No. At least, not so far. I like my hypothesis, and now I'm gathering field data, as you know. So I'd say everything is going along very well."

Professor Jolicoeur had hoped he would find his student confused about what to do so that he could gallantly come to her rescue. But since this wasn't the case, he resorted to his second ploy.

"I've been invited to go down to Marseilles to give a lecture," he told her. "Perhaps you'd like to attend?"

"What's your talk going to be about?"

"It's about the terrible influence of North African native Arabic speakers on our contemporary French language," he replied, trying to make his lecture sound interesting. "It will contain information that will be useful for your thesis," he added, as if to punch home the selling point.

"In that case I'd be glad to attend," Kate said, noticing the implication that not to attend could be a costly academic mistake. "What time should I be there?"

"It's at two o'clock in the Humanities Lecture Hall at the university. If you arrive fifteen minutes earlier you'll be sure to get a good seat."

"All right. I'll be there."

"Good, then. Please stop by after my talk to say hello," Jolicoeur said before hanging up.

Kate couldn't help feeling that destiny was closing in on her. Thus far she had avoided any embarrassing rejection scenes with an amorous teacher who could affect her grades if he decided to retaliate. She had attributed this to the fact that he had made a fortuitous oversight in her case, since he was involved with so many other students. She had heard rumors that his calendar for female student office hours was very full. Her take on the situation was that her turn had come, and that in some way or other this professor was going to come on to her no matter what she did.

Pierre Mondragon was annoyed to have been called in to see his boss in the middle of his lunch with Kate Evans. He knew that it lowered him in her opinion. To have to interrupt a meal because someone snaps his fingers was embarrassing to him. His male ego had been compromised, but refusing a direct order from this caller was unacceptable. He made his excuses to Kate, and she seemed to take it pretty well.

Although she had said nothing about it, he was unsure if Kate had seen the body of the dead man in the confessional booth as they left the basilica. It was obvious that she hadn't connected him to the dead man, or she wouldn't have gone to lunch with him. Nevertheless, the cops might get around to interviewing her, and she could place him at the scene. His background was far from savory, but he had never been convicted of any major crime, and he wanted to keep it that way. The last thing he wanted was to be suspected of having committed the murder in the church. He was sure there were no eyewitnesses or any evidence that would enable the police to charge him with the crime, but if he could be placed at the scene they would harass him, hoping to trip him up or maybe force him to confess.

Pierre Mondragon's boss was the equivalent of a don in a Mafia family. His territory was Marseilles and its environs. His name was Henri Casanova, the most common surname in Corsica. His crime family called him "Henri l'homard," not because he looked like a lobster, but because, as any fisherman knows, lobsters eat their young. Casanova was said to have reached his vaunted position in the Corsican Mafia as a result of cannibalizing two of his brothers who challenged his leadership. He shared no relationship, either familial or in character traits, with his famous namesake, the Chevalier Giovanni Giacomo Casanova. Henri wasn't in the least bit interested in fame, however, and seldom traveled far from Provence. He would never publish *his* autobiography, but if it were to be published it would be more shocking and less amusing than the Chevalier's.

The Lobster was not political, but he was nationalistic in one respect: his ties to close business associates were limited to those who originated in Corsica and could speak to him in Corsu about covert matters. Pierre Mondragon barely made the cut in Henri's opinion, as he was only half Corsican on his mother's side. The crime syndicate that Henri was part of had begun on his native island, and like the more famous Sicilian crime families, it had also expanded over time to include people who were not Corsican. Casanova was not in favor of admitting others into his Corsican private club. He was pathologically suspicious of everyone, and although he trusted no one completely, those whose veins pulsed with Corsican blood could achieve a greater position of trust with him than those without the Corsican connection. Mondragon fell between the cracks of his boss's prejudices, and he knew it right from the start. He felt the way a bastard grandson would feel in the presence of a stern grandfather who never quite accepts him.

Casanova used Pierre in matters that required violence and that were tangential to his business. He awarded him tough assignments and paid him well, but he never discussed his reasons for asking Pierre to perform his dastardly deeds. Mondragon realized that he was in the position of a servant who would never be invited into the family he served. Even though he spoke Corsu with his boss, his knowledge of the Corsican language of the island was insufficient to gain his trust. Mondragon knew that he was destined for anonymity within the Casanova crime family. He also knew that their code was "once in, never out." The only way he could hope to achieve fame was to lead a successful coup some day and accede to a position atop the Lobster's hierarchical realm of bottom feeders.

Henri Casanova was sixty, and at the top of his powers. His connections within the French Syndicate were strong and undeniable. The young aspiring criminals all feared him, and Mondragon was no exception. The Boss could read the minds of the young hoods, and he knew which of them presented a threat to his hegemony. Pierre Mondragon came under Henri's perpetual scrutiny because of his coolness in dangerous situations. Casanova was certain that one day this half Corsican bastard would make a move against him, and he resolved not to be surprised. In the meantime he would employ Pierre's unique talents for his own purposes. When the brash young veteran criminal arrived at Henri's house he was told to take a seat until the Boss could see him.

"Come in, my son," Henri said, opening his office door after having intentionally kept Mondragon waiting.

"I was having lunch, but I came as quickly as I could," Pierre hissed, as if to insinuate that evidently he needn't have hurried since he had been kept waiting for half an hour.

"I have several reasons for calling you away from your assignation," Casanova said pleasantly, making it clear that he knew about Mondragon's penchant for the ladies. "Tell me everything you know about this business at the basilica."

"There's not much to tell," Pierre replied. "I arranged to meet Luciani in the basilica. We sat in a confessional booth. I told him you suspected him of being light in his kickbacks.

He denied it. I told him that you had proof. He still denied stealing from you, but he was squirming in a guilty sweat. I realized you were right to suspect him, so I shot him in the head through the talking hatch. I used a silencer so nobody heard the shot, especially with all the noise of the tour guides talking to their groups and the crowds walking on the marble floor."

"The police got wind of your work awfully fast. How did that happen?" Casanova asked.

"When the bullet hit Luciani, he slumped down and his foot pushed the door of the confessional open. It wouldn't have been safe for me to arrange the body, so I just left. Someone must have discovered his body because his shoe was protruding."

"And how did you make your escape?"

"I picked up a female tourist, and we left as a couple."

"That was convenient for you, wasn't it?"

"In this business you have to improvise sometimes."

"Yes, but too much unnecessary creativity can be a bad thing," Casanova said, resenting this kid for telling him how to run his business. "Did the woman see Luciani's corpse?"

"I don't think so. Only one foot was sticking out, and not very far. If she did notice she would have thought the man was a drunk who passed out in the booth. It was dark, and she couldn't have seen into the confessional because the door was only open far enough to let a shoe out."

"How come the police got involved so quickly?"

"It must have been just a coincidence that somebody found the body so quickly," Mondragon said. "Don't worry, nobody can connect the killing to me, or to you, either."

"Guessing is not good enough for me. How can you be so sure that the woman didn't see Luciani's foot? She could have heard about the murder the same way I did, and she could have connected the dots. How do you know she's not in the police station right now telling them how she saw the foot as she was leaving the basilica with you?"

"It's not possible. We went to lunch together and she didn't show the slightest sign of suspicion at all," Pierre said, growing more defensive.

"Where did you go out for lunch, and how did you get there?" Henri's questions were coming thick and fast now.

"I took her to Massalia in my car."

"Of course, where else can you eat so well, and so free?" Casanova said sarcastically. "Driving around in that pussy wagon of yours, I suppose that was to impress this woman who can now connect you and your car to the scene of the crime. Who is she? And where is she staying? You said she was a tourist. Do we have to start killing tourists now in order to keep your hide out of jail?"

"Her name is Kate Evans, and she's an American who's studying French at the Sorbonne. She's here just visiting Marseilles. I took her to the Hotel de Ville in the Old Port where she's staying for a few days. I was planning to find her there after you were finished with me."

"Take care, my friend, that I don't become finished with you," Casanova said, dragging his hand across his throat to indicate what could happen to Mondragon if he displeased his master. "I had another assignment for you, but in view of your carelessness I'll send someone else. You will keep an eye on this tourist until she leaves Provence. If she goes to the police, kill her. Is that clear?"

"Yes, Boss."

"Call me often. I want to know what's happening before the police find out this time."

After Pierre had dropped her off at her hotel, Kate decided to have a rest during the hottest part of the afternoon when the dependable, furnace-like mistral wind from Africa blew dry air over the Midi. She picked up the remote and idly turned on the TV. An excited newscaster was reporting breaking news about the body of a man that had been found in a confessional booth at the basilica. The police were asking anyone who had been there during the past ten hours to come forward if they had any observations to report.

After hearing this announcement, Kate sat up and went over the events of the day. She wondered if she'd really seen anything important enough to report to the police. In her mind's eye she saw the image of the murdered man's foot sticking out of the confessional booth. Yes, she thought, but was that a matter that would change anything as far as the police were concerned? The victim must have been already dead, and she hadn't seen his face, so she couldn't identify the body. She had no desire to involve herself in a police investigation, especially in a foreign country. She lay back on the bed and imagined the questions that a gendarme might ask her. Whatever they were, she would have to mention Pierre Mondragon, and he wouldn't be at all happy to be involved. Who would be? She was sure Pierre had nothing to do with the killing. He had merely been in the basilica, just as she had been, around the time of the murder, and that was no crime. She decided against making a police report.

She remembered that when Pierre had answered the call from his boss he had spoken to him in a strange language. She had meant to ask him about that, but she hadn't gotten around to it because Pierre had so abruptly interrupted their lunch. She hadn't totally believed him when he told her he was an off-duty tour guide. She couldn't be sure, but she had the distinct feeling that underneath all his bravado he was scared to death of his boss. Kate couldn't imagine why he would be so afraid of his boss if he was just a tour guide.

Kate's thoughts moved on to Leslie Jolicoeur. He was an older man with short, sandy hair and handsome features. He was what most people consider to be an ivy-league type in both appearance and demeanor, but the trouble with him was that he had an unmistakable eye for the students in his class, and this disqualified him as a potential suitor as far as Kate was concerned. Living with infidelity in her life was out of the question for her. Areas of mutual intellectual interest were fine as far as they went, but infidelity was a deal breaker. Leslie was an addicted roué, and she knew he would never change. As for Mondragon, he was completely out of the question. She would have to look longer and harder if she was going to find a suitable male companion. Just then her thoughts were interrupted by a phone call.

"Good afternoon, Kate, it's Pierre Mondragon," said the caller. "We missed dessert when I was called away at lunch time, but I'd like to make it up to you. How about I come over this evening and take you to a wonderful bistro that serves authentic Provençal dishes fit for the gods?"

Kate was tempted to take him up on his invitation, for she was dying to hear his version of the deadly incident in the basilica. After letting a few seconds go by she decided to reply in the affirmative.

"I would enjoy talking to you about a few things, but I must tell you in advance that I'm not interested in starting any sort of romantic alliance. I'm too busy with my work and I don't have time for anything else. If this condition is acceptable to you, I'd be happy to have dinner with you."

"No problem. I understand completely."

"I hope so, Pierre. You're a generous, hospitable man," she added. "It's nothing personal, but I just wanted to be up front with you."

"I appreciate your candor. But not everything between a man and a woman has to be about sex, does it?" He spoke blithely to indicate his indifference. "I'll meet you in the hotel lobby at eight."

Pierre laughed inwardly as he hung up the phone. How often had he heard women say that kind of thing, and how often had they really meant the exact opposite? He actually believed that no woman sincerely meant "no" when she said it. To him it was all a game they played to simulate virtue. The confident Mondragon was convinced that no woman could resist his masculine presence, and that they wanted to submit to him regardless of what they said.

Later that evening Kate stepped out of the elevator and immediately saw Mondragon standing nearby.

"Ah, good evening, Miss Evans," he said, offering her his arm and leading her to the front entrance. "The bistro that I mentioned is just a few blocks away. We can walk. It's a nice evening and I believe you will like the food. Besides, the owner is a friend of mine and he needs the business."

"Now that it's getting dark out, the harbor looks magical with all the boats lit up like stars in the sky," Kate said.

"There, you see? You're more romantic than you think you are," Pierre smiled. "Marseilles is mostly an industrial city, though, with a large commercial port. It still harbors a fishing fleet, a yacht marina, and many historical points of interest, but it's principally a modern business hub."

"Well, I'm more interested in the history and culture of Marseilles than I am in the contemporary success of its businessmen," Kate admitted, confirming that she was an academic and not a fan of modern development.

"Very well then, I'll treat you like one of my tourist clients and fill your head full of stories that have taken place here in Marseilles," Pierre said. "Would you like me to tell you about the origin of the French National Anthem?"

"La Marseillaise? Sure, tell me about it," Kate said, as they turned from the Old Port onto the Rue de la Republique. "Then I'll tell you about the Star Spangled Banner."

Pierre didn't reply directly to her offer because he didn't give a damn about the American anthem. He'd learned to hate it after watching the Olympic games on TV when the winning country, too often the USA, had its anthem played.

"Kate, I hope you won't be disappointed to know that the Marseillaise was written by a sapper military officer from Alsace. It was composed in Strasbourg and called the war-song of the Army of the Rhine. It got its name from the 500 volunteers that were sent by the City of Marseilles to help establish the Republique during the French Revolution. Before the departure of the volunteers, each was given a copy of the song. They sang it in unison and it became an instant success. They sang the song everywhere they went until they became a specialist choir, and then the electrified crowds named the new hymn La Marseillaise."

"What part did Marseilles play in the Revolution?" Kate wanted to know. "It seems to me from my study of French history that Marseilles was called the "city without a name.""

"Well, aside from supplying the anthem, the inspiration, manpower, and the most important and sanest revolutionary leader, Marseilles had nothing to do with it."

"Who was this sane leader?" Kate asked.

"Why, the Comte de Mirabeau, of course."

"And what sane things did he do?"

"Mirabeau was one of the great figures in the National Assembly, the body that ruled France at the time of the Revolution," Pierre said, hoping Kate wouldn't ask for any details he couldn't supply. "He advocated a constitutional monarchy for France, but the king and the revolutionaries were suspicious of each other and wouldn't go along with Mirabeau. If they had, perhaps all the aristocratic bloodshed could have been avoided."

"So you're saying that if the wiser heads of Marseilles had prevailed, France could have had a peaceful revolution?"

"Just so," said Pierre, "we could have had a negotiated settlement, but instead we got Robespierre and the Jacobins with their blood-thirsty Reign of Terror, the guillotine, and the radical anti-religion extremists."

"Wasn't Robespierre himself executed by guillotine?" Kate vaguely remembered this from her history class.

"Yes, and it served him right," Mondragon said firmly. "The only good thing that came out of the Revolution was that we got some Corsican influence into politics."

"Do you mean Napoleon?" Kate asked him, looking surprised. "You like Napoleon, do you?"

"Yes, I do. He brought glory to France and to Corsica, but ever since then it's been downhill for us."

"Why do you care about Corsica so much?"

"Because I'm Corsican," Pierre said proudly. "Mirabeau himself spent years in Corsica as a soldier."

"So was that the Corsican dialect that you were speaking over the phone to your boss?" Kate asked.

"No, I was speaking Corsu, the language of Corsica. It's not a dialect of French. It's its own language," Pierre replied, with nationalistic pride. "You should know that," he said critically, then immediately regretted saying it, as it could well offend her and kill his chances for an intimate interlude with this young woman whom he regarded as a choice piece of American academic fluff.

Their walk had taken them to la Canebière, the main street and the hub of commerce of the city of Marseilles. Pierre led Kate onto this great street with its plethora of fish restaurants.

"I'd like to try the real bouillabaisse that the local people eat," Kate said. "Can we do that, please?"

"Of course, what kind of guide would I be if I didn't take you for a bowl of bouillabaisse?" Pierre replied. "Oh, by the way, the guillotine stood on this very site and many a federalist's head rolled in this street during the Rebellion when the Convention supporters took the city by assault. But don't worry," he added with a snicker, "none of the heads dropped into the bouillabaisse."

"That's a horrible image!" Kate exclaimed, recoiling at the thought. She would certainly have reacted even more strongly had she known that this man had dispatched his own share of the citizens of Marseilles.

"Don't think about it then," Pierre said with a shrug. "I'm taking you to L'Ecailler, a restaurant that specializes in bouillabaisse. It has a very interesting décor. Just wait and see."

CHAPTER THREE

The restaurant was located on rue Fortia and, true to Pierre's description, it had unusual furnishings. The interior was an accurate Victorian period design, and Kate was surprised to find such a charming place in the gritty city of Marseilles. She liked the character of the city because it had no pretensions. As Europe's second largest port city, its sixteen districts occupy twice the land area of Paris. The heterogeneous population makes for a very lively place, but it would be disappointing for those looking for the gentility of other French cities. Kate found the people on the street to be colorful and spirited, but although she liked Marseilles, she recognized that it was a city where one had to be careful. Oddly enough she felt safe with Pierre Mondragon.

They were both seated along the wall at a table for two. Pierre ordered a bottle of Bordeaux, and the waiter brought a basket of bread.

"No matter where you go in France, you can always depend on the bread," Kate said to her companion.

"And the wine," Pierre replied.

"Yes, and the wine," Kate agreed. "Now let's talk about this language of yours – Corsu."

"Very well, what do you want to know?" Pierre asked confidently, believing that since he was a native speaker of the language, he was therefore an expert.

"I want to know what the Corsicans consider to be the etymology of their language."

Kate was far from granting Pierre's request that Corsu be given the status of a language. She regarded it as a dialect in spite of his protestations, but she resolved not to overtly challenge him on this point.

"I was taught in school that Corsu derived from Latin in the Middle Ages, but I believe our language was influenced long before that by Greeks, Etruscans, and Carthaginians who were in Corsica before the Roman conquest in 259 B.C. Then you have to consider the scrambling contributions to the language by the Vandals, Lombards and Saracens in the Dark Ages."

Pierre was quoting the words of a previous conquest of his – a Parisian scholar of a certain age who, three years earlier, had fallen for his line and willingly admitted him into her hotel room. Scholars and educated women were Pierre's preferred sexual prey. He used to tell his friends about his bedroom exploits with the intellectuals he picked up in the museums of Marseilles. His Corsican background never failed to interest these women. He didn't know why they were so curious about it, but he had used the conversational topics of Corsican history and culture many times to soften their resistance to his subsequent advances. His friends loved his stories and thought he was some kind of genius lady-killer. This kind of admiration extracted from his peers assured his status within his circle of associates, so he worked hard on creating the legend of his irresistibility to women. His boss was less impressed and preferred that he stick to business and find himself a wife.

"Language is a constantly growing, evolving vehicle of communication," Kate said, "so tell me, what changes have come about that trace their origins to the last few centuries?"

"The struggle for control of Corsica has been a perennial one," Pierre said sagely. "The city states of Genoa, Pisa and Aragon all had their kick at the can and exerted power over parts of the island until France finally ended up annexing it in 1769. I say 'parts of the island' because in the interior, up in the mountains, the frequent changing of the guard in the coastal areas meant nothing. My people are from the highlands and weren't affected by what happened along the coastline. Our familial background is made up of ancient, independent tribal alliances. The Mondragons have always regarded ourselves as free, even after Bonaparte quelled the separatists and Corsica became a province of France," Pierre proclaimed proudly.

The waiter brought the bouillabaisse, and the unlikely couple began eating hungrily. The arrival of the food slowed the conversation. Between delicious mouthfuls and sips of wine, Kate only managed one other question about language.

"Do you think you speak Corsu with a different accent than those from the seaports of Corsica?" she inquired.

"I do," he said proudly. "I always know by the accent whether a speaker is from the mountains or the coast."

"How interesting," Kate mused, as she stared across the table at his dark eyes and crude features.

As Kate's eyes flicked from Pierre's peasant face to her now nearly empty bowl, she was startled to catch a glimpse of a familiar figure crossing the room. It was none other than her professor, Leslie Jolicoeur. His aristocratic features atop his tall frame were unmistakable. Evidently he had arrived a day earlier than Kate had expected. That was understandable since he was accompanied by a statuesque young blond woman whom Kate also recognized. She was Tiffany Chance, a first year student in the same international program in which Kate was completing her studies.

Kate watched as the maître d' led the handsome couple to a table not far from where she and Pierre were seated. There was no question but that she would be recognized. She anticipated that moment with dread, although she was sure that Leslie would be totally nonchalant about it. It made for an uncomfortable moment for Kate, as now she had caught the roué red-handed. She tried to rehearse what she would say to him, but she was unable to think of anything that made sense except the truth. She would probably have to introduce Pierre to Leslie and Tiffany.

It was not surprising that they should be eating at the same restaurant, because L'Ecailler was popular and famous. An experienced traveler like Leslie would know that. She also foresaw that he would rate Pierre, with his gangster suit and Corsican accent, as well below her in social status. He would assume the worst, of course, and conclude that Pierre was merely a sex toy for her. She knew how she would have responded to that misconception if she had been with Leslie alone, but in front of Pierre she couldn't say that he was a subject for her thesis.

Tiffany was patrician in appearance. Tall and willowy, she looked the part of a Southern California co-ed. She might have been controlling her weight by purging, as she seemed to be the type in Kate's opinion, but she was clearly the best looking girl in the international university program. It would have been out of character for an experienced lecher like Leslie to let a tasty morsel like Tiffany escape from his orbit untouched. Kate had to admit that they made a striking couple. They wouldn't have stood out in Cannes or one of the other playgrounds for the rich and famous, but in the buzzing, busy old part of the seaport of Marseilles, two tall blond gods like Tiffany and Leslie attracted a considerable number of envious stares. The handsome couple was not averse to turning a few heads when they entered a room. They would have been disappointed, in fact, if their presence in a room hadn't created surreptitious glances and whispered comments. Even Kate couldn't help staring, but then she had reason to, as she wished to avoid having to speak to them.

She needn't have worried, as Leslie and Tiffany would be at least equally anxious not to be seen together by another student at the university. Reputations and enmities were born in such circumstances. Leslie had his academic position as a serious scholar to protect. He had no idea that his female students had him perfectly pegged as a typical predatory male pedagogue, an opinion shared by his colleagues. His successes came with those students who wanted an older man experience, or who thought that they could improve their grades and lessen the academic work expected of them by permitting an assignation to occur with their professor.

Leslie Jolicoeur was a wily old fox, however, and he had handled little embarrassments like this chance meeting many times before. His eyes were always darting around any room he happened to be in. Usually he was taking inventory of the possibly available women who were present. This time it was to avoid being seen by Kate Evans, whom his discerning eye had immediately recognized.

He pretended not to have seen her, and made sure that Tiffany was seated with her back to Kate and her low-class escort so as to minimize the damage. Being seen with the beautiful, naïve Tiffany was probably not going to enhance his chances of seducing Kate, but it added a little additional challenge to the situation. In fact, it could have a propitious affect on his role as a Don Juan if it encouraged Kate's female competitiveness or piqued her curiosity about him as a lover. Leslie Jolicoeur continued his pretense of not having noticed her by putting a menu in front of his handsome face. He would sort out the issue of whether she had seen him later, but for the moment he just hoped Kate was at the end of her meal and would soon be leaving the restaurant.

For her part Kate's problem was more complicated than the professor's. She would have liked the opportunity to use the occasion of a chance meeting with friends as a way to get rid of Pierre after dinner without hurting his feelings, but in this case, of course, that ploy wouldn't work. She didn't look forward to provoking Pierre's rage when she refused to invite him to her room at the end of the evening. Now she would have to find some other way to reject the advances that she was certain he would make.

She hadn't yet had sufficient time to note all the linguistic anomalies of the Corsican's speech. Kate had just begun to realize the affect that Corsu had had on standard Parisian French, which the Alliance Française promoted as *the* correct vocabulary and pronunciation for proper spoken French. Corsu was enough of an anomaly to help fuel her thesis, so she didn't want to end her conversations with him entirely – only those that led to physical intimacy.

When the check came, Pierre dealt quietly with the waiter. He seemed to be signing the bill without presenting a credit card. While Pierre was busy with the waiter, Kate had a moment to think of an excuse that would keep him around as a subject for her research while simultaneously removing the inevitable sex issue. She rummaged around in her purse while Pierre's attention was distracted. She found a package of tampons and moved it to the top of the pile so it would be visible when her purse was open. It was a ruse she had used several times before, and it had always worked.

After the bill had been settled Kate opened her purse and pulled out her notepad, making sure that Pierre was able to see the tampons.

"What are you doing?" he asked, looking at the notepad.

"I thought I'd ask you a few questions about Corsu, if it's all right with you."

"Never mind that," said Pierre peevishly. "I think you should get an early night. You've had a long day."

"Well, thank you so much for the lovely dinner," Kate said, delighted that her ploy had worked yet once again. "I've eaten the world's best bouillabaisse, and now I think I should take your advice and retire early."

"After you," Pierre said gallantly, indicating the main door of the restaurant. Kate turned her back on Jolicoeur's table and walked in front of Pierre to the exit. Once out in the street she accepted his arm, although she would have preferred to be a little less friendly and encouraging. She was surprised by the thickness and hardness of his arm, which was well beyond what she would have expected from a tour guide.

For his part Pierre was on his best behavior, but he had assessed Kate's bodily attributes the minute he'd seen her in the basilica. He thoroughly approved of her muscular calves, firm thighs, and tight, round buttocks, but he was not very impressed with her décolleté. She had the breasts of an athlete – young and firm, but not particularly womanly. Nevertheless, he continued to feel that she would do nicely for his intended purpose, even if it had to be put off for a bit.

"By the way, what did you think about the murder in the basilica?" Kate asked him as they strolled along observing the boisterous crowds on the street.

"What? There was a murder in the basilica?" Pierre said incredulously.

"Yes, didn't you know? I heard all about it on the TV in my room this afternoon."

"Tell me about it," Pierre said, eager to find out what she knew before adding any comments of his own.

"Well, I don't know much about it, only what I heard on the news. The newscaster said that a murdered man's body had been found in a confessional booth, and they're asking everyone who was in the basilica that morning to come forward and make a statement about what they might have seen."

"So did you go to the police station?" Pierre inquired casually, as if it were of little interest to him either way.

"No, of course not. I don't have any information that would be helpful to the police. Did you see anything unusual while we were there?"

"No, nothing," Pierre replied quickly.

"As I think about it now, it seems to me that I did notice a man's foot sticking out of one of the confessional booths at a strange angle. At the time I didn't think anything about it," Kate mused. "But maybe it's an important clue. Do you think I should volunteer this information to the cops?"

"Not unless you want become a suspect in the crime," Pierre said. "You'd be letting yourself in for a whole lot of bother unless you witnessed the crime or could identify the killer. As it is, I think you should just forget it. You're only a visitor, after all. Why get involved?"

"I guess you're right, Pierre. But if I did see the shoe of the murdered man, shouldn't I report it?"

"So you saw a shoe. How would that help the police to find the killer?" Pierre asked.

"Well, for one thing it could help them establish the time of the crime," Kate replied, as if that might be an important piece of information. "How about you, didn't you see the foot sticking out of the booth? We passed right by it on our way out."

"I'm sorry, but I didn't notice a foot anywhere on the scene," Pierre lied. "I guess I was too interested in the lovely lady I had just met."

"Why thank you," Kate said, pretending to be flattered. "I guess you're right. I'll try to forget it too."

"I'm sure that's the best thing to do," Pierre agreed. "I'll call you in a couple of days. Perhaps I may be allowed to take you to see some of the extraordinary sights that can be found in the nearby small, but historic cities of the Midi."

"That's very kind of you," Kate said, in a parting lie that was one of those things that are said, but not meant, when mere acquaintances part for the last time.

When they arrived in the lobby of the hotel Kate went to the desk clerk and asked for the key to her room. The man picked the key off a board that hung on the wall behind him and handed it to her. He was surprised to see the couple say goodbye, and even more surpised when Pierre left the hotel. The night clerk had never seen Mondragon politely withdraw before. He had always gone up to the rooms of his lady friends. Sometimes he came down in a couple of hours, and at other times he left in the morning.

Kate took the elevator to her floor, walked to her room, opened the door, and entered her hotel room. She was glad to have gotten rid of Pierre without any fuss, muss, or bother.

Pierre, for his part, was already making his plans for Kate's seduction. He would give her a couple of days to get over her period. Then he would call her and offer to take her for a driving tour of the Côte d'Azur. Part of Pierre's job was to make the monthly collections from a number of his boss's clients in nearby Nimes, Arles, and Aix-en-Provence, and as he had to go anyway, he thought the company would be pleasant. Pierre felt sure that by the time they returned to Marseilles, Kate would be only too glad to yield to him. In the meantime, he would have one of his subordinates follow her to make sure that she didn't go to the police.

Leslie Jolicoeur was an experienced professor, and was quite comfortable speaking to audiences in the lecture format. His speaking engagement in Marseilles was open to the public, and the Alliance Française, the sponsors of his talk, hoped that it would be well attended by public and press alike. The Alliance had been fighting for years against the continuing pollution of the French language by Muslim immigrants to France from North Africa. The population of France had been declining for a long time except among the Muslims, where the opposite phenomenon had already put them into the majority in several centers, and was trending in that direction all over France. It was predicted that by 2050 Muslims would constitute the majority religion in heretofore Catholic France. Jolicoeur and the Alliance Française were attempting to be politically correct about the situation, but they were actually angry and hostile, and found the situation untenable. They didn't want the basic standard French to be corrupted by immigrants, and the Alliance Française was using Leslie Jolicoeur as its point man in its advocacy.

In Courneuve, a suburb of Paris where the effects of this outnumbering was already very evident, non-Muslim women were feeling pressured to veil themselves for fear of being raped – one of the prescribed Koranic punishments for those who opposed the najaf (compulsory wearing of the burqa for women). The liberal culture of France that was summed up by the revolutionary cry of "Liberté, Egalité, et Fraternité" was being eroded and displaced by obedient submission to the principles of Muhammad.

Professor Jolicoeur was angry about the situation, but he couldn't argue against it without seeming to be a bigot, so he had made up his mind to fight against the corruption of what he felt was *his* language by championing French linguistics. His approach was similar to the one employed by educators in the United States when they were being pressured to make

Ebonics a legitimate area of language study in the regions where African-Americans were approaching the numerical majority.

Jolicoeur had designed his lecture to appeal to laymen. He had organized his talk to contain just enough technical linguistic terminology to assure the linguists that he was one of them, and at the same time guarantee that the press and the general public at large would understand him.

Kate sat in the middle of the large auditorium. She was impressed and surprised by the content of his talk, and by Leslie's delivery of the lecture. Kate had, mostly because of his misogyny and predatory womanizing, dismissed the possibility of Jolicoeur having any real academic weight, but on the strength of his performance during the lecture, she found herself to be more favorably disposed to him. He was definitely a handsome, educated, and poised man of the world. She could now understand a bit better what all the female students at the university liked about him.

At the back of the room, standing by the exit door, was a man who seemed out of place in the academic environment. He was swarthy, informally dressed, and too young to be interested in the subject matter of the lecture. He was a teenager on a mission, and he was not listening to the lecture at all. His focus was on one of the members of the audience – Kate Evans.

His name was Didier Albertini. He was a Corsican boy, eager to follow in the footsteps of his mafia-connected hero, Pierre Mondragon. He came from the mountains of Corsica like most of the recruits that found their way into the cell headed by Henri Casanova. For hundreds of years his family had been connected to the secret criminal brotherhood that had made its own sub rosa laws and whose creed trumped all other allegiances. From early childhood Didier had been programmed to serve the gang. Disinterested in schoolwork, he began a life of crime at an early age. He was loyal to his capo, Henri Casanova, and idolized Pierre Mondragon. He had no other desire in life but to obey them and move up in the organization.

Kate listened to the presentation by Professor Jolicoeur without knowing she was being watched. When his speech was over and the applause had died down, members of the enthusiastic audience surrounded the professor as he stood at the podium, graciously receiving his post-lecture adulation. Kate, who felt obligated to extend her congratulations, had a difficult time going against the traffic. It was obvious to Didier that Kate knew the professor and that she was going to the front of the lecture hall to speak to him. The boy took this opportunity to call Pierre.

"Salut," Pierre answered in the Corsu accent that Leslie Jolicoeur would have instantly recognized and hated.

"It's me, Didier. I followed the woman to the university. She sat in the hall for about an hour listening to some dandy speaking about what he called the *French Correction*. Now she's gone up to the front to speak to him. She seems to know him quite well. When she shook his hand after his speech, he didn't let it go for a long time."

"Stay with her till you see me," Pierre Mondragon said. "I'm nearby. I'm coming now. When you see me you can leave and go for lunch. I'll call you later if I need you."

Pierre arrived a few minutes later. He saw Didier and dismissed him with a subtle nod in the direction of the exit door. The boy left quickly and unobtrusively. As usual he had no idea why he had been ordered to follow the woman, but knowing Pierre, it probably had something to do with sex. All he did know was that he was a soldier and he was obeying orders. His aspiration was to be the one giving the orders someday, but for the moment he had to be concerned only with pleasing the officer above him.

Kate was one of a group of admirers who surrounded Jolicoeur and who evidently didn't want him to make his escape. The tall, handsome professor was in his element as he charmed the mostly young women around him. Pierre sat down in one of the theater seats and silently watched Kate.

He was trying to establish the degree of intimacy in her relationship to the professor from her mannerisms and expressions. Finally he came to the conclusion that she was tentatively exploring her options with the man. From his long experience observing people and attempting to discern their motives, Pierre was very good at reading faces. He was exploring his own options with Kate as he focused on her every movement. Then suddenly he knew exactly what he had to do. He got up from his seat and walked to the front of the hall, joining the groupies at the podium.

Leslie Jolicoeur noticed the new masculine addition to his circle of admirers. He raised an inquiring eyebrow in the direction of Pierre in the same manner as a bull in a field of cows would sniff the air at the sight of another bull in his pasture. Pierre, for his part, gathered his suit jacket around himself. This little hitching action was reassuring to him, because in performing it his fingers touched the 9mm pistol that was in his shoulder holster beneath his jacket. Pierre didn't much care what became of Kate Evans after he had had her at least once, but he was not about to let this upper class fop have her before he did.

CHAPTER FOUR

Kate was astonished to see Pierre Mondragon in such an out-of-context location as an academic lecture hall. She couldn't imagine what he was doing there, listening to a speech given by Leslie Jolicoeur on the topic of the pollution of the French language.

"Pierre, what on earth brings *you* here?" she asked him, secretly disappointed that she hadn't gotten rid of him after all.

"Since it was a public lecture, and I'm part of the public, I thought I'd attend," he said. "You've made me want to know more about my own language. I admit I was hoping to impress you with my newfound knowledge the next time we met. I had no idea you'd be here too."

"You two know each other?" Professor Jolicoeur asked, surprised at the Corsican accent that he detected in Pierre's speech pattern.

"Yes," Pierre said. "We've had a few dates."

Kate wouldn't have called them dates, but she couldn't deny the fact that Pierre had showed her around Marseilles and bought her a couple of meals. She was angry with Pierre for mentioning the "dates" in front of Leslie and his fawning female fans. For his part, Leslie hadn't yet figured out the nature of Kate's relationship to Pierre. Was she his mistress? Pierre struck Leslie Jolicoeur as a tough low-life who wasn't suitable as an escort for an upper-class American student. Perhaps Kate didn't know any better than to take up with a type like Pierre, or perhaps she liked rough sex, which is what Jolicoeur believed was the only kind of sex that Pierre could provide. As he stood there evaluating him, the crowd of admirers began to thin out, for they could see that Kate and Pierre were known acquaintances of the great man.

"Professor Jolicoeur, my name is Pierre Mondragon. My charming friend here has neglected to introduce us," the tour guide cum gangster said. "I'd like to hear your thoughts about Corsu. Do you believe that Corsican is also one of the polluters of the French language?"

"Excuse me, I don't mean any offense, but yes I do feel that Corsu is one of the dialectical culprits that are having a deleterious effect on the French language," the professor said loftily, as if taking it for granted that an uneducated Corsican could never begin to understand the damage he was doing to the mother tongue every time he opened his mouth to speak.

It was obvious to Kate that these two men would never get along. It was also clear that each of them had some kind of design on her, but not having been asked how she felt about that, she was loath to hurt either's feelings by verbally dispatching them, and in any case she certainly didn't wish to do it in front of both of them. She wondered how it had come about that the two men had suddenly taken such an interest in her.

"I think I should invite the two of you for a drink so we can all discuss the issue of Corsican influences on the French language," Pierre said. It never occurred to him that he was out of his depth in the present company.

"That's kind of you, old chap, but I have many things to discuss with my student, so I must decline your offer."

He spoke with a certain air of proprietorship for Kate and for his beloved French language. He felt quite certain that neither wanted to be abused by this coarse Corsican.

"Where is your hotel, my dear?" he continued, turning to Kate. "Perhaps we can go there to have our discussion."

"I'd like to hear you two argue the issue out," Kate said, not wishing to be alone with either of these men. "Why don't you accept Pierre's invitation, Professor Jolicoeur? He has insider knowledge about the best restaurants in Marseilles, you know. Pierre, can you recommend a good place for our little debate?"

"Certainly, my dear," Pierre replied. "There's a small, elegant café called Le Coq D'Or very nearby."

"Yes, let's go there then," Kate said, directing her plea toward the professor.

"Oh, all right then," he said unenthusiastically. He felt that as long as he was the one to escort the lovely student back to her room, it would be bearable to spend some time with this Pierre fellow.

"Good then, follow me," Pierre said cheerfully, leading the way and thinking the very same thing as his rival had thought about being the one to end up in Kate's room.

As long as a threesome could be maintained, Kate knew she was safe from their sexual predations. Some societal rules still applied, but why did women have to suffer the continual pressure of unwanted attentions from men? She wondered if it might be possible to discover some sort of communication system which would allow women to control and direct their attractiveness so that only the object of their affection got their message. She had to admit that for most women this wouldn't be acceptable. Huge industries are devoted to enhancing the beauty of women. Flashy fashions, spas, and cosmetics are designed for the purpose of making a woman physically attractive to the largest possible number of men. Kate wondered why this was necessary.

As she walked with her two unwanted companions, she found the idea of mating with either of them to be distasteful. Whether her grounds for rejection were based on moral or physical reasons, the two men seemed totally disinterested in her feelings about the matter. Kate could almost feel the heat coming off their bodies, and she didn't like it. Many women would have felt that the rivalry of two men for their affections was exciting, but Kate didn't.

She knew that this problem had existed for thousands of years, and she was disappointed that the human species hadn't found a better way to handle gender relationships in all that time. She believed that the situation had worsened in recent generations. The women's liberation movement and the popularization of the many kinds of birth control had upped the opportunities and reduced the penalties associated with promiscuity. Modern prophylaxis and more accurate medical counsel supposedly reduced the risks of acquiring a sexually transmitted disease, but these so-called advances had done nothing to improve the condition of the heart. In Kate's experience all these developments had worked solely to the advantage of men in the battle of the sexes.

Kate thought that by inventing methods and devices that promoted safe promiscuity, men had altered human sexual mores in favor of the male's perennial desire for more and freer sex relations with women. Now they could influence women to have intercourse with them by saying that women could at last have the pleasure without paying the price, just like a man. Kate thought that the modern liberated woman, by insisting on having pleasure equal to that of men, played into the male libido pattern, which is what men wanted all along. Men had at last succeeded in making the "why not?" case stronger than the "why?"

Kate Evans, like most girls, had fallen for the argument. Conveniently for teenage boys, girls were now putting out for anyone they called a boyfriend. Kate had done her best to fit in with the generally accepted moral behavior patterns of university life. It wasn't until her senior year that she belatedly began to question the common perception of what male/female relationships should be. She was unwilling to accept the assumption that virginity was something that needed to be eradicated. She recognized that all people have sexual needs, but she had now put her desires under the supervision of her brain. As she looked at the faces of the men at the café table she knew she was the only one present for whom abstinence was even a possibility.

"Corsu is a dialect, not a language," Leslie was stating with his usual scholarly self-assurance, as though Pierre had to be an ignoramus to think otherwise.

"Whether you call it a dialect or a language," Pierre said indignantly, "it's a living method of communication shared by hundreds of thousands of Corsicans. I agree that Corsu has had a lot of input from other languages. We've woven them into our speech and made them our own. So what's wrong with that? Is it any different with other languages?"

"Look, Mr. Mondragon, Corsica is a province of France and has been for centuries. French is the language of France, therefore you should be proud to speak it and impelled to speak it well," Leslie said, in his lofty French.

"I speak it perfectly well," Pierre insisted. "I don't know anyone in France who doesn't understand me. Even you seem to understand me."

"Yes, I understand you, but that isn't the point," said Jolicoeur. "For one thing, your accent in French offends my ears. Why can't you pronounce your vowels without turning them into diphthongs? Even a duck quacks without making diphthongs, so why can't you?"

"I may not know what a diphthong is, but I can cut your offended ears right off so you'll look like a duck," Pierre said menacingly.

"Please, gentlemen, show some decorum," Kate said, trying her best to cheerfully quell the nasty atmosphere that was developing between the two men.

Kate looked at them thoughtfully. They were different from each other in every way possible. Physically they were opposites, Leslie being tall and Nordic while Pierre was average in height and olive-skinned. Jolicoeur was a man not to be argued with because he was verbally skilled and educated in the ways of debate. Mondragon was a man not to be argued with either, because his anger was barely being contained. Kate imagined that if it were released it could be terrible. The man of letters wouldn't have a chance against the man of action, she mused.

"Let me ask you this, my irritable Corsican friend," said Leslie. "How can you tell if a naked man is a king or a peasant?"

"You can't," Pierre fired back.

"No, you are wrong," said Leslie haughtily. "You can tell by his bearing and by his speech. A cultured man will always shine through in every circumstance. It's the same with language. If you use French in an educated way you will be perceived as a gentleman. If not, you will be thought of as a boor. On a national scale it's the difference between being respected and being looked down upon."

"I disagree," Pierre said vehemently. "If you expect France to be respected in the world, then France will have to start winning wars instead of losing them. Diplomatic talk is not worth the paper it's printed on. Power gets respect."

"Let's not get into politics," Leslie said. "We're talking about language here. Don't you think that an Englishman using Oxford English will be more highly regarded than one speaking with a Cockney accent?"

"I think the one who has the biggest balls will be the most respected," Pierre said.

"I can see that your mind is not subtle enough to grasp the finer points of my argument," Leslie said in his loftiest, most dismissive manner.

"I think I'd like to go back to my hotel now," Kate said, hoping to separate the rivals by changing the subject, and assuming they would all go their separate ways afterwards.

"That's a good idea," Jolicoeur agreed. It was obvious, he thought, that in spite of the fact that he was intellectually superior to this Corsican dimwit, he was even more eager to win the battle over who was to accompany Kate. "I will take Kate in a taxi."

"Very well," Pierre agreed, to the amazement of both Leslie and Kate. "I'll just take care of the bill and call a taxi for you."

"That's very kind of you old chap," Leslie said. "Kate and I have some matters to discuss concerning a paper that she's writing for one of my classes."

"All right then," Pierre said as he stood up and marched ahead of them toward the door.

On his way out of the café Pierre paused to have a word with the waiter. Kate noticed that once again he seemed not to pay the check, but he did place a tip in the fellow's hand. The waiter hustled out into the street and hailed a cab. While they all waited for the taxi to pull up, Pierre leaned over and whispered in Kate's ear.

"I'll call you in the morning. Perhaps I can take you in my car to see some of the other famous parts of Provence. Think it over and let me know what you decide, all right?"

"Will do," Kate smiled.

"Professor," Pierre Mondragon said, opening the door of the cab for them, "it was nice to meet you. Good luck with your work of converting the unwashed of the Mediterranean to your point of view."

"Very nice to have met you too, Monsieur Mondragon," Leslie answered politely, hoping it would be the last time he ever saw the cretin.

Kate was still stunned by how easily Pierre had agreed to let Leslie take her back to her hotel, but she thanked him for the coffee and the conversation. She let the answer to his offer of a motor trip slide without acknowledgment, hoping he would get the hint. Then, as the professor took his place next to her in the taxi, she started to think about how she could let him down equally easily.

As soon as the cab was out of sight, Pierre reached for his cell phone and punched a number on his autodial.

"Hello, Boss," said Didier Albertini, answering his cell almost immediately.

"I've got a job for you," Pierre hissed. "Get your pistol. Make sure it's loaded. Use a silencer. Go to the hotel of the Evans woman. In a few minutes she'll arrive in a taxi. She'll will be with a tall blond man. He's the mark. She's to be unharmed. Wear a mask so you can't be identified. This is the most important job I've ever given you. Hit him just as I've trained you to do it. Got all that?"

"Yes, Boss," Didier replied. "Do you want me to repeat your instructions?"

"No. It's simple enough. Just make it quick. Call me when the job is done."

"Yes, Boss."

Pierre went back to the café and sat down at the same table, which had not yet been cleared. When the waiter returned he was a bit surprised to see Pierre back again.

"Bring me a cognac," Pierre said. "What time is it?"

"Eight o'clock," said the waiter, looking at his watch.

"Are you sure your watch is right?"

"Yes sir," the waiter said, trying not to sound irritated.

"Good. Then bring me the cognac, and be quick."

Mondragon sat for a full hour watching the pedestrian traffic mill about as he smoked and sipped his drink. Finally his cell phone rang.

"Yes?"

"It's done, just as you ordered."

Kate Evans and Leslie Jolicoeur had been taken by surprise by the loud knock at her hotel room door. The professor had convinced her that the papers and books he had in his brief case couldn't be spread out and discussed properly anywhere but in her room. She had agreed, albeit with a degree of reticence, to allow him to come up. Kate was having one of her bouts of indecision. On the one hand she wanted nothing to do with this academic Lothario, but on the other hand she was curious about what made this particular man capable of successfully seducing so many young and attractive women. Female competitiveness made her unwilling to be the one that was left out – to be the wallflower, so to speak. It was the Don Juan fascination, she told herself, and she should resist both her urges and his.

Jolicoeur had indeed brought some relevant documents that could be helpful to Kate. He had the papers spread out over the small desk that was in the economy-class room, and he was sitting at the desk with his back to the door when the knock came. Kate had been sitting next to him on a chair that she had pulled over so she could look over his shoulder to see what he was talking about. He had planned it that way so that she was forced to be close to him. He was just about to make his move on her when she jumped up to see who was at the door.

"Who is it?" Kate asked through the closed door.

"It's the hotel porter, Ma'am," Didier Albertini called out in his distinctive Corsican accent. He was wearing a mask and holding a pistol fitted with a silencer in his right hand. "I've got a package for Miss Evans."

"Just a minute," Kate said, looking around for a few francs with which to tip the man.

Leslie remained seated at the desk while Kate answered the door. He didn't see her open it, nor did he see the masked man put his hand over her mouth to silence her. He was also unaware that he was holding his gun against Kate's midriff as he pushed his way into the room. Holding her tightly with one strong arm, the intruder marched her silently backwards into the small room. When he was within a few inches of the back of Jolicoeur's head he quickly moved the pistol away from Kate's stomach and casually discharged a single bullet into Leslie's head. The slug took a downward course as it slammed into the professor's brain and exited through his mouth. Leslie Jolicoeur was dead before the force of the shot shoved his face down onto the desk.

The masked Didier casually glanced at the bloody mess his action had created. Blood had spattered across the desk and against the wall. It continued to ooze from the body, forming a puddle that soaked the books and papers. A tooth had fallen on the floor. Dazed and frightened, Kate had gone partially limp in the killer's grasp. He threw her onto the bed and withdrew a roll of duct tape from his coat pocket. His mind was working overtime. Under the same conditions he might have raped and then killed the woman, but Pierre had specifically ordered him not to harm her. He wondered what was so special about this woman that a man had been killed over her.

The revolting sight of Leslie Jolicoeur's execution and its bloody aftermath had Kate terrified. Her only thought was to stay alive in any way she could. Before she had a chance to beg for her life, the intruder slapped a patch of tape over her mouth, then took some heavy cord from his pocket and tied her hands and feet behind her and threw her onto the bed. Then he tied her to the bedpost so she couldn't wiggle off the bed later and get to the phone. He took a few quick snap-shots of her, then looked around as though reassuring himself that everything was in order. When he was certain that he hadn't overlooked anything, he left without a word.

Kate had expected the worst, so she was amazed when the killer put away his gun and left the room, closing the door gently behind him. He had been a little free with his hands when he tied her up, but she was amazingly untouched considering the drama that had taken place. For a few minutes she expected the murderer to return, but gradually she began to realize that he wasn't going to come back. Though she struggled to free herself, it was no use. She would be tied to the bed until the housekeeper came to make up the room the next morning.

To keep her mind busy she tried to remember everything she could about the killer so she could tell the cops. It had all happened so quickly, and the man had been masked, so she didn't think she'd be much help to the police. The only thing she could say about him was that he was certainly a Corsican. His pronunciation and phrasing were exactly like Pierre's, so she was sure that he also came from that nearby island. She managed to wiggle around enough to see Leslie, who was still slumped over the desk. She wanted to cry out in despair, but the duct tape muted any expression of grief.

When Didier Albertini returned from his mission he found Pierre in the back room of the bar that Casanova's boys used for a clubhouse. As soon as Pierre saw him, he left the table where he'd been sitting with his friends and led the young man away to another table where they had some privacy.

"How did it go?" Pierre asked. "Did he put up a fight?"

"No. I surprised him," the young killer said. "He was dead before he knew I was even there."

"And the woman?" Pierre inquired. "What about her? Was she there when you did it?"

"Yes. She was in her hotel room with him," Didier said, enjoying his boss's curiosity. He thought it was nice to have more answers than his superior for a change. "I wore my ski mask so she couldn't identify me."

"How did you keep her quiet?" Pierre asked, thinking that it was like pulling teeth to get the story out of him, and wondering if he was intentionally doling it out slowly so that he could be given more credit for his workmanlike job.

"I put some duct tape over her mouth and tied her up," Didier said, "then I threw her down on the bed. I also tied her to the bedposts so she couldn't wiggle off the bed and get to the phone. She'll be there when the maids come in the morning to make up the room. We'll never be connected to this hit. Don't worry, Boss."

Didier Albertini had one small satisfaction that he withheld from Pierre Mondragon. When he had tied up Kate Evans her skirt, which had an elastic waistband, was pulled out of place in such a way that it revealed a small tattoo on an area of her body that very few men would ever have seen. Didier was sure that Pierre hadn't seen it, at least not yet. He had snapped a picture of it with his cell phone. It was a detail of one-upmanship that he kept for future reference in case he ever wanted to use this piece of information against Mondragon, whose weakness for women was well known to his colleagues.

The next morning the maids knocked on the door, and when they got no response they admitted themselves with their passkey. Their attention was centered on the bed, which was the focus of their mission. When they discovered Kate's predicament they mistakenly attributed it to a vengeful lover. While one of the housekeepers began to free Kate, the other looked over at the desk to find a phone with which to report the incident to the head housekeeper. When she saw the body of Leslie Jolicoeur slumped over the blood-soaked desk, she let out a terrified cry.

The head housekeeper hurried to the room after paging the hotel manager to ask him to come immediately. They arrived at Kate's room almost simultaneously. The manager was a nervous little man who compensated for his lack of height by affecting an attitude of haughty authority. He immediately called the police to report the murder. Then he turned to Kate and asked her if she had an explanation for what had happened in his hotel.

"I prefer to wait for the police to come before giving my statement," Kate said, not wishing to have to relate the horrible story more than once.

"My dear young lady," the pompous man said, " I have a right to know what transpired on my property." Seeing that Kate was not cowed, he broke away and asked the maids for their version instead.

The maids had no choice but to comply with their boss, so they reported the situation to him and to the head house-keeper as they had found it when they had entered the room. Except for a brief glance in the direction of the desk, the hotel manager did his best not to look at the body of the unfortunate Mr. Jolicoeur. Finally he stated rather too loudly the obviously unnecessary order that nobody was to touch anything until the police arrived.

CHAPTER FIVE

A loud knock at the door announced the arrival of the police. The manager had made sure the door had been tightly closed so that his other guests would not get the idea that his hotel was unsafe because of the presence of the police and the crime scene activity. One of the maids opened the door, and a phalanx of men quickly entered, with Inspector René Martin at the fore.

"I want everyone out of here," the inspector said. "Is the room next door empty?"

"Yes, inspector," said one of the maids. "We just made up that room before we came to this one."

"Very good, then I want all of you to go next door with Assistant Inspector Benamou. He will take your statements," Martin said, directing the people out with hand motions like the traffic cop he had been in the years before his many promotions. "The coroner will be here soon to collect and examine the body. I'll let you know when it's permissible to clean the room." This last instruction he directed to the hotel manager and the head housekeeper.

The inspector walked around the hotel room making mental observations before focusing his attention on Kate, who had been asked to take the chair near the bed. He looked at her for a moment without saying a word, then he pulled a chair over so that he would be facing her when he sat down.

"I'm Inspector René Martin, Mademoiselle," he said, extending his hand. "Now, please tell me what happened here," he added in a friendly voice. "Take your time, but leave nothing out, not even the smallest detail. I prefer the anecdotal style to the more formal legal question-and-answer method. I've placed a few officers at the elevator door to prevent the news hounds from butting in, so you can, for the time being at least, be calm as you relate the events that led to this murder."

There were still a couple of plainclothes policemen in the room gathering finger prints and looking for any clues to the identity of the killer, but they weren't paying attention to the conversation between Kate and the inspector. For some reason she liked this policeman, and felt relaxed about telling him her story. She resolved to try to figure out what it was about him that she liked, but a deeper analysis would have to wait until afterward.

"My name is Katherine Evans. I'm an American student studying in Paris. The dead man's name is Professor Leslie Jolicoeur. He's... I mean he was my mentor and my thesis advisor. Before this happened we had been having a coffee at Le Coq D'Or café with a friend, after the professor had delivered a lecture at the university. We chatted for about an hour, and then he and I shared a taxi here. He told me he had some material that might be of interest for my thesis, so I invited him up to my room to discuss it. We had just spread all the papers and books out on the desk the way you see them now, when a knock came at the door. I went to see who it was. As soon as I opened the door an armed man in a black ski mask forced his way into the room. He grabbed me and covered my mouth with a gloved hand, so I couldn't make a sound. The professor was seated as he now is, with his back to the door. The assailant pulled me along with him and shot the professor in the head from behind. Then he threw me down on the bed and bound me with duct tape and gagged me. After that he tied my hands and feet to the bedposts and left. And that's exactly what happened."

"Well, I accept what you say, but I'm rather sure it's the abbreviated version," Inspector Martin said patiently. "Now I need the unexpurgated version."

"What do you mean?" Kate asked, playing dumb for a reason she didn't understand.

"Well, for instance, who else were you talking with at the café?" Martin asked, trying to be sensitive to the sexual aspects of the case by not getting into those details right off. "You did say you were with someone else at the café, didn't you?"

"Oh yes, of course. It was a Mr. Pierre Mondragon, a tour guide I believe," Kate said reluctantly, fearful that the inspector would also connect them to the death of the man in the basilica. "He was also at the professor's lecture," Kate said casually.

"How do you happen to know Mr. Mondragon?" René Martin asked.

"I met him in my capacity as a tourist."

"Do you mean you were on a guided tour, and he was the guide?" the inspector asked, knowing perfectly well that Pierre Mondragon was anything but a tourist guide.

"Not exactly," Kate replied, still trying to keep her cards close to the vest. "He told me he was a tour guide, but he was off duty at the time we met. What difference does it make how we met? He wasn't the killer."

"How can you be so sure it wasn't Mondragon, if the killer was masked?" the inspector asked.

"That's easy," Kate said. "The assailant was taller and lighter in build. Believe me, I could tell the difference between their voices as well. The only similarity was their accents, which are definitely Corsican."

"You speak French surprisingly well for an American," the inspector remarked. "But do you expect me to believe that you can identify a Corsican when he speaks French?"

"You can depend on it," Kate said, with a bit of prideful vehemence. "I have a good ear for accents."

The inspector was a little taken aback by her accurate diagnosis and her feisty confidence in her talent. He hadn't failed to notice Kate's physical charms, but of course he had to maintain an attitude of total professionalism, if only to give his crew a good example of a crime scene investigator.

"Why do you think this brutal killer did you no harm?" The inspector posed the question to hear what conclusions she had drawn about the murderer, but also to offer her a chance to explain why she'd been found tied up on the bed, yet wasn't complaining that she'd been sexually assaulted.

"I don't know. He had the opportunity to rape me, if that's what you mean, but he didn't. I guess he just wanted to get out of there as quickly as possible. After all, he had just committed a murder. Maybe he didn't want to take any chances."

"No, I guess not," the inspector conceded. "But I find it strange that having you at such a disadvantage, and being a man capable of cold-blooded murder, that he didn't rape you when he had the chance."

"You sound disappointed, inspector. Is that what you'd have done?"

"Not at all, Miss Evans," he replied defensively. "But we're not dealing with a moral member of society here. This killer is obviously a sociopath. His behavior is typical of a man without a conscience. Why would he just walk away from such an opportunity?"

"I don't know," Kate said. "*You* tell *me,* or don't you investigate non-rapes? Perhaps you can ask him when you catch him."

"It's true that I'd prefer to catch this villain and convict him of murder," the inspector said, "rather than the lesser crime of conspiracy to commit rape. But you can't hold that against me, can you? I find it peculiar that a beautiful young woman like you should be intentionally spared."

"Intentionally spared?"

"Yes, Miss Evans. The intruder had the opportunity, and presumably the interest, to commit a sexual assault while he had you at his mercy, but he didn't follow through."

"Inspector, you make it seem as though I was a choice morsel rejected by a gourmand," Kate smiled. "Can *you* think of a reason why I was rejected as a sex object – one one that doesn't hurt my self-esteem?"

"Perhaps you were raped, but have your own reasons for not accusing the man? Or maybe this was a gang killing and the murderer was a hit man ordered not to touch you?"

"Well, your gang killing theory makes sense to me," Kate acknowledged. "But as to why I wasn't molested, I can't say. Maybe he didn't want to leave behind any semen samples that could be used to identify him. I don't know. I can only swear to you that I was not harmed in any way except for being tied up, which was not too comfortable, I can tell you that much."

"Very well then," the inspector said, wishing to move on to other questions concerning the peculiarities of the case. "Tell me everything you know about the victim. What kind of man was he?"

Although she had had a certain amount of disrespect for Leslie Jolicoeur, Kate certainly didn't wish him dead. She was aware that he was the type of man that some women get involved with, and who then get bitter later on when they are spurned. She considered the possibility that some woman had paid a hit man to kill the professor, but dismissed the idea as far-fetched.

"Professor Jolicoeur was an able teacher," Kate began. "He was very knowledgeable about his subject, which was French as a language. He was a principal mover in the Alliance Française's effort to keep the French language pure and grammatically correct."

"Tell me about him personally," said Inspector Martin. "I'm less interested in his professional qualifications. Did he have any enemies?"

"No, none that I know of," Kate replied. "But he was a professor, and all professors have jealous colleagues."

"But you don't know of anyone who would resort to the ultimate act of jealousy?" Martin persisted. "How about his relationship to his students? Was he a tough grader? Do you think any of the students might have killed him because he was failing them in one of his courses?"

"It's possible, of course," Kate admitted, "but not very probable, I should think. I've never heard of such a case."

"I agree with you, Miss Evans, but it's best not to leave any stones unturned. Stranger things have happened."

"Well, that's true, I suppose. But I'd be more inclined to believe that the motive had something to do with sexual jealousy rather than despondency over a failing grade."

"Why is that, Miss Evans?"

"Well, for one thing 90% of his students were women, and Professor Jolicoeur was quite the ladies' man."

"With a gender ratio like that a male instructor could get into trouble, couldn't he?" Martin said thoughtfully. "Do you know of any specific individual that the professor might have been involved with?"

"His reputation among my fellow students was that he was a player," Kate said evasively, hoping she wouldn't be expected to tattle on her colleagues.

"Do you have any personal experience with him in this regard? Since he was alone with you in your hotel room, do you think he had certain... aspirations for the evening?"

"You put it very sensitively, Inspector," Kate said. "I can only say that he had bona fide information with him that was of interest to me in preparing my thesis, and as of the time he was killed he hadn't made any improper advances. I can't testify as to what he might have done if he'd lived."

"That sounds as if you anticipated that he would make a pass at you," Inspector Martin suggested.

"Well it had occurred to me," Kate said. "I'd be a fool if that sort of thing had never crossed my mind."

"It appears from your statement that your virtue had two close brushes with compromise last night," the inspector said sincerely.

"You could say that," Kate said, amused by his quaint way of putting things.

The other policemen had finished examining the body for clues, and had taken fingerprints and DNA samples. A gurney had arrived and the body was placed on it, covered with a sheet, and wheeled to the service elevator on the instructions of the hotel manager, who was making every effort to protect the other hotel patrons from the sight of a dead guest being wheeled out of the main entrance of the hotel. At the lower floor delivery entrance the coroner's van was waiting to pick up the corpse and take it to the morgue. The inspector was anxious to confer with his assistant to see what the maids and other hotel personnel had to say, and to hear if it conflicted with what Miss Evans had told him.

"I guess that's the end of my questions for the moment," Inspector Martin said. "But please don't leave town without telling me where you can be contacted. I might have further questions for you as my investigation proceeds."

"I expect to be here for a few more days, Inspector," Kate said. "Then I'll be traveling in other parts of France in search of data relative to my studies."

Kate had to admit to herself that she hoped the inspector would call her. She liked his sincerity and his consideration of her feelings. He seemed sensitive and caring, as well as smart and earnest. Her interest in the inspector was purely outside of his professional bounds, however, so she didn't really expect to hear from him again unless he needed her to discuss or identify any future suspects.

Inspector Martin was interested in Kate Evans too, but he was aware of the risks involved with getting personal with a principal in one of his cases. He was attracted to her on several levels, which included her looks and her intelligence. After questioning her he was certain that she had given him only the bare facts. It was as if she knew more than she was saying, or perhaps she was protecting someone else. He believed he was dealing with a professional hit, probably carried out by the Corsican mafia. But he still had many questions concerning the case. Why, for example, would the syndicate want to kill a language professor?

Pierre Mondragon wondered if he could call Kate for a date right away, or if he should wait a day or two. He was sure that he couldn't be connected to the murder of Professor Jolicoeur, but he didn't particularly want to appear at the hotel while the police inspectors were still hanging around. The news of the professor's murder had just become public knowledge. Pierre decided he should call Kate immediately because she would appreciate having someone in her corner to fend off the news hawks, and to commiserate with her on her loss. Choosing to call at this stressful time would amply demonstrate to her, and to the police, that he had nothing to do with the killing. With the press circling around the scene, now would be the perfect time to get her out of Marseilles and show her the Côte d'Azur. Mondragon felt she could hardly refuse his generous offer under the circumstances, so he dialed the hotel and waited for her to pick up.

"Hello," Kate answered. "Who's calling, please?"

"It's Pierre. I just heard the news on TV. Are you OK?"

"I guess I will be. The police just finished questioning me, and I'm a bit shaky. I've never had anyone in my circle die before. He was shot right in front of me. I couldn't believe my eyes. Thanks for calling. It's very kind of you."

"Think nothing of it, my dear," he said soothingly. "What you need is to get away from the hotel, the police, and all the questioning. How would it be if I picked you up in my car and gave you a private tour of the Côte d'Azur?"

Kate, who thought she'd seen the last of Pierre, now considered his offer. Perhaps she had misjudged him. He couldn't help being a little primitive – after all, he had no way of choosing his own genes. Having no other options, and not wishing to spend her time in Provence ducking the media people, Kate consented to go with him.

"Listen carefully to me now," he said conspiratorially. "If the media people see you leave the hotel they'll follow us and ruin our time together. If you do what I say, I think we can make a clean get-away. So in fifteen minutes, take the elevator down to the basement parking area. Don't enter the garage. Open the unmarked door on the opposite side – it's the kitchen storeroom of the hotel. Go in that door, and walk about ten steps. You'll see an unmarked door on the right. It leads to the loading dock that's used by the commercial vehicles when they make their food deliveries. I'll meet you there with my car. If we're lucky the media will think you're still in your room. Have you got that? Can you do it?"

"Yes, I think so," Kate replied. "Thank you so much for trying to get me away from all this."

"You're welcome," Pierre said. "Bring a small bag, pack a bathing suit and a change of clothes. You may want to test the famous waters of the Riviera. I'll see you out back in fifteen minutes. OK?"

"OK. I'll be there."

Inspector René Martin was intrigued by the case of the murdered professor because there was apparently no motive for the killing. In the course of his own education he had felt like murdering the occasional professor, but he had turned himself into a modified autodidact instead. His good instincts were inherited from his mother, and his problem-solving from his father, who was an engineer/inventor. His superiors in the police department held him in high regard because he had common sense, which was all too often an uncommon commodity in the gendarmerie, and this particular trait was most responsible for his promotion to Inspector at his age.

As he rose within the ranks of the department, several transfers had conspired to keep him single. His marital status made him the butt of jokes by his colleagues, and he was sensitive about it. He understood better than most the role that sexual attraction played in crimes. His experience and his common sense were lined up against getting involved with a subject in an investigation. In spite of all this René had to confess to himself that he was drawn to the American girl, Kate Evans. He tried to figure out exactly what his fascination for her was all about. She was attractive, but then so were many other women with whom he had come into contact in his life as a policeman. She was intelligent, but that was often a problem for a detective on duty. He had to remain objective, he told himself, if he was to solve the case. Martin felt that the young woman hadn't been entirely forthright when he questioned her. But if she was criminally involved in the murder of the professor, he hadn't yet been able to uncover even a hint of complicity in the killing. If he had come up with any evidence against her, he would have turned it over to the prosecutor, regardless of her allure.

René Martin had watched Kate carefully while he was questioning her. She was convincingly upset, but many actresses can create believable lies. Taking statements from people immediately after their ordeals had both its good and bad side. Their remarks were quick and spontaneous, but on the other hand these comments could be emotionally charged and possibly confusing. When he was questioning Kate, he felt there were some things she hadn't been candid about. It could have been because she was shocked by the recent events and unable to think clearly, or she might have been trying to protect a third party – perhaps the killer. The inspector had no doubt that he would have to speak to her again, at which time he would expect a calmer, more rational explanation of what had taken place in her hotel room.

He had asked her not to leave the area of his jurisdiction until the criminal investigation had been concluded. He was therefore rather surprised when he went to the hotel to find Kate and was told by the manager that she had been seen by kitchen personnel leaving the loading dock area with a man in a dark-colored BMW, and that she had taken a suitcase with her. The manager also stated that she hadn't checked out of the hotel.

René Martin didn't know what to conclude from this last bit of information. Either she had not checked out because she expected to return, or she had neglected to check out because she was running away with the man in the BMW. He sincerely hoped it was the former.

All he could do at that moment was leave a message with the concierge asking that he be called immediately if Miss Evans returned to the hotel. He realized that he was just as interested in whether Kate had stayed out all night with the owner of the Beemer as he was anxious to ask her some additional questions concerning the murder. He felt uncomfortable about the effect this foreign woman, whom he hardly knew, was having on the passionate side of his nature.

He decided to blot out his thoughts about Kate Evans by getting back to the other aspects of the case that needed investigating. Among the things they had found on the body of Leslie Jolicoeur were his driver's license, some credit cards, and his ID card from the university. The inspector called the administrative office of the university and was given Professor Jolicoeur's address and phone number, as well as that of his next of kin. Inspector Martin informed the university of the death of Professor Jolicoeur, and told the human resources official that he would inform the wife. His next call was to Marlene Jolicoeur.

"This is Inspector René Martin of the National Police in Marseilles. I'm sorry to have to tell you that your husband, Leslie Jolicoeur, has been murdered."

There was a short period of dead air over the phone until Marlene Jolicoeur recovered sufficiently from the shock.

"Would you tell me the circumstances?" she asked in a slightly shaky voice, but one that continued to be controlled.

"Of course," Martin replied, not sure of how specific he should be about the details of her husband's death. "We were called to the Hotel Belvedere this morning. We found the professor's body in one of the rooms. He had been shot in the back of the head. We are searching for the perpetrator now, but so far unsuccessfully. We understand the professor had delivered a lecture at the University in the afternoon."

"Was he alone?" Marlene Jolicoeur asked timidly.

"No Madame, he was found in the room of an American student named Kate Evans. Do you know her?"

"No, he never told me the names of his students," she answered in a world-weary way that made Martin think that it wasn't the first time the professor had fooled around, but it was certainly the last. "Was the student also murdered?"

"No, she was tied up, but uninjured," Martin said. "I'm sorry to have to ask, but what would you like us to do with the body?"

"I don't know. How are these matters usually handled?"

"If I were you I'd call a mortuary in Paris, if that's where you'd like him to be buried. I'm sure they can arrange to have the body transported. Just tell them it's being held in the Marseilles coroner's department, and as is customary in cases of unnatural death, an autopsy is being done prior to the issuance of a death certificate," Martin said in a matter-of-fact way. "Do you have any idea who could have killed your husband? Did he have any enemies that you know of?"

"None that I think would have murdered him," she said, in a way that suggested that he had many enemies, but just not ones that were serious enough to commit murder.

René Martin knew what she was insinuating. In his experience, professors were an envious bunch. They hated one another, fearing that others might gain some modicum of academic advantage. Their jealousy was akin to the kind displayed in the Old Testament. What else could one expect from those whose professional lives were wholly given over to criticizing the work of others? René had hoped that he would find enlightenment to be the objective, but he had been disappointed to find that at least in the humanities, the primary goal had shifted to personal aggrandizement. To discover an arcane fact and present it in obfuscated, high-flown language, and then to get it published in an academic journal, was the ambition of university faculty members in the humanities. Those lucky enough to be given positions in the academic field of their choice were given incredible freedom to do as they pleased in the tradition of elite gentlemen scholars, but latterly the majority had become usurpers and no longer deserved the lofty honors they heaped upon themselves and their profession.

Inspector Martin, during his time at university, shared the general view of his fellow students that most professors were an arrogant, pompous, spoiled class of egotists who were suckling on the public sow. After he graduated he decided he'd had enough of formal schooling, and that from then on he would educate himself. René believed that those who had been foolish enough to give professors the power to affect the lives of students, deserved to be chastised for it. As a result of his personal experience, he had developed a prejudice against professors, but he would have to overcome his bias in order to do his job as an investigator of the facts concerning this murder. He could see how a student could be driven to desperation by a self-centered professor with ulterior motives. He was, therefore, forced to consider if Professor Jolicoeur had been killed by one of his students – perhaps one not too unlike himself.

It wasn't possible that Kate Evans could have killed him, disposed of the weapon, and then tied herself to the bed to make it appear that she was innocent of the crime. Since Kate had said that the killer was masked, he could have been a student, but most of the professor's students were women. Could one of his students have killed him? He would ask Kate the next time he saw her, but for now he would ask the professor's wife.

"Madame Jolicoeur, you have suggested to me that your husband was seeing other women. Can you elaborate on that a little bit for me?"

"We had a modern, open marriage," Marlene told him. "It was the only kind my husband would have tolerated."

"So he had a mistress, then? Can you tell me her name?"

"I've always had trouble with the definition of the term *mistress,*" Mrs. Jolicoeur confessed. "To my understanding a mistress is a woman other than a man's wife with whom he is having ongoing sexual relations. By this definition I'd have to say that my husband had no mistresses. What he had was a series of adulterous relationships with co-fornicators, most of which were one night stands."

"I see," the inspector replied.

"I'm sorry, Inspector Martin, but I'm afraid you don't see," Marlene Jolicoeur said in an ironical tone that revealed the deep hurt that she had often suffered because of her husband's affairs. "I think my husband had a mental illness. If he'd been a woman, it would have been nymphomania, but I don't know what that sickness is called when a man has it. My husband was a French professor, but his obsession was young women. He was a very good French professor I'm sure, but he held his position mainly in order to feed his obsession. Every school year he was presented with a bevy of new female students who were away from their homes and lonely. Being the comforting professor was the perfect occupation for a man with a fixation such as his."

"I understand," Martin said sympathetically. "However, that doesn't help me to solve the mystery of who killed your husband, because from what you say it might conceivably have been any of his students, including any that once were his students but aren't any longer."

"I'm afraid that's the situation, Inspector Martin."

"I thank you for your frankness, Mrs. Jolicoeur. I hope to be able to contact you again if I have any more questions, or better yet, to advise you that I've arrested the culprit."

"Good luck to you, Inspector."

CHAPTER SIX

Henri Casanova was beginning to show the effects of the tribulations he encountered by being a mob boss. He was aware that his occupation was dangerous, but he contented himself with the thought that it was more dangerous for those who opposed him. Nevertheless, the stress of the job and the measures he took to relieve it had had a deleterious effect on his health. His skin was sallow, probably from his habitual smoking. His thinning gray hair was sparse and matted even when it was newly washed. His deeply lined face with its perpetual five o'clock shadow gave him a sinister expression. His body had gone flabby, but his memory refused to recognize that fact. He still strode around in a pugnacious fashion, wore expensive suits, and spoke in a croaky voice reminiscent of an actor in a gangster movie. Anyone could have told him that he resembled a stereotype of a Mafioso, but no one would dare.

What Henri Casanova had that made him so successful wasn't visible to the naked eye. He had managed to live through half a century of illegal experiences that had played themselves out in his psychopathic, conscienceless mind, and had resulted in the creation of the ultimate criminal. In other words he not only looked the part, but his personality was perfectly suited to the role. In a world that was built on taking advantage of the weak, Casanova was an opportunist without parallel. Even the other bosses in the syndicate, mostly younger men now, gave him a wide berth as long as he stayed in his territory and abided by the decisions of the council. His younger cohorts would have preferred to see him dead, along with the rest of the criminal dinosaurs that had preceded him, but they recognized clearly that the old snake was still venomous, so they had resolved to be patient rather than risk any incursions into his territory. As the syndicate's boss in Provence, Henri had total control over organized crime on the Côte d'Azur. He ruled his minions with an iron hand and demanded absolute obedience from his underlings.

Henri Casanova had only a couple of rules that his men were expected to follow. One was familial in nature, and required that his criminal soldiers had to be from Corsican families that were known to him. In this way, if he were crossed, he could wreak vengeance on the members of the sinner's family. This tactic helped keep the troops in line, both in Provence and Corsica as well. Another of Casanova's requirements for gang membership was absolute loyalty. If caught, his men were never to cooperate with the police or give testimony against their fellow conspirators.

Henri's nature was to be suspicious of everyone, starting with those closest to him. He was ever watchful of character flaws in his gang members. Disobedience was not tolerated. Ambition was a trait that he watched especially closely. So when it got back to him, as everything always did, that one of his men had performed an unsanctioned offing, Henri was furious, but he had learned long ago to contain his fury until he was ready to dispense his version of justice.

Henri Casanova was conducting an investigation that was similar to Inspector Martin's. Both men were looking for the same murderer, but the sentence for being found guilty wasn't at all the same. France had forsaken capital punishment many years before, and had recently amended its constitution to specifically prohibit the death penalty. But Casanova's unwritten constitution had no such clause. In Casanova's version of justice the ultimate penalty could be exacted for any number of crimes, and there was no need for a jury trial. If convicted by the one-magistrate Corsican judging system, the guilty party's sentence was carried out quickly but not always painlessly. The civil court was the justice system of choice for the innocent amateur or the guilty professional criminal, but for Casanova's men there was no choice, and they all knew it. They were not safe even in a government penal institution, so the onus was clearly on the Mafiosi to stay in the good graces of Henri Casanova.

When it got around that Casanova was interested in finding out who had knocked off the French professor, the boys clammed up. Didier Albertini, the culprit, developed a particularly severe case of lockjaw. He may not have been a genius but he realized that if word got out that he was the one who had bumped off the professor, he could be a goner. He had felt from the moment he had received the go-ahead to make the hit that the motivation was jealousy on the part of Mondragon. He doubted that Casanova had sanctioned the killing, but he performed his part anyway, just in case the order had come from higher up than Mondragon. If the syndicate wanted him to obey his superior without question, then he would do so. He counted on using the hierarchy of command as his excuse, should Casanova ever question him about the killing. The photo of Kate Evans tied to the bed was to be his ace card with Mondragon should he dare to try to place the responsibility for the murder on him alone.

Pierre Mondragon was not at all concerned about being connected to the murder, as he wasn't the one who pulled the trigger. He was sufficiently self-confident to think that he could justify himself to Casanova, in the unlikely event that he should be taken to task over the matter. Anyway, what the hell difference did it make to Casanova if a professor got himself knocked off? Pierre honestly thought that the clever way he had removed a rival would have impressed Henri. After all, Casanova would have done the same thing himself if he were interested in a woman. In fact, Pierre would have bet that Henri had done such things in his own past, so he would understand the convenience and finality of getting rid of a rival quickly and permanently. In the unlikely event that the police questioned him as a suspect, he could always give Didier Albertini up.

He hadn't chosen Didier to be his right hand man. He had been assigned to him, and Pierre had never liked him

very much. He felt he was too ambitious for his own good.
Didier played the part of a stupid hood very well, and few
thought of him as clever, but he was not as dumb as Pierre
and Henri thought. Didier was well connected, too. In the
Corsican mafia, the Albertini clan was second only to the
Casanovas. Over the centuries the two families had honed a
certain partnership that had cut down on the tribal feuding
and brought prosperity to both clans. The birth records of
the island showed that the two most popular Corsican
surnames were Casanova and Albertini. Mondragon had no
blood connection to these families, and he underrated their
importance to his future. Didier had the benefit of the
unspoken loyalty of family, a never-to-be undervalued
support factor for a Corsican mafioso.

Didier considered it his job to watch Pierre's back. His
mentoring process was part of the initiation ceremony that he
had to go through to move up in the gang's fraternity. It was
his clever contribution to the process to take surreptitious
photos of his mentor, which he would show to the leader of
his crime family if he were asked about the progress of his
internship. Unknown to Pierre, Didier had taken a number
of photographs of the American woman in the company of
his boss and tutor. His purpose in secretly taking shots of
Pierre in action was two-fold: first to refresh his own
memory, and secondly, to illustrate the highlights of his
training for his paranoid big boss. Didier subscribed to the
adage that a picture was worth a thousand words. The new
miniature camera technology made taking secret photos
much easier, and the suspicious mob boss loved to see the
results of Albertini's spying sprees, particularly when they
involved Mondragon.

Once Pierre got Kate comfortably settled in his car, he sped
out of Marseilles in a northeasterly direction along the road
toward Aix-en-Provence. He chose this route mainly because
it was on the way to Cannes and Nice. His plan was to make
a fast circuit in the car, during which he would point out the

majesty of the avenues and the loveliness of the fountains and squares without having to leave the car. He assumed that an American girl would prefer to see Cannes, with its film festival reputation, rather than the more historic sites in Aix or in Avignon. But Kate wasn't an ordinary American tourist – she was deeply interested in the history of Provence. Before long Pierre wished he had paid more attention to his history classes in school. He only recalled enough to put on a brief and shallow presentation of the place of Aix in French history.

He explained to Kate how the Roman general Marius had defeated the barbarian Teutons at the end of the second century, and how in memory of that battle many Provençal parents still named their sons Marius. The gory details appealed to Pierre more than the political results, and so he dwelled on how 100,000 Teutons had been slain, and how the Barbarian warriors had killed themselves after strangling their children rather than allowing them to be captured by the Romans. Kate reminded him of the importance of that victory to France, as their future was welded to Gallic Rome from that time on. She pointed out to Pierre that the event had the effect of making French a Romance language with its origins in Latin, which wouldn't have been the case had the Romans been defeated. Pierre received her input sullenly, as he didn't like females contributing to his knowledge base.

He continued with his limited recitation concerning Good King René, the most famous of the citizens of Aix. Pierre couldn't have known, nor had he made any effort to find out, that during her studies Kate had become very fond of Good King René. She knew a good deal more about René than Pierre did, and that created an unpleasant situation for him. Kate was innocently unaware that her rendition of the Good King's talents and reputation would be taken as an assault on the Mondragon family jewels.

When Kate recounted some of the other achievements of Good King René, including his gift for musical composition, the painting of illuminations, and verse writing, she noticed that Pierre's expression had darkened. Kate had seen this reaction on the part of males before. Misogynists of both the overt and covert variety often sulked when confronted with a female in possession of knowledge greater than their own. The syndrome is widespread in academia, and pervades the atmosphere of the student body and the members of the faculty. Kate decided to do what she always did, which was to ignore the males who felt threatened by an intelligent woman, but being alone in a car with one of them certainly limited her options.

"Don't be such a pill, Pierre," Kate said, still believing that he was a bona fide tour guide and should therefore be interested in learning more about the history of the area about which he was informing tourists. "Scholarship is my area of expertise. You needn't feel threatened by that."

"Believe me, I'm not threatened by you," Pierre said, inwardly thinking that it was the other way round, and that Kate was the one in jeopardy. "What else do you think I should know about Good King René?"

"Well, for instance, did you know that he was married when he was twelve years old?" Kate asked him. When she got no response, she shrugged and kept going. "He was happily married to Isabelle of Lorraine for thirty-three years, and they had a daughter, Margaret, who married Henry VI of England."

"Well that was nice for him," Pierre said sardonically. "Are there any other domestic tidbits you'd like to add?"

"Only that a couple of years after Isabelle's death he married Jeanne of Laval, who was twenty-one at the time. Apparently this was a very happy marriage, and she was just as popular as her older husband."

"Obviously René had a taste for young women," Pierre said, with a suggestive sneer. "It seems that only good things happened to René, is that why they refer to him as Good?"

"Not at all," Kate replied. "During his life René lost his son and two grandsons. Besides that, he was criticized for imposing heavy taxes and having weak monetary policies.

The poor quality coinage that he struck was referred to as *parpaillots*, which meant *counterfeit*, and was an offensive term the Catholics used for Protestants."

"Do you think the casual tourist is going to remember or care about Good King René? I think they would be more interested if he'd been Bad King René. People are cynical and more attracted by evil celebrities like Ivan the Terrible, or Vlad the Impaler, than good ones like René."

By this time Mondragon's blood was boiling, but Kate paid no attention. She was too busy explaining the history of Provence.

Inspector René Martin decided to go over to the hotel where Professor Jolicoeur was a registered guest. He wanted to go through the dead man's things to see if he could find any clues that might help him find the killer. He dispatched his assistant, Maurice Benamou, to the police station where he was to do a background check on the professor and any of the male students in the present class, as well as any that had been his students in the past five years.

Inspector Martin thought of Benamou as his ferret. He used him to dig into the histories of criminals, suspects, and interested parties. The inspector didn't enjoy that part of the job anyway, and he was only too glad to pass along the detail work. For his part Benamou was not very interested in the process of gathering evidence, conducting interrogations, and interfacing with prosecutors, so their partnership was good for both of them.

The inspector sought out the manager of the hotel and advised him that his guest, Professor Leslie Jolicoeur, had been murdered in another hotel. He requested his permission to enter the dead man's room to search for clues, and it was duly granted. The house detective accompanied Martin to the dead man's room. The detective knocked on the door, and expecting no response, he inserted a passkey into the lock.

"Who's there?" came a confident female voice.

"It's hotel security," the detective said. "May we speak to you about a private matter?"

The door was opened a crack, and a pair of lovely green eyes peeked out and blinked at the two men. Inspector Martin pushed his identification card and badge through the opening. In a few seconds the chain was removed and the door swung open to admit the men, but the inspector barred the hotel employee from entering.

"Thank you very much," René Martin said to the house detective. "I can take it from here."

"Very well then," the disappointed security detective answered, for it was obvious that he had hoped to be privy to Martin's questioning of the beautiful woman. "You know the hotel must have the name and credit card information for all the occupants of its rooms."

"I realize that," the inspector replied. "I'll see that it's taken care of later, but for now the nature of my inquiries must remain private."

The inspector stepped into Jolicoeur's room and shut the door behind him, leaving the other man outside in the hall. Now he could see the whole person who had opened the door for him. She was a remarkably lovely young woman of the much-idolized California beauty queen type. Martin had tried all his life to judge the appeal of women by taking into consideration their inner characters, not just their physical attributes. But that was difficult in this case, just as it's hard to think of a thoroughbred racehorse in the same way as a workhorse. His snap opinion was that although this purebred young woman had class and breeding, she might not be able to go the distance.

"Mademoiselle, may I know your name?" the inspector inquired. "May I also ask what you're doing in Professor Jolicoeur's room?"

"My name is Tiffany Chance, and I'm sharing this room with Professor Jolicoeur," she replied self-righteously. "Is there something wrong with that? And do you know where the Professor is?"

"What is your relationship to the Professor, may I ask?" said Martin, ignoring the judgmental issue and attempting to assess in advance what her response would be when he told her about the killing.

"We were lovers," she said, without the tiniest element of shame. "Now, would you please tell me where he is?"

"I'm sorry to have to tell you that he's dead," Martin said in a subdued and respectful fashion.

"Dead?" she repeated, as she continued packing.

"I can assure you he is. He was murdered yesterday, and I'd like to ask you a few questions about it."

"Murdered? My God, who would do such a thing?"

"That's what I'm trying to determine," Martin replied. "When did you last see him, Miss Chance?"

"The night before last. We had dinner alone together on the Canebière, then we came back here and spent the night together," the girl said. "The next day he gave his speech at the university. After it was over he went someplace with his associates, and I went out with a few friends. That was the last time I saw him. He never came back to the hotel."

"Can you tell me who these associates of his were?"

"I only saw two of them. One was a graduate student in our program. I think her name is Evans. The other was a guy I never saw before."

"Can you describe the man?"

"Medium height, olive skin, dark hair. He didn't look like a scholar. He looked more like a dressed up fishmonger from the port. That's all I remember about him."

"Any idea where they went after the lecture?"

"Out for a drink, I guess," Tiffany replied. "I never ask a guy where he's going. They don't like to have to report to a woman. But I did expect him to return to the hotel that night. I still can't believe he's dead."

"I'm sorry for your loss," Inspector Martin said. "You can rest assured that I'll do everything in my power to catch the murderer. Will you remain in Marseilles, Miss Chance?"

"I don't know," she replied. "I'll have to see how I can finish my course now that the professor is gone."

René didn't have any more questions for Miss Chance. What she had told him had gelled with what he had learned from Kate Evans. Tiffany's description of the dark man fit Pierre Mondragon, but Kate had been positive that he was not the masked killer. The opportunity to conect Mondragon with the murder would have to wait until evidence became available from another source. He would get back to Kate about this piece of the puzzle. As for Tiffany Chance, she could go on her merry way. It was obvious that she had no special fondness for the dead professor, or she would have stopped packing when she received the news of his death. In fact, her total self-absorption was revealed clearly when her concerns about her schoolwork took precedence over the news he had just given her.

"Miss Chance, I'm assuming you've finished packing your things and that every article left in this room belonged to the professor," the inspector said. "Please check with the clerk at the check-out desk when you leave. They'll want to know that the room is empty. I'll pack up the professor's things and see to it that they're returned to his wife."

"His wife? I didn't know he had a wife," Tiffany said. "He was a rogue, but nobody knew he was married."

With that Tiffany left the room lugging her suitcase, an activity to which she was unaccustomed as she usually had a male friend to carry it for her.

CHAPTER SEVEN

Pierre and Kate arrived in Cannes. The International Film Festival had come and gone for the year, and most of the glitz with it. Pierre had collections of graft to make for Henri Casanova, and he wanted to get them over with so he could concentrate on having his way with Kate. He drove straight to the Hotel Le Suquet, which sits atop a hill overlooking the old port. His intention was to park Kate there until he'd finished making his rounds. He pulled up in front of the elegant old hotel and stopped.

"Kate, we'll be staying here for the night," said Pierre in a tone that left no doubt that they would be spending the night together. "In the morning we'll see the beaches, the Palais des Festivals, and then we'll move on to Nice and Monte Carlo. If you're good to me we can go to the casino tomorrow night. You go in and register, and I'll have the bellboy bring up the luggage. In the meantime I'll take care of the business that brought me to Cannes. I'll be back in time for dinner. You can have a bath if you wish, and get fixed up to eat where the movie stars dine, if there are any here at this time of year."

Pierre didn't wait for her reply. He hopped out of the car and collared the doorman to explain what he wanted done. The man removed the luggage from the trunk while Kate got out of the car. Pierre got back into the car and took off. The throaty sound of the BMW's engine was still in her ears as Kate approached the registration desk.

"Good evening Madame," the reservation clerk said. "How long will you be staying with us?"

"Just tonight," Kate replied. "I'd like two rooms that don't adjoin, please. My friend, Pierre Mondragon, will be coming in later. The bellboy can put one bag in each room."

"Very well, Mademoiselle," the clerk said, trying not to show his surprise about her request for separate rooms.

Mondragon was well known to the staff, as Pierre often frequented the hotel. He was usually accompanied by a series of different foreign ladies, but this was the first time in the clerk's experience that he'd be staying in separate rooms. Kate was determined not to have obligatory sex with Pierre, and she hoped the room arrangements would make that clear to him without her having to turn him down flat. She hoped that she hadn't misled him into thinking she was interested in him in a physical way. She reasoned that he needed to make the business trip to the towns they were visiting anyway, so merely having her tag along shouldn't be a commitment on her part to have sex with him. She was certainly willing to go Dutch on the expenses, as she had been planning to visit the same places without him.

Kate decided to follow Pierre's suggestion and take a nice hot bath while she was awaiting his return. She intended to read one of the books that Leslie Jolicoeur had brought her from Paris. He had written it on the topic of Provençal, the language of the troubadours, which preceded modern French. It had been the professor's PhD thesis, and it was close to his heart. He wanted to show Kate how he had handled the question of the effect of one language on another. When she opened the book, Kate saw some small dots of bloodstains on the pages. Her mind was once again forced back to the scene in her hotel room. She could still see the professor slumped over, with his dark, thick blood oozing out over the contents of the desk.

She had only read a few pages of the book when it occurred to her that she should finish bathing so that she would be dressed when Pierre returned. It would be difficult enough to fight off his advances without trying to do it naked. She toweled herself off, managing to be fully dressed and ready to go before he showed up. When he knocked on her door, she opened it and stepped out into the hall.

"I'm ready to go," she said, catching Pierre by surprise and closing the door behind her. "I took your advice," she added. "I bathed and got ready for dinner as you suggested."

"Let's go then," he said, all other options having been removed. "I've picked out a place that serves the best rock lobster in Provence."

The ill-matched couple walked in the old part of Cannes. The scale of things was considerably smaller than in the port of Marseilles, but the character and period of the buildings were similar. Kate knew that the intrinsic charm and flavor of Mediterranean France had attracted famous American and British writers to settle there, and she could understand why Laurence Durrell, Graham Greene, F. Scott Fitzgerald and H. G. Wells had taken villas in Provence. The area had enchanted writers from the troubadours in the tenth and eleventh centuries, to the masters of the succeeding centuries such as Petrarch, Mistral, Zola, and Pagnol. Most of these authors' works were unknown to Pierre Mondragon, so Kate thought it best to lead the conversation around to things that might be of more interest to her tour guide. She had found that when chitchat declined because of the disinterest of one partner, it was best if the other partner changed the subject to focus on the issues closest to the heart of her companion, so Kate launched into the topic of Pierre's life, hoping to spark a dialogue.

They had arrived at the restaurant, been seated, and ordered their dinner according to Pierre's recommendations.

"How did someone with the name Mondragon ever get to Corsica?" Kate asked. "It's not a Corsican name, is it?"

"My family had no interest whatsoever in coats of arms, family trees, and genealogies," Pierre snapped. "They were too consumed by the daily problems of scratching out a living in the mountains of Corsica to be concerned with that sort of nonsense."

"Do you think having pride in one's family name is sheer nonsense?" Kate asked.

"Yes, I do," Pierre replied, "but I recognize that some people take it very seriously."

"A name says a lot about a person," Kate said, realizing that she seemed to have touched a nerve with him. "A person with a knowledge of languages can usually tell what a man's ethnic background is, and his probable religion, and occasionally what diseases he may be susceptible to."

"I can agree that we can tell some people's nationality and religion from their name," Pierre replied, "but predicting what illness they can get seems ridiculous to me."

"If you're a black man living in Africa, for example, the chances are high that you have sickle cell anemia."

"All right, so what are you likely to get that goes along with your name?"

"My name is Welsh," Kate recounted, "and in that part of the British Isles, we have the greatest susceptibility to something called Dupuytren's disease."

"What's that?" Pierre asked, hoping it wasn't a venereal disease that he hadn't heard of.

"It's a genetic condition that causes the fingers to curl because the tendons keep getting progressively tighter," Kate said. "My dad has it but they released his fingers surgically. He calls it the Viking's revenge because they've traced the gene back to the time when the Scandinavian countries raped and pillaged the British Isles."

"That's actually very interesting," Pierre replied, before he answered his cell phone, which had started buzzing in his pocket. "Excuse me, I have to take this call. It's business."

"Please. Go right ahead."

"Mondragon here," he said, trying to sound important and businesslike.

"Where are you?" came Casanova's voice.

"I'm in Cannes making my collection rounds," Pierre replied, hoping that it would satisfy his boss. "Tomorrow I'll collect in Nice."

"No you won't," Casanova said. "I want you back here at once. Something's come up."

"Can't it wait till tomorrow?" Pierre asked.

"No, I want you here now," Casanova said impatiently.

"Very well then," Pierre said, as his plans for spending the night with Kate vanished. "I'll start back in one hour, as soon as I've finished my dinner."

"No, you'll have to eat later and do the Nice run another day." Henri Casanova was aware that Pierre had a woman with him. He always knew these things. Besides, young Albertini had already told him all about Kate Evans.

"All right, I'll start back at once," Pierre sighed.

"You do that," Casanova replied, getting pleasure out of disrupting his inferior's plans.

"I'm afraid I've got to go back to Marseilles right now," Pierre told Kate, "My boss is on the warpath. I don't know why, but when he's in this mood it's no use arguing."

Kate was not in the least bit disappointed. She had had a lovely day of sightseeing and a great dinner, and best of all now she wouldn't have to fight her escort off. She couldn't imagine why a tour guide's boss needed to see his employee immediately and at night, but in this case she was glad that he had the power to summon Pierre. They decided to skip dessert, and after they got back into his car they returned to the hotel to pick up their luggage and cancel their stay. When they were back in the car and on their way to Marseilles, she began telling Pierre about the Occitanian dialects that had evolved from Vulgar Latin and developed into langue d'oïl in the north of France, and langue d'oc in the south of France, which would eventually form the basis for modern French. She could have gone on for an hour, thanks to what she had learned from her dead mentor, Leslie Jolicoeur.

She noticed that Pierre was distracted by his own thoughts, and wasn't paying much attention to what she was saying, so she spared him the rest of the lecture. For his part, Pierre was thinking that an intellectual woman like Kate was sometimes interesting to talk to, but he was afraid that she might turn out to be all talk and no action. He was glad when she finally shut up.

Once in Marseilles, Pierre drove directly to Kate's hotel and let her out of the car with a cursory formal good night and an unwanted promise to call her the next day. She watched him hurry off to see his boss. The receptionist had given Kate a different room, correctly assuming that she wouldn't want to stay in the same room in which her friend had been murdered. There was really no choice anyway, as the police had sealed the old room in order to complete their crime scene investigation. Kate went to the desk to get the key to the new room. The desk clerk recognized her and gave her the key along with a number of telephone messages.

Kate took the elevator up to the fourth floor and found her new room. When she opened the door she discovered that her things had already been moved there. They had also provided a bouquet of fresh flowers with a note from the hotel manager stating that he hoped she'd find the room to her liking, and apologizing in advance for any inconvenience the move entailed. After a quick look around, Kate sat on the bed and began to look at the messages. One was a routine request from her mother, asking her to call home to let them know how her trip was going.

She realized that she hadn't told her parents anything about the murder, because they would have insisted that she get on the first plane and return home. Kate knew that if she did that, she might have to give up on her current thesis and start all over again, this time with an unknown professor. She felt she had gone too far to start again. Since she had an approved thesis subject from her deceased faculty advisor who was the only language expert in the department, the university would be bound to allow her to finish her degree under the guidance of some other professor. No, she decided, she would say nothing to her folks about the murder, and continue to pursue her degree by completing her thesis.

The second message was from Inspector Martin, who was asking her to call him to arrange a meeting, as he had some additional questions to ask her concerning the death of her professor. She had nothing to hide, so she wasn't worried about meeting the handsome police detective again, and she resolved to call him early the next morning. She couldn't help wondering how his investigation was going, and if he would soon arrest the killer. She had no idea what more she could add to what she had already said, but as a courtesy she would grant him another chance to ask her for a date, which was what she hoped he would do.

The third message was a little more mysterious. It was from a man called Henri Casanova, who claimed to be Pierre Mondragon's boss. It had been hand delivered to the desk clerk, and was written in old-fashioned script with a flowery style. The message was simply that he wanted to see her about a delicate matter. He was inviting her to lunch with him at his villa, and informing her that he would have his chauffeur pick her up at noon. Kate had the feeling that this Casanova, unlike his namesake, was not interested in affairs of the heart. She wondered how this stranger was able to command Pierre so easily, and why he now thought he could command her as well. She decided to ignore the man and simply not call him.

The fourth message was from Tiffany Chance. It stated that even though they hardly knew each other, they were Americans attending the same university, and since they were both strangers in Marseilles and both knew Professor Jolicoeur, it might be nice if they met and got acquainted. Tiffany's message said she would call Kate the next day to arrange a meeting.

Pierre's BMW convertible screeched to a halt outside Henri Casanova's sprawling villa. Trying to appear as dutiful as possible, he rang the bell and waited. A minute later Carlo Santori, Casanova's large and trusted long-term Corsican bodyguard, opened the heavy wooden door. No words were exchanged when Carlo stood aside so Pierre could enter. He didn't have to be told where he would find the boss. Henri was always in his office at his huge black desk. None of his henchmen knew what Henri found to do at his desk all day every day, and they often joked about it.

"I came as quickly as I could, Boss," Pierre said, trying to gauge Henri's mood. "The traffic is getting heavier all the time. Mostly drunken tourists and wannabe big shots on the coastal road these nights."

Pierre tried his best to read Henri Casanova's mind from the expression on his face. This was of no use, as Henri's face revealed nothing of what he thought. He had spent his life hiding what was truly on his mind, and he never gave any facial hints that would tip a person off as to whether he was to be shot or patted on the back. A better way to read the boss's disposition was to see if there was a chair in front of the desk. If there was a chair, you might be asked to sit down, if there was no chair, a visitor could tell he was going to be leaving soon, one way or the other. There was no chair when Pierre arrived.

"You'd have been here sooner if you hadn't dropped the woman off at her hotel first," Henri said, making it clear to him that he knew his every move. "I would have liked to meet this woman that you think is worth killing for. Don't you know I'm the one who authorizes the hits around here?"

"I didn't kill that guy in her room."

"No, but you ordered Didier to do it," Henri said, with venom spewing from his lips. "No one dies on the Côte d'Azur without my permission. You should know that. Do you deny that you told Albertini to whack that professor? And are you telling me that it wasn't done so that you could have her yourself without a rival?"

"No, I don't deny it, but it was not for business reasons, so I didn't think you'd care," Pierre stammered, hoping his logic would be accepted. "Anyway, we got away with it, so what's the difference – one hit more or less."

"The difference, Mr. Mondragon, is that *I'm* the one who orders the hits, not *you*. As for getting away with it," Casanova paused for effect, "when it comes to murder, there's always a backlash. You kill someone, and his brother or his father, they kill you back. The police never forget a murder, either. They're still looking for Jack the Ripper. I like my murdering to be done according to my rules, not because of some petty jealousy over a woman you just met. The gendarmes get even more suspicious of us when a civilian is assassinated in the Corsican style. They drool at the chance to get famous by hanging the crime on us. You should know this. How do I know that if you're implicated you won't roll over on the rest of us? I'm told that Inspector Martin is handling the case. He's young and hasn't yet tasted the flavor of our graft money that's so irresistible to cops. He's working on the Luciani business in the basilica too, and if he can connect the two killings to us he can make himself a hero, and take us all down in a frenzy of prejudicial media publicity."

"They can't connect those two deaths," Pierre protested.

"They better not," Casanova said malevolently. He had already decided what the penalty for Pierre's unsanctioned hit should be. "I'm suspending you for six months. Effective immediately. Albertini will take over your book."

"No! Boss, I've killed many men for you. It's not fair to penalize me for one little indiscretion," Pierre whined.

"I know it may seem harsh to you, but in our thing we have to obey the orders of the one in command, just like it's done in the military ranks."

Henri spoke in a paternal fashion intended to encourage the young Turk to think that he would be restored to his position after he had served his time. "And that includes not doing hits that haven't been ordered."

The faithful Carlo Santori had mysteriously reappeared and Pierre, face flushed with hurt and anger, was silently escorted out. The truth was that Henri liked Pierre because he had chutzpah, but like all over-confident gangsters, they had to be reined in sometimes for the organization's sake. The ever-suspicious Casanova had also decided to verify Pierre's assertion that the two hits couldn't be connected. Behind all his doubts about Pierre was Henri's distrust of his loyalty. Casanova just couldn't believe that a man with the name Mondragon was a true Corsican. He decided to see for himself, and as a start, he made a mental note to speak with the Evans woman in the morning.

The next day Kate went down to the dining room to have breakfast. The hotel personnel were beginning to know her, and she felt at home. The French servers liked her because she spoke their language well, and didn't try, as the usual American tourists did, to impress the serving staff with the few words of French that they knew. As she waited for her Croque Monsieur and coffee to arrive, Kate thought about how she'd handle her messages, and decided that she would make the obligatory call to her mother first. It would be easiest to handle that call, as her mother would be quickly assuaged by a modest apology for not having called sooner, and she would be happy to know that things were going well with her daughter. It was also unlikely that she would have heard about the death of Kate's professor and mentor.

Calls to the Inspector and to Tiffany were merely for the purpose of making appointments, which wouldn't take long. She decided to ignore the call from Henri Casanova, as she felt she had nothing to say to him, and she didn't understand what he could possibly want from her. Besides, she wanted to disassociate herself from Pierre Mondragon before his unwanted attentions became unpleasant.

Without some prior knowledge of Henri Casanova's history, Kate couldn't have foreseen the strength of the man's will. A sample of his tenacity was demonstrated when she received a telephone call from him the minute after she had finished her breakfast and returned to her room. She had just taken a seat at the desk in her hotel room, and had been thinking about Leslie Jolicoeur's cowardly assassination that had happened while he had been seated at just such a desk. The outgoing calls she wished to make had to be delayed because of Casanova's unsolicited incoming call.

"Hello, Miss Evans?" came Henri Casanova's voice.

"Yes. Who's this?" Kate asked.

"My name is Henri Casanova," the husky voice said in a distinctly Corsican accent. "I'm the employer of Pierre Mondragon, with whom I believe you are acquainted. I've been trying to reach you. Didn't you get my message?" he asked, trying to be patient in spite of her having ignored him.

"Yes, but I hadn't gotten around to answering yet," Kate said. "What is it that you want from me?"

"I want to invite you to lunch," Henri said, anxious to placate her irritation, and also attempting to be mysterious, as he had found curiosity to be a powerful tool in enlisting interest. "I understand that you have skills that might suit a temporary position that I'm trying to fill at the moment. Please allow me to give you a nice lunch and we'll talk about it. I feel it's always preferable to meet with people face-to-face when I'm discussing important matters."

"I'm flattered that Pierre has said nice things about me," Kate replied. She did wonder what in fact he had told his boss about her, but since she could see no reason to turn down an opportunity to make some badly needed extra cash, she agreed to meet him. "Very well, I guess I have nothing to lose. When did you want to see me?"

"In exactly three hours my car will call for you at your hotel," Henri said, in his usual authoritative manner, and he abruptly hung up without waiting for Kate's acquiescence.

Kate decided to put off calling her mother because it was only five a.m. at home in the U.S. She called Inspector Martin instead. After being connected and identified, Martin asked if he could come over to the hotel immediately to question her further about the murder she had witnessed. Kate decided it must be important if the detective insisted on seeing her urgently, so she agreed to meet him.

While she was in the phoning mode, Kate returned Tiffany Chance's call.

"Tiffany, this is Kate Evans returning your call."

"Oh yes, Kate, thanks for calling back," Tiffany said in English, as though she were glad to be speaking her native language again. "As you know, we're in different years of the same program at the university. I'm sorry we never got to meet socially before, but I thought perhaps now might be a good time to rectify that. How about we get together for a drink tonight?"

"That would be nice," Kate said insincerely, as she was sure she had little in common with Tiffany Chance. "I've got a busy day, so let's make it after dinner."

"Perfect," said Tiffany, oblivious to Kate's insincerity. "Shall we say nine o'clock?"

"Your place or mine?"

"I could meet you in the lobby of your hotel at nine."

"I'll be there," Kate said, grateful not to have to run all over Marseilles to meet someone she didn't particularly like.

CHAPTER EIGHT

K ate found herself pacing nervously around the room as she waited for the inspector to show up. She recognized a certain mixture of feelings within herself that she identified as the kind of instinctive attraction that a woman feels for the occasional man that she randomly meets. Kate knew exactly what the feeling was, and what it meant. She had learned the most important lesson in inter-gender relations at an early age. In brief, it was that the female makes the decision about which male she will mate with. Whatever the mysterious reasons, whether genetic, physical, or sociological, a woman knows instantly which men she might mate with and which she would never couple with under any circumstances. In Kate's case the inspector was in the first category, and Mondragon in the second. Men in the first category didn't come into her life very often, and never to the degree that Inspector René Martin had.

The inspector walked up to the hotel desk clerk and inquired about Kate Evans' new room number. He knew that her room had been changed because the old one was still being treated as a crime scene by his police officers. He took the old rickety elevator up to the fourth floor and found the room number that he was looking for. He knocked.

"Who is it?" a voice called out.

"Miss Evans, it's Inspector Martin."

After peering through the peephole in the door, Kate confirmed that it was indeed the inspector. She opened the door to admit him.

"Come in, inspector," she said. "What can I do for you? Please have a seat."

"Thank you, Miss Evans," Martin said as he accepted her offer to sit down. "I'm afraid I still have some questions in regard to the murder of Professor Jolicoeur."

"Oh? I thought I'd told you everything the last time we spoke," Kate replied.

"I don't believe that you've told me everything yet. For instance, since you were in the basilica when the unfortunate Mr. Luciani was killed, and then you were in the hotel room when Mr. Jolicoeur was dispatched, I think it's only natural to ask you if you believe there's a connection between these two murders."

"I have no idea," Kate replied. "It never occurred to me that there might be a connection."

"Well, is it a customary thing in your life to be present at the assassinations of two individuals?"

"Hardly," Kate said, nodding. "And anyway, I don't know that I actually was present at the time of the killing in the cathedral. I just happened to notice a foot protruding from one of the confessionals, but I didn't know it belonged to a dead man, and I also didn't know how long he'd been there."

"So you never saw Mr. Luciani enter the booth?"

"No," Kate replied. "I never saw the dead man's face before or after he died. I only saw his foot sticking out of the booth at a peculiar angle."

"But you never called the police to come investigate, did you?" Martin asked, raising one of his eyebrows to indicate his incredulity at her indifference to the man's predicament.

"I didn't want to get involved. After all, I'm just a visitor in Marseilles," Kate protested, feeling annoyed by the implication that she didn't care about the welfare of another person. "Besides, I was distracted when I left the basilica."

"Distracted? Why were you distracted?" Martin asked, with more than casual interest.

"I was talking with a tour guide that I met inside the basilica, that's all."

"This tour guide, did you get his name?"

"His name is Pierre Mondragon," Kate said. She didn't think his name was relevant to anything, so she didn't feel guilty about revealing it to the inspector.

"Pierre Mondragon!" the inspector exclaimed, raising his voice. "Pierre Mondragon is no tour guide, unless you're touring the River Styx. He told you he was a tour guide?"

"A part-time tour guide, yes," Kate replied, wondering what the big deal was about that.

"I see," Inspector Martin said, omitting any additional commentary that would warn Kate that he had been pursuing Pierre for suspected homicides over a long period of time. "So how well do you know Mr. Mondragon?"

"I don't know that it's any of your business, but we're just friends. Is that a police matter?"

"No, it doesn't interest me who your friends are," René admitted, "unless you're helping them to commit crimes."

The inspector was secretly hurt, and felt that Kate was defending a false friend. He couldn't pursue the attraction he felt for Kate if she was mixed up with Mondragon and his crime family. She might be just a duped naïve foreign girl, or she could be an accomplice. She evidently doubted his statement that Mondragon wasn't a tour guide. He told himself that all he could do at this point was to keep his sentiments hidden until his investigation was over.

"I'm not helping anyone to commit crimes," Kate said adamantly, "unless having a meal with Pierre Mondragon is a crime."

"To your knowledge, did Mondragon know, or have any contact with Professor Jolicoeur before he was killed?" the inspector asked, figuring he would get more information if he backed off the accomplice insinuation.

"We three had coffee together in a café on Le Canebière the other night," Kate said. "As far as I know that's the only time they met."

"How did that go? Were they on friendly terms?"

"They had an argument, but nobody came to blows or anything like that," Kate said.

"What were they arguing about?"

"Well, the professor had just given his public lecture at the university. He had stated that all French-speaking people should adopt standardized Parisian French. He supported the position of the Alliance Française that the French language was being corrupted by the influx of people from other French-speaking areas such as Algeria and Corsica."

"Since Mondragon is Corsican, my guess is that didn't go over very well with him."

"No, Inspector, it didn't," Kate agreed, "but if you're suggesting that Pierre was the one who killed him, you're wrong. I would recognize Pierre's voice anywhere, and the man who tied me up wasn't Pierre. The murderer was taller and thinner than Pierre."

"What was Mondragon's position in the argument?"

"He said that language is a living thing, and as such it would keep on changing no matter who wanted it to remain standardized."

"Whose side were you on?"

"I didn't take sides. I just let it be known that I wanted to go back to my hotel."

"So you chose to leave with Professor Jolicoeur"

"Yes, as I mentioned before, Inspector, we had work to do," Kate replied. "I was a bit surprised by how easily Pierre gave up insisting that he take me. He must have believed that the professor and I did indeed have work to do."

"Or he had a different plan," the inspector suggested.

He resisted the opportunity to speculate on what Pierre's plan could have been. He was nearly convinced that Kate was completely innocent, and he was equally convinced that Mondragon had had something to do with the professor's untimely death, but proving it was another thing. In Martin's mind the Luciani killing in the basilica was clearly done by Mondragon. If he could convict him of that crime he could take him off the streets. And if he could prove him guilty of that, maybe he could persuade him to give up the perpetrator in the hotel killing, in return for a reduced sentence. He refocused his attention on Kate.

"When did you first notice Mondragon in the basilica, Miss Evans?" he asked. "Was he there all along, or did he come in after you arrived?"

"I really don't know, Inspector. He came up behind me, and I didn't notice him until he spoke to me. He could have been there before me, but I can't say for sure. I do know that we left at the same time, because we left together."

"All right, Miss Evans, I think those are all the questions I have for the time being."

The inspector left Kate's hotel room and went across the street to a coffee bar and ordered an espresso. He stood at the bar and wistfully looked across the street at the hotel entrance. He was thinking how sad it was that when he found this interesting girl, he couldn't ask her out because of official protocol. Martin had let his suspicions of Kate relax, and he was now willing to believe that she had nothing to do with the killings or the Corsican Mafia. As he was staring at the hotel, a long black limo pulled up in front. He was shocked when Kate Evans came out of the hotel and got into the limousine. Inspector René Martin knew the vehicle well, for it belonged to Henri Casanova, the leader of Corsican Mafia operations in Marseilles.

Kate sat in the padded black leather interior of the limousine, feeling guilty about being treated so specially. She reflected on the nature of a man who could own such a vehicle. Was he a show-off who had no conscience about the effect that a vehicle such as this had on ordinary people? Was he just an ostentatious egotist out to impress her with his wealth? That wouldn't work on her, she promised herself. How could a man who owned a tourist guide business, which is all she knew about Casanova's dealings, earn enough to merit a magnificent car like the one she was riding in? When the limo pulled into Casanova's private driveway, which led to the entrance of his palatial Mediterranean villa, the question of affording a limo became moot.

The chauffeur, who had remained silent until their arrival, now asked Kate to follow him. He mounted the flight of marble stairs that led to the impressive ironbound wooden door. He pushed the hand-sized doorbell, which was shaped like a woman's breast, and stood aside so she could pass when the door opened. Kate found that little bit of rococo ornamentation to be offensively ostentatious, and she felt that piece of nonsense didn't bode well for a woman about to discuss business with Mr. Casanova. Carlo Santori opened the door and invited her to follow him inside. She trotted along behind him, padding over the immaculately clean, cream-colored tile floor until they reached a double set of beige doors. Carlo opened a door to admit Kate, and then closed it after himself, leaving her alone in what used to be called a drawing room, but now served Henri Casanova as an over-sized office. He sat behind an enormous desk which dwarfed him, although he was not a tiny man by any means.

"Ah, Miss Evans, how good of you to come," Casanova said, in the oiliest version of his croaking Corsican French. "Please have a seat here," he said, indicating the chair which had been placed there, unlike the night before, when Pierre Mondragon had had to stand throughout his inquisition.

"Thank you, Mr. Casanova," Kate said politely. "You have a beautiful house," she added.

"Why, thank you my dear, but you haven't seen very much of it yet," Henri said, rising from his chair behind the desk with the intention of giving Kate a tour of the house and grounds. "Why don't we take a walk around and I'll show you some of the special features of my villa while we talk?"

"That would be very nice," Kate replied. "How could I refuse such a pleasant tour, especially one led by the owner of a tourist guide business?"

"Let me show you around inside the house first," Henri said, extending an arm so that she would take it and thereby establish a degree of familiarity. "The room we are in is the former drawing room. I have converted it into my office because I like the feeling of space, and I spend more time at my desk than anywhere else."

"I agree that it's nice to have space, but this room is large enough to be a condominium in New York City," Kate remarked, allowing herself to be led out of the room and back into the foyer. "That's a magnificent chandelier, Mr. Casanova."

"Yes, I agree. It's Italian and formerly hung in the Corsican Governor's house," Henri boasted. "This is the dining room," he said, as they entered another room. "The table can accommodate thirty people."

"Do you often have so many guests?"

"Only occasionally. I use this room mostly for business conferences. I operate my businesses from my home, you see. You'd be surprised how efficient that is. I never have to waste time traveling to get to work, and I don't have to maintain offices elsewhere."

Casanova opened the French doors, and he and Kate went out onto the terrace. The view of the Mediterranean was breathtaking. Casanova seemed in no hurry to get down to business, so Kate waited for him to bring up the subject. She wondered why a man as obviously wealthy as Henri Casanova would want to employ a young, inexperienced, foreign woman like her. As they proceeded down to the water's edge, Kate observed that there was a small marina where a number of speedboats were moored. There was also a fairly large boathouse. When she looked back at the house from the water she noticed what seemed to be a parking lot to the east of the house. In it were a sizeable number of cars, but Kate hadn't seen any other people except the chauffeur and the manservant, so who owned these cars and where were the owners?

Henri Casanova had been a rough man in his youth, but he was older now and had developed a considerable amount of surface savoir-faire, but below the smoothened exterior was the temperament of a wild Corsican mountain goat. He had learned that life was a continuum, and even in the criminal world one had to keep up with the changing times. The result of this dichotomy was that Henri Casanova could be charming in the old world European sense, and also as dangerous as a lion that has suddenly been awakened from its sleep. When the world moved into the information age, Casanova saw the potential it had for his crime syndicate. He was an early user of computerized telecommunications equipment, and he marched to the tune of a very different drummer – a digitized one – right from the beginning.

Henri had hired a couple of Corsican geeks and set them up in a secret location. He gave them all the latest equipment, and then offered them the task of becoming his intelligence service. His early talent identification system had found him the best brains on the island, and their tribal family heritage provided the moral turpitude to blend with the strong-arm methods of the Mafia. Over time people credited Casanova with having a brilliant, intuitive mind, but in reality it was the hacking and prying of his personal CIA that earned him the reputation of being a clairvoyant. At first Giovanni Rossi and Guido Mattei, Henri Casanova's resident telecommunications geniuses, tapped into the affairs of every friend and enemy of the Casanova crime family, but eventually they expanded into broader, white-collar crime activities. In fact, in the past year the income from secret electronic operations had exceeded all the other operations of Casanova's criminal gang. Best of all, none of the income was known to the other syndicate bosses.

As Kate and Henri sat on the terrace admiring the view, she would have been shocked if she had known how much Casanova already knew about her. To satisfy his paranoia, his two G-men (Guido and Giovanni), had tapped into the personal computers of his own gang members. He'd made a gift of a PC to each of his employees, which was nominally in the nature of a bonus for their good work. In reality the two G-men had given themselves access to the computers' contents in spite of the P.I.N. selected by the individuals.

This little feature enabled Henri to know everything about his gang members. He knew when they were using the internet, and when they were watching pornography. He could look at their personal data and the digital photos they had stored in their computers. In the case of Albertini, it was this last surreptitious peek that captivated Henri Casanova.

The photos that Didier had taken of Kate Evans when she was tied to the hotel bedpost were in his hard-drive, and unknown to him, Henri Casanova had access to anything on his employee's hard-drive. The photographs were stark, and revealed an interesting anomaly. Kate had, in an effort to gain acceptance as one of the sisters in her sorority, a tattoo on a private place on her body. True to her undergraduate major in English, Kate had the tattoo artist ink a quote from Dante's Inferno on her lower belly, just above the top of her hairline. This location ensured that her parents would never see it, but her parents didn't have Casanova's spying ability.

When two individuals stare at the same scenery, it is often amazing how different their thoughts can be. Here they were, Henri and Kate, sitting on his terrace looking out at the Mediterranean Sea, yet neither of them noticed the natural beauty of the seascape that lay stretched out before them. Instead, Henri was thinking of the photo of the tatoo for its arousal potential, and trying to make up his mind what Kate's fate would be. Would he have her killed, or would he hold her hostage while he dallied with her, or would he use her to find out about Pierre's loyalty to him? Before making up his mind, he decided to see if he could learn what she knew about his operations and Pierre Mondragon's part in them. He was afraid that Pierre, in his braggadocio style, might have spilled too much information about the Corsican Mafia. As for Kate, she was only thinking about when Mr. Casanova would get around to discussing the mysterious job offer he had wanted to see her about. He finally broached the subject, but in a round-about way.

"What has Pierre told you about his responsibilities in my business?" Henri asked, trying to shake the picture of the peculiar tattoo from his mind.

"Practically nothing at all," Kate replied truthfully. "He said he's a part-time tour guide, and that he also manages the collection of receipts from your various businesses on the Côte d'Azur."

"I see," said Henri, tempted to believe her, because he judged her to be too naïve to lie to him. "So your interest in Pierre is romantic?"

"No, not at all," Kate protested. "We've only met on a casual basis. I have no interest in Pierre as a lover, if that's what you're asking me."

"I'm not hinting at anything. I've had some difficulties with Pierre's loyalty. I'm trying to find out if he's a good employee or not. Do you have any opinion on that subject?"

"All I know is that twice now, when we were eating in restaurants, you called him," Kate said. "On those occasions he dropped everything and went immediately to see you."

"And what is your conclusion about that behavior?"

"Well, either he's very obedient, or he's afraid of you."

"What do you mean, he's afraid of me?" Henri asked.

"It was just a feeling I had," Kate responded. "Sort of as though he was afraid you might fire him, perhaps."

"That's all?"

"That's all I know, Mr. Casanova."

"What do you think Pierre's intentions toward you are?"

"I guess he's interested in me as a woman," Kate said, "but I can assure you, just between us, that I'm not at all interested in him, at least in that way."

"Good," Henri said, patting her hand in the manner of a maiden aunt who has just been relieved at the news that a favorite niece is still a virgin.

"In fact," Kate went on, "I was very glad that your calls came when they did, as I wasn't looking forward to fending Pierre off."

"You think he was going to try to have sex with you?"

"I certainly thought it was a possibility," Kate replied. "It's every woman's nightmare, having to turn a man down while trying not to damage his ego."

"I imagine that's a continuous problem for someone as beautiful as you are, Miss Evans," Henri said, in a flattering manner.

"You're very kind, Mr. Casanova, but you should meet my classmate if you wish to see someone truly beautiful."

"I'd like that, though I doubt someone more beautiful than you can exist. Perhaps I can hire you both."

"I'm meeting her tonight at my hotel at nine o'clock. You could come along accidentally on purpose if you like."

"Well, I think I'll do just that, and I thank you for the recommendation. I look forward to meeting your friend. But right now there's something else I want to ask you. Did you happen to see anyone suspicious at the basilica the day that man Luciani was shot? It was the same day you met Pierre, wasn't it?"

"Yes, it was the same day, but we didn't see anything out of the ordinary. It's a huge church, and many tourists were passing through at the time," Kate said. "I did observe that a foot was sticking out of one of the confessional booths, but I didn't think anything of it then. Later it occurred to me, after the news of the killing hit the media, that the foot might have belonged to the dead man."

"Did you report that to the police?"

"No, I didn't want to get involved. I'm a foreigner, after all, and I really didn't know anything. If I had told the police it would also have unnecessarily involved Pierre Mondragon, and I was sure he didn't have anything to do with the affair."

"What made you so sure he had nothing to do with it?"

"He was with me around the time it happened, and he was relaxed and natural. I'm sure that if he had just killed somebody I would have noticed something unusual about his behavior. He would have been sweating, and nervous, and worried, or something of that sort. But he wasn't. He was perfectly calm and chatty."

"That's good. I wouldn't have wanted an employee of mine to be involved in a police matter."

"Mr. Casanova," Kate ventured, changing the subject, "I wonder if you'd mind telling me about the job that you asked me to come here to discuss."

"I've been thinking about that, and I've decided to wait until tonight when I can also meet your friend," Henri said. "That way I shall only have to explain it once. I'll be at your hotel at nine o'clock."

As if by magic, Carlo Santori appeared.

"Please have the chauffeur drive Miss Evans back to her hotel," Henri said.

CHAPTER NINE

Inspector René Martin had, for the moment, no other life but his police work. He was young to have advanced to such a high rank within the gendarmerie, but the fact that he was still unmarried was creating questions in the minds of his superiors. His superintendent believed that a man of René's age should be married in order to have stability in his life. He was of the opinion that his young inspector couldn't possibly handle the challenges of the job unless he had a settled and mature sexual life. The superintendent's way of pressuring René was to frequently ask him questions about his love life. The continual probing was a source of irritation for the young inspector. Martin felt that his superior wasn't satisfied with his performance as a man because he wasn't married. Naturally he took the position that his personal life had nothing to do with his job performance, and was outside the purview of his boss.

The situation was an irritant that was affecting his mood the way an oncoming low-pressure front affects the weather, but other things that were bothering him even more than this. His usually cheerful behavior was clouded over by suspicion and worry about Kate Evans' association with Mondragon, and now with Henri Casanova as well. His main concern was that she might unknowingly be getting involved in something from which she couldn't be extricated. Not only was his investigatory curiosity piqued by her association with these known Mafia criminals, but his initially favorable judgment of Kate's character would be shaken if she were figuratively, or worse, actually in bed with these gangsters.

In an effort to prove his theory that the young American was innocently unaware of her involvement with criminals, he had been conducting a personal surveillance of her hotel.

On his own time, and without notifying his boss, he had begun to keep tabs on Kate's comings and goings. He also had other matters to resolve in connection with the murder of the professor. He was not too surprised, then, when he saw Tiffany Chance enter Kate's hotel, for he remembered her from his questioning session. But he was troubled when, a few minutes later, Henri Casanova alighted from his familiar limousine. He wondered if the Mafia boss had managed to recruit yet another good-looking American woman into one of his nefarious activities. He moved his position so he could watch Casanova without being seen.

The dapper Corsican went directly into the bar. He spotted Kate and Tiffany talking to each other as they sat at a corner table. He moved purposefully in their direction, and a few moments later he was sitting with the two women and chatting amicably. He ordered drinks and seemed to be very comfortable with his two foreign women. Unfortunately Inspector Martin could not make out what they were saying, but if he had been able to eavesdrop on their conversation he would have heard Henri Casanova describing a position that he was trying to fill in one of his companies.

"Years ago I acquired a tour bus company," Casanova was saying. "I grew the company by a process that you Americans like to call *vertical integration.* In other words, I acquired other tourist-related businesses and started a few new ones, finally putting them all together to form a large holding corporation that with its many entities is a leader in the tourist business," Henri told them proudly.

"That explains what Pierre Mondragon's job is," Kate interjected, relieved that at last she was evidently going to hear the details of the position that Henri had in mind for her.

"Yes," Henri said doubtfully, not at all sure what Pierre had told Kate, but certain that it exaggerated Mondragon's importance. "Well, as you know, there are many classes of travel, and likewise there are many classes of tourism. Some tourists are squired around by the busload, and shepherded by a tour guide with a microphone. High-class rich people don't go for that kind of treatment. They expect individual services provided by cultured, intelligent, English-speaking guides who also speak other languages."

"Oh, so you want us to be up-scale tour guides for your rich clients?" Tiffany blurted out.

"Yes, my dear, but more than that I want you to be tour *leaders*," Casanova responded.

Henri Casanova had for many years been taking his Mafia family into legitimate enterprises, and trying to use his influence with his peers to get them to follow his lead. He had discovered that the differences between operating a mob business and a legal one were slight. The attractive part of legitimacy, from Henri's perspective, was the vastly reduced chances of criminal conviction for operators of ordinary businesses. He had noticed that the sums involved in the swindles of the relatively few white-collar executives who were caught, were considerably greater than those of the thieves and gangsters convicted for operating in the much more dangerous Mafia mode. He was fond of the quote attributed to the notorious American bank robber Willy Sutton who, when asked by a reporter why he only robbed banks, replied with the now famous statement, "Because banks are where the money is."

"Rich people have the money to pay for things. As tour leaders you'd be expected to take them where they can spend it. I can help you with those choices."

"So the position you're offering us requires us to lead wealthy clients on private tours of Provence, is that right?" Kate asked.

"Exactly," Casanova confirmed.

"Not to be crass about it, but how would we be paid?" Tiffany asked.

"Good question," Henri said. "I try to pay all my people according to the value of the contributions they make to the organization. If you lead these clients to the places that I will list, you will be paid a 10% commission on all sales that are made."

"And what if these clients don't buy anything?" Kate asked. "Are we then working for nothing?"

"No, you will be earning the going hourly rate of pay for tour guides. The commission is in addition, a sort of bonus," Henri explained. "I need people of quality that can interface with our special clientele. I believe you two young women are of the type that can do very well in this kind of work."

"I see. And there are no other hidden requirements of the job?" Kate asked, a bit suspiciously.

"No. What you do or don't do is entirely up to you," Casanova said, fully understanding the implications of her question. "Believe me, I understand your concerns, but the clients have been pre-screened and informed that our tour leaders are to be treated with respect at all times. You must, of course, be knowledgeable about the history of the Midi, and the places of interest here."

"And what is the going rate of pay for tour guides?" Tiffany wanted to know.

"Don't concern yourselves about that. It's standardized within the industry. What is truly exceptional about this job opportunity is the earnings potential on the commission side of the ledger," Casanova bubbled. "I can already see that you'll be among my highest earners if you do as I say."

"You know that we're students in Paris," Kate reminded him. "We can't stay down here on the Riviera indefinitely. What about our studies?"

"What you decide to do about your studies is up to you," Henri replied. "I think you owe it to yourselves, however, to try my proposition. You may find that you prefer the real world to the academic one. After all, what good is a higher education if it doesn't provide you with a satisfactory living? Besides, now that your professor is gone, your program may be discontinued. I think you should consider my proposal, and let me know your decision tomorrow."

With that, Casanova rose, made his excuses, and left the young women to discuss his proposal.

"It's true what he said about Professor Jolicoeur, you know," Tiffany said. "The program might be discontinued, or at least postponed until next year while they look for a replacement for him."

"Yeah, we might be left high and dry for months," Kate agreed. "But how did he know our professor was dead?"

"How should I know?" Tiffany asked. "Didn't you tell him?"

"No. Maybe Pierre told him," Kate replied. "I guess it isn't important, anyway. What do you think we should do?"

"I'm thinking we should give it a try, at least."

"Then I'm willing to give it a shot too," Kate said. "I'll call him tomorrow morning and tell him we accept his offer. Then we'll see where it takes us. Deal?"

"Deal."

Inspector Martin decided to see if he could find out what the two American beauties had been talking to Henri Casanova about. He casually wandered into the bar after Casanova had gone and pretended to accidentally come across the women sitting there.

"Hello, ladies," he said. "I don't know if you remember me. I'm Inspector René Martin. We spoke about the dead professor."

"Of course I remember you," Kate replied, sounding a bit annoyed, but not for the reason that René supposed.

"I remember you too," Tiffany piped up. "If you're not busy, why don't you join us for a drink?"

"Thank you," the inspector said. "I'd like that. Please note that I'm off duty now," he said, with a pleasant smile. "I wouldn't want you to think I was tailing you."

"We'd be flattered if you were," Tiffany said enticingly. "You're the only man we know in this part of France, which makes you rather special, don't you think, Kate?"

The reason why Kate didn't want to meet René Martin at that moment was amply typified by Tiffany's relaxed, but flirtatious banter. Kate Evans' self-effacing nature had her convinced that if she and Tiffany were seen together, most men would be more attracted to Tiffany's California surfer type of beauty than to her reserved New England intellectual appearance. Since she was developing an interest in René Martin, she didn't want Tiffany working her physical wiles on him before she had an opportunity to see if the man's brainpower was all she hoped it would be.

"Sure," Kate replied, resigned to the fact that she would have to play out the unspoken rivalry role. "Have a seat and tell us how things are going in the detecting business."

"Suffice it to say," Martin answered, sitting down across from them, "that we're working on the case."

"So we're still persons of interest," Tiffany remarked, intending her observation to be a clever double entendre. "Nothing turns a woman off like disinterest, you know."

"I'd have to be visually impaired if I were disinterested in two such beautiful women as the ones sitting at this table," Martin said, playing along with Tiffany's kittenish repartee.

"Inspector, do you happen to know a man by the name of Henri Casanova?" Kate asked, wanting to change the subject to something other than Tiffany's flirtatious banter. "He's just offered us a job, and I'm afraid we don't know much about him."

"I don't know him personally," René said, equally glad to get away from Tiffany's sophomoric conversation. "But I know of him. What kind of job has he offered you?"

"The job title is Private Tour Guide," Kate replied. "He wants us to conduct private tours for the rich and powerful – those who can't allow themselves to be demeaned by being lumped in with the hoi polloi on a bus."

"I see," Inspector Martin said thoughtfully. "Well, that seems like a reasonable use of your talents."

"Yes, but what can you tell us about this Casanova guy personally?" Tiffany asked, inserting herself squarely into the conversation. "Like, does he live up to the reputation of his family name?"

"Well, one thing I know is that he's often seen in the company of beautiful women," the inspector replied, fending off another of Tiffany's not too subtle innuendoes. "As for his reputation, I'd say it's spotty at best."

"Are you saying that we should turn down his offer?" Kate asked pointedly.

"No, I wouldn't go that far," Inspector Martin replied thoughtfully. "I'd be careful, though. Keep an eye out, and if he does anything, or asks you to do anything questionable, then report it to me at once."

"You're serious, aren't you?" Kate said.

"Yes, I am," René replied, his mind divided between not wanting to spread gratuitous gossip, and his concern for the young women's safety and welfare. "We have no evidence to support any charges against the man, but he's involved in so many things that I can't bring myself to give him a clean bill of health."

"I hope you're not asking us in a roundabout way to be informants for you, are you?" Kate inquired suspiciously.

"Perhaps not informants, just interested observers," the inspector replied.

"Like peeping Toms," Tiffany interjected.

"No, not at all like that," Martin said. "Just call me if Casanova gets out of line with either of you, that's all."

"So then, would we be considered persons of interest?" Tiffany asked.

"I suppose then you would be, in a manner of speaking," the inspector replied.

"I did ask him specifically if he was expecting us to be anything other than guides," Kate said. "But he assured me that wasn't the case, and he resented the insinuation that he had such a thing in mind."

"He can resent anything he likes," the inspector replied. "All I'm interested in is whether or not he breaks any laws or hurts anyone."

"The only thing he said to me that had the slightest suggestion of hanky panky to it was that he wanted me to lead my client visitors to certain tourist shops," Kate told him. "I assumed that was just business. No doubt he has financial interests in some of the places we'd be expected to go, and he's offering a commission for all sales that occur as a result of our guidance. Isn't that sort of normal? After all, the clients don't have to buy anything they don't want."

"That's true," Inspector Martin agreed, "but I'd like it if you'd provide me with a list of those places."

Short of placing herself in danger, the inspector hoped that Kate would do what she could to help him out, which would give them an opportunity to meet occasionally under the ostensible heading of business. If she were willing to do this, it would also satisfy him that she wasn't a willing participant in any of the Corsican Mafia's activities. Martin knew that there was a protection racket operating in his district, but no one would talk about it. He suspected that Henri Casanova was behind the blood-sucking racketeering, but he had to have proof. The inspector believed he could leave Tiffany out of it, as no doubt she would have the same list of places to bring her clients to. Besides, he judged her to be too silly to be of use to him in his investigations.

Kate had been considering her options as they chatted. She had not yet committed herself to taking the position with Henri Casanova. She had felt a bit embarrassed by the idea of being a shill for Henri's businesses, and now she was feeling rather guilty about the inspector asking her to inform on her soon-to-be boss. On the personal side she felt even more attracted to the detective now, especially since he had so clearly seen through Tiffany's unsubtle come-ons. It was rare, she thought, for a man to resist the obvious charms of a beautiful, available, obviously willing woman in favor of one with a head on her shoulders, so Kate felt loath to let her chances with him pass her by.

"We had just about decided to take up Casanova's offer on a trial basis when you happened along," Kate explained. "Off hand I don't see anything wrong with telling you where

I'm leading my tourist clients. I'll make it perfectly clear to them that they're under no obligation to purchase anything."

"Good, then," Martin said, as he prepared to leave the table. "I've got an early day tomorrow. We'll be in touch in a few days, Miss Evans. Good night, Miss Chance. It was nice to see you again."

He shook their hands, giving Kate's an invisibly firmer squeeze, and walked away from the table, stopping only to pay the bill at the bar. He left so precipitously that Tiffany didn't have a chance to give him her number, or deliver one of her suggestive remarks in parting.

Pierre Mondragon was on tenterhooks. He didn't know what to do. He knew he'd better keep his nose clean or Casanova might take it into his head to remove him permanently. He thought often of calling Kate Evans, but he'd heard that she had been to Casanova's villa, and he decided not to take the chance that she might say something to his boss, particularly if Pierre did to her what he had in mind. He felt that Kate owed him sex, and that she had escaped without paying her debt. He wasn't particularly good at clear thinking, but he knew that on the two occasions when something could have happened between them it was he who had been called away, and both times it was Casanova who had called. Perhaps this was no coincidence. If there was any chance that his boss had designs on Kate or in some way was in cahoots with her, then the risk for him was too great to contemplate. He could only ponder the possibility of getting even with them both somehow, but he had no suitable plan to get revenge on Casanova for suspending him, or on Kate for wriggling out of what in Pierre's mind was obligatory sex.

When he heard through the grapevine that Casanova had hired both Kate Evans and Tiffany Chance, Pierre couldn't abide having them see him in his present demoted state. He decided to go to Corsica to visit his mother. He couldn't afford to stay in Marseilles for six months without earning some money, and Casanova had closed off all the monetary venues on which he counted. Pierre notified him of his plan to return to Corsica, and receiving no objections from him, he left for his family home.

By living cheaply at home, he thought he could stretch the money he had under the mattress until Casanova took him back. Pierre Mondragon thought it was peculiar that his boss didn't consider him to be a true Corsican just because his name wasn't one of the traditional six family names that composed the majority of the population of the mountainous Mediterranean island north of Sardinia. Pierre Mondragon considered himself to be as completely Corsican as the goats his family raised for a living.

It wasn't long after he arrived in the village near his family home that he was embroiled in a typically Corsican property dispute. A French family from the mainland had bought some land from a Corsican peasant who was distantly related to the Mondragons. The purchasers were city folks from the north of France who had come to find some sun and peace among what they thought were the benighted but morally good people of Corsica. It wasn't the first time that mainland back-to-the-landers had mistakenly assumed that the island was in need of gentrification. For the first few months the interlopers were totally ignored. When shunning failed to send them back where they had come from, sterner measures were contemplated. That was when Pierre came into his own, for he had learned from his boss how to encourage unwilling folks to come around to the Corsican point of view.

Because of his age and reputation, Pierre was expected by the locals to be in charge of repelling the latest wave of foreign invaders. For a thousand years or more the native residents of Corsica had beaten back all the efforts of those from away, as they called them, to settle on their land. In the old days invaders would simply be killed, but in the modern era there were many discouragements that could be doled out to resolute foreigners before resorting to the final solution. Neighbors could get nasty, crops fail, animals die, fires break out, and a host of other unpleasant things could beset the new landholders. When all these tactics had taken their toll, the new owners would be made an offer – a low one – which they were told they couldn't refuse, and in no time flat the dastardly foreigners would be on their way home again.

Corsican citizens had a deep loyalty to one another that transcended all other possible loyalties. Most people would have identified the cause of the peculiar Corsican standards of behavior as corruption. The local citizenry thought little about it, accepting it for what it was – the Cosa Nostra, *our thing*. The police kept things from becoming chaotic, but their sympathies were always on the side of the locals in any dispute with foreigners, who were defined as anyone not descended from generations of Corsicans. Thus the unspoken code of tribalism resembled those of the Arabs, Afghans, and other Middle Eastern peoples who permit all kinds of local criminal activity in the battle for hegemony, but who oppose any influences, even progressive ones, if they are introduced by foreigners.

It wasn't surprising that the practice of nepotism became so ingrained in Corsican society. Family loyalties were seen to be the strongest of all human bonds. The exercise of power as demonstrated by the Bonapartes had given way to the modern sub rosa pattern typified by the silent dons of the Mafia. It was ironic that the current don in charge of this old system should be called Casanova, or *new house*. It was also ironic that when Corsicans went to the mainland and gained wealth and notoriety, the double standard of success was accepted and held in the highest regard at home in Corsica, where people from away were castigated and driven off.

Pierre Mondragon's final speech to the neighboring foreigners before they packed up and left the island consisted of classical Corsican logic. He informed them that he had been delegated by the people of the village to speak for them, and that he had come in peace. Mondragon told them the history of the district with an emphasis on the not-too-subtle lessons learned by those who had tried to usurp land from the local people. Without threatening or bullying, he was able to convince the unfortunate French family of the wisdom they would be showing if they withdrew gracefully and returned from whence they'd come. The plethora of ills that they had suffered since they had arrived in their village would end as if by magic, if only they would pledge to be gone by the end of the week. Pierre Mondragon hadn't needed to precisely document what would happen if they refused his invitation to depart. The folk of rural Corsica deemed that he had acted bravely and wisely in bringing the situation to a peaceful solution.

Richard Nixon put it well when he said, "The greatest honor that history can bestow is that of peacemaker."

CHAPTER TEN

Henri Casanova, like the Caesars before him, was battling in the provinces, but he was simultaneously maintaining his influence in Rome. At home in Corsica, where he maintained the family estate in which his wife and children still lived, Casanova was the patriarch. To his neighbors and the politicians of the island, he was the eminence grise. Little happened in his realm that didn't get back to him, and so he was made aware of Mondragon's feat on behalf of the forces of the status quo. Actions such as his redounded to the credit of the don, and kept the Mafia in control generation after generation. As a result, Casanova decided to commute Pierre Mondragon's sentence and allow him to return to his old job.

The decision to restore Pierre to his former place in the organization was popular with all the boys except Didier Albertini, who would now have to step back into Pierre's shadow. He felt he had done a good job in taking over for the newly-acquitted Mondragon, and therefore he shouldn't have to be forced now to retreat into the background. Henri Casanova, the wily don, knew quite well how Didier felt, but he liked to encourage edginess between the men. His theory of management was to keep his men lean and competitive with one another and with the rest of the world. In this way Henri suppressed any potential coups, and the gang members themselves kept one another in check.

While Pierre was playing defense by not contacting Kate and also trying not to commit any blunders that could get him back into hot water with the boss, Didier was on the offense, scheming to get rid of him. The tension between the two men was palpable and thinly disguised. It was Didier's turn to make a mistake, and it was a big one. He had an opportunity to sell the photos of Kate that he had taken while she was tied to the bed in the hotel. He had no idea that Casanova had an electronic intelligence group, or that it had access to all the digital photos on his laptop.

Once again Casanova's paranoid, suspicious nature paid off, for yet another of the unsanctioned, perfidious activities of his men was revealed. It turned out that Didier had told a shady porn producer that the photographs were of an aspiring actress, so he put the images in a bondage magazine. This came to the attention of Henri's G-men during a periodic electronic search of the hard-drives in the laptops he'd given to his underlings. The unique tattoo was indelible evidence that Kate Evans was the subject in the hotel pictures, and that the photographs had been taken in the room where Professor Jolicoeur had been murdered. This was irrefutable evidence that the photographer had had the opportunity to commit the murder before taking the pictures. Although the evidence was only circumstantial, the only thing now that could keep Didier from being positively identified as the killer was the mask he wore that night.

Accepting Henri Casanova's job offer had turned out to be a sinecure for Kate and Tiffany. They had learned that their course at the university was going to be postponed due to their professor's demise, so they had time on their hands. Since neither girl wanted to go back home to the States, they devoted themselves to their work. It turned out that Henri Casanova had correctly identified the latent talent of these young women for being tour guides to the rich and powerful. Since Kate was a bit older and had been the first one to meet Casanova, she was the nominal supervisor and distributor of the assignments. Kate Evans was the one who handled the calls, scheduled the appointments, and created the itineraries. Tiffany Chance had only to lead the tours that Kate assigned to her. Casanova had said that what they did with the clients was up to them to decide. Kate stood back and hoped that the California sex bomb wouldn't get into trouble.

Kate selected for herself those clients who were older and seemed more intelligent, and she personally led them around the Côte D'Azur. It was easy work for her, as she enjoyed talking about France, its history, and culture. She met people of stature, and some she knew would become, if not friends, then at least remembered acquaintances. Just as France had always had an attractive "je ne sais quoi" quality for Kate, so it had for most of her clients. Tiffany seemed to be having a good time too, but Kate never asked her for details. Maybe her lack of curiosity was based on jealousy over the easy way Tiffany had of going from one person to another like a bee seeking to sample all the nectars in a field, or perhaps Kate just didn't want to know. After a while, when their commission checks began to come in on a regular basis, they actually began doing very well financially. It was a temptation to just forget about going back to school, and continue to earn money and enjoy life.

Although they worked for the same boss, Kate never met Pierre again during this time. She heard that he had gone to Corsica to visit his family, and she was happy that he was gone and out of her life. Even when she learned that he had returned to work for Casanova again, they never met, and he never called her. It made Kate wonder what had motivated him to drop her like such a hot potato. She would learn later what the cause of his sudden lack of interest was all about. But for now a new chapter in her life was opening, and life was better than ever.

Inspector René Martin had given up any thought that Kate Evans was plugged into the Corsican Mafia. He was resigned to the fact that she just happened to work for the don, in the same way that a person could be the servant of a tycoon without being wealthy. His logic may have been influenced by the fact that now Kate had agreed to go out with him. It had all started when Kate began to meet with René Martin to tell him where she was expected to take her clients. The meetings took place in Kate's hotel bar, but this time there were just the two of them present.

René Martin was very businesslike to begin with.

"Thank you for meeting me and doing this for me, Kate. I've no doubt that it will help with my investigation. The world is a perilous place to live, not because of bad people, but because good people don't do anything about them. I'm very happy you're not one of those people."

"Which people, the bad ones, or the good ones?" Kate joked. "Anyway, I'm glad I can make you happy."

"Let's go over your list, shall we?" Martin said, missing the opportunity to engage in a bit of repartee that might have gotten personal. "It's more extensive than I thought," he added, reading quickly down the list that Kate had provided.

"What do you hope to find out from it?" she asked.

"I think we can assume that the shops on this list are paying a kickback to Casanova," the inspector remarked, as if it were a matter of fact. "With this information, perhaps I can persuade them to testify that it's protection money for the Mafia. Casanova, of course, will maintain that their payments are a commission for sending them customers."

"The Mafia?" Kate said in surprise. "I thought they operated in the States or in Sicily, not here in France."

"I'm afraid we French have also caught the malady, only here it's the Corsican version of the Mafia."

"And are you insinuating that Casanova has something to do with it?"

"My personal view is that he's *the* man responsible," the inspector said gravely. "Unfortunately, I don't have enough proof to arrest him. I need witnesses who are willing to talk, but so far the victims are too timid to speak up. With your list, at least I know who to talk to now. If one of these small business owners gets fed up with the graft, or shows up injured, perhaps I'll be able to persuade him to talk."

"Do you think I should start looking for another job?" Kate said, but seeing the blank expression on René Martin's face, she added, "I mean, if you put Casanova in jail I may be out of a job."

"I have no doubt that a brilliant, attractive young woman like you will have no problem getting another job. Besides, putting him in jail is easier said than done. Casanova has never even been arrested, and if I do collar him, his lawyers will probably get him off."

"Ah, so you think I'm attractive and brilliant. Is that your professional opinion?"

"No, it's my personal opinion. If it were my professional opinion I'd have to take you to headquarters for observation and interrogation."

"That doesn't sound too bad. Is that how you get most of your dates?"

"No, sometimes I get lucky and don't have to resort to subterfuge."

"Let's go back to the attractive and brilliant stuff," Kate said with a wink. "Tell me more about that."

"I'd rather do that at another time, when I'm off duty."

"When will that be?" Kate asked.

"How about tonight? I'll pick you up at seven. We can have dinner, and this time you can do the interrogating."

"That's fine," Kate said. "It'll give me time to prepare my Q & A."

During the time that Pierre Mondragon was in Corsica taking his imposed time out, Didier Albertini had taken over his collection route. Once a week he would make the drive around the circuit as he had been instructed. Because of his newness on the job, his relative youth, and his desire to make a good impression on the boss, Didier was projecting a very tough face to his unenthusiastic clientele. His clients didn't appreciate being leaned on by a strange new kid collector, but most were too timid to complain.

The jeweler Steinmetz had recently sold his business to a young Israeli, and had just retired. The successor, Shlomo Litwak, had been in the diamond business in Israel, spent some time in the diamond centers in Amsterdam and New York, and also served his time in the Israel Defense Forces. During the business sale negotiations, Steinmetz hadn't been forthright with Shlomo about his business connection to the Corsican Mafia. So when Didier arrived to make his first collection, both he and Shlomo were equally surprised.

"Is Steinmetz around?" Didier asked, as he confidently sauntered into the jewelry shop.

"No, Steinmetz is gone. He retired, and I bought the business," Shlomo replied. "My name is Shlomo Litwak. What can I do for you?"

"I'm here to collect the commission you owe us," Didier said. "I suppose you're going to tell me now that Steinmetz didn't inform you about our agreement?"

"That's right. What agreement are you talking about?" Shlomo answered, disappointed that the swarthy young man wasn't a customer.

"I think you know that Steinmetz paid us a commission on the sales that were generated as a result of the customers that our tour guides bring to the shop," Didier explained impatiently.

"I know nothing about any such commission," Shlomo insisted. "And I'm not paying anyone anything until I have a signed agreement outlining the services performed, and how much is being charged for them. So you can go right back to whoever you work for and tell him what I said."

"Be careful, my friend," Didier said, as he opened his jacket, revealing the gun he had in his belt. "Mr. Casanova doesn't permit people to welch on him."

"Unless you're fully prepared to use that gun in broad daylight with witnesses all over the place, I suggest you turn around and go back where you came from. Tell your boss Don Juan, or whatever his name is, to come and see me like a businessman and we'll discuss it face to face. If his deal is reasonable I'll consider it, and if not, don't ever come into my store again and try to muscle me. Do you understand? Now get out of here."

Didier wanted to shoot the Jew where he stood, but he was only there to collect money. Because of the way Pierre had been banished for ordering the hit on Jolicoeur, Didier was well aware that Casanova wanted to be consulted before anyone was offed. Didier decided to tell his boss that the jewelry store owner was new and didn't know the system, so he had given him a little leeway this time with the collection. He would let Casanova decide what to do. If the Israeli was stupid enough to give his boss a hard time, he would be more than happy to carry out any necessary hits. So he buttoned his jacket and left without another word.

Later that same day, Kate Evans was scheduled to take a couple from Moscow around Cannes on a shopping tour. She picked them up at a five-star hotel in Henri's stretch limo as planned. The driver was the same stony-faced, silent man who had taken her to Henri's villa, and to whom she had now become accustomed, as he often drove her and the upscale tourists around the Côte d'Azur. Kate shepherded her charges into the limo, then they drove off toward their destination. She pointed out the sights to them in French, the language they had chosen in spite of the fact that they spoke it poorly and with a heavy Russian accent. Kate had ample opportunity to take stock of the strange pair as they sat in the rear of the limo. She was seated facing them in back, so she was able to observe her clients closely while she delivered her tourist spiel.

The man was a short block of masculine impertinence squeezed into an expensive suit. Kate could imagine him as the commissar of a Soviet agricultural co-op, but not as the billionaire oil magnate which she had been told he was. The woman with him was a caricature, but of what? Kate finally decided that she reminded her of a praying mantis. She was taller than the man by several inches, and weighed perhaps half what he did. She was dressed in a sleek, grass-green dress that displayed her long, stick-like legs, which she kept folded to one side as she sat in the back seat of the limousine listening uncomprehendingly to Kate's commentary, and idly fooling with her ridiculously ornate purse. The Mantis had large black eyes that were made up by an expert cosmetician, but they still managed to bulge like those of a hungry insect.

After bouncing around the French Riviera for a few hours ogling the locations having to do with the film festival and the ballyhoo surrounding it, the Mantis announced that she wanted to go shopping and asked to be taken to a jewelry store.

Kate instructed the limo driver to take them to the shop owned by Mr. Steinmetz. She had been there before, but not recently, so she was surprised to see that the store was now called Le Bijou Sabra. She introduced herself to Mr. Litwak, who told her that he was the new owner. While her Russian clients looked around, Kate explained that she worked for Mr. Casanova, and she assumed he knew what that meant.

Litwak waited on the Russians, speaking to them in their native language. From their gestures Kate was able to figure out that the Mantis liked diamonds and wanted to see several pieces of diamond jewelry. Litwak seemed knowledgeable about diamonds, and the sales talk went along smoothly. In the end he sold the Muscovites a few pieces containing some large stones, and they seemed to be satisfied. Kate was also pleased because her commission from the sale would be a good one. While the Mantis was admiring herself in the mirror, Litwak turned and spoke to Kate.

"I have no arrangement as yet with Casanova," he said, realizing that she was going to suffer a loss of commission. "I'm sorry for you, but perhaps he will make it up to you. Mr. Steinmetz never told me about his deal with your boss. Please tell Casanova to come see me to discuss a deal. OK?"

"I'll tell him what you said," Kate replied unhappily, imagining that Henri would be angry when he heard that Litwak expected him to go to his store to negotiate a deal.

Kate had the mute chauffeur drive the couple back to their hotel in Marseilles, and then take her to Henri's villa.

After cooling her heels for about ten minutes, she was finally ushered into her boss's office.

"Mr. Casanova, I was asked to give you a message from the new owner of the Steinmetz jewelry store. He said that Steinmetz never advised him before he bought the shop that there was a commission arrangement with our tour company to bring customers to his store. He asked me to have you stop by his shop to discuss the matter."

"I'll take that under advisement," Henri said, in his usual noncommittal manner.

"You'll be pleased to know," Kate continued, "that the Russians purchased some expensive diamond jewelry from Mr. Litwak, the new owner. And they've asked me to take them to the Casino tomorrow night. They seem to be rolling in money."

"I'm glad to hear it, Kate. By the way, would you like to see the upper level of the villa? As I recall the last time you were here you didn't get to see upstairs."

"No, not this time, thank you Mr. Casanova. I have a date this evening and I'd like to get back in time to change for dinner," Kate replied quickly, not unaware of what he might have been suggesting.

"That's all right, my dear, another time," Henri said. "Tiffany was just here anyway."

Kate didn't need to be told what that meant. She was grateful to Tiffany for her efforts, because she was spared the embarrassment of having to reject Mr. Casanova's advances. She had no desire to emulate Tiffany under any conditions. Just as a precaution, she resolved never to go to Casanova's villa alone again.

Inspector René Martin hadn't been a uniformed policeman for several years, and as a plainclothesman he always wore a suit and tie. On the night he picked up Kate for their first date, he showed up with a fresh haircut and wearing his new, dark blue suit. For an ordinary date he probably wouldn't have made these special efforts, but this time it was different.

He arrived at the hotel fashionably on time – about ten minutes late. He called Kate's room on the house phone, and she told him that she would be down shortly. While he was waiting for her he spoke to the concierge, wrote a card, and asked that it be put with some flowers that were to be placed in Kate's room after the couple left the hotel.

CHAPTER ELEVEN

When Kate emerged from the elevator, the inspector waved to her from across the lobby. She tried to think what it was that looked different about him. She finally realized that he'd had a haircut. That was it. He looked very attractive in his blue suit, which she thought was like a slightly informal uniform. She liked uniforms and men's dress suits because they obviated the need for her to look at a mismatched tie or an ill-fitting suit of clothes for a whole evening. That way she could be free to enjoy the man inside the clothes, and when the clothes were all the same she could forget the superficial issues and concentrate on the character of her escorts.

Kate went up to René and took his arm, and they walked out of the hotel into the cool Marseilles evening. He opened the door of his car and helped Kate into the passenger seat. Then he walked around and got into the driver's seat. He started the car and moved into the traffic, headed she knew not where. It was strange, she thought, that she didn't mind not knowing where she was going with René, whereas with Pierre or Henri she would have hated not knowing their destination. That was it – she felt safe with René, and very unsafe with the others. In fact she felt safer with him than all the other men she had known, except possibly her dad. Her confidence in him increased when he stopped in front of a small family restaurant that was off the beaten path for tourists and wealthy, pretentious patrons.

They were greeted by the chef's wife, who recognized the inspector but wasn't well acquainted with him. Kate felt it was a good sign that René hadn't been there before with many other women.

The restaurant was a bistro in size and informality. It catered to local people who liked really good home cooking, and knew the difference between good food and mediocre, overpriced meals. Kate was pleased and impressed, even more so than if he had taken her to Maxim's in Paris. Not that the meal would have been bad at Maxim's, but what was required for for getting acquainted on a first date was quiet and privacy. The fact that René understood this was piling up points for him with Kate. They sat at an out-of-the-way table, and he ordered a bottle of the house wine – another point in his favor. She detested the whole process of wine selection. How could anyone outside of the wine business keep up with all the fine details of wine production? She was thrilled to hear that René felt the same way.

When they were finally settled in behind their glasses of rich, ruby-colored Bordeaux, they relaxed and tried to learn as much as they could about each other.

"What's it really like to be a detective, René?" Kate asked him, à propos of nothing in particular. She wanted to give him a chance to talk about himself, and she also took the opportunity to call him by his first name.

"Why, are you contemplating a career change, Kate?" he asked her, consciously switching the attention back to her, and showing her at the same time that he was happy to be on a first-name basis.

"Strangely enough, I've sometimes thought that I might be good at police work," she confessed. "What do you think? Am I tough enough to be a cop?"

"You don't have to be tough to be a detective," René replied. "There are many tough policemen out there who aren't suited to being detectives," he added. He carefully avoided the word "cop," as he hated being lumped in with traffic cops and other poor relatives of the detective. "Now let me give you a little test. How many people are in this restaurant at the moment?"

"I don't know, do you?"

"Yes, there are forty-one people seated, and one is in the washroom."

"How can you tell there's one in the washroom? Maybe that person is just eating alone at one of the tables."

"I saw him go in there just now," he said with a smile. "You see, it's not so hard to be a detective."

They both laughed and began looking at the menu.

"Do you know what their specialty is in this restaurant?"

"Not really. I've only been here once before, so I'm not an expert on their menu."

"Was she beautiful?" Kate asked.

"Who?"

"The girl you were with the last time you were here," Kate said, pretending to be jealous.

"If you must know, I've never been here before with a woman," René said.

"Do you do any other detective's parlor tricks besides counting restaurant patrons?" Kate asked him, changing the subject so he wouldn't notice how pleased and relieved she felt at learning that he had never been to the restaurant before with another woman. He had scored huge points with her for not trying to make her jealous on purpose – a ploy which always struck her as hurtful and unkind and which, in her case, never achieved its intended goal.

"Well, these days I'm sorry to say that most of our tricks are classified because of the terrorists, but because you are unlikely to be a terrorist, I can tell you one secret that could destroy this restaurant if it were known."

"My God, what is it?"

"It's the lobster tails Fra Diavolo. The dish is so good here that if word gets out, the place will be overrun with addicted crustacean-eating mobs who will soon devour every lobster in France, causing riots that rival the storming of the Bastille, leaving this place totally ruined."

"I see. That would be horribly catastrophic. And how did you come to know about the excellence of this dish?"

"My associate Mr. Benamou and I had lunch here one day while we were working a case in the neighborhood. I called it the case of Brother Devil's lobster tails, and I swore I'd return again to the scene with someone I found worthy enough to appreciate it with me."

"And I'm to assume that I'm that person?"

"Yes, so you see you've solved the mystery. You are indeed a detective, Kate Evans."

"Very well, shall we take our chances on devastating this very nice homey restaurant, and order two of these meals that are fit for the devil?"

"I think we really should, Kate. The odds are with us, as we have the lobster population of Nova Scotia to fall back on if we finish off all the French lobsters."

When the owner's wife came to take their dinner order, René asked her if it was true that she had been found guilty of murder.

"What? Murder?" the surprised woman asked.

"I'm Inspector René Martin of the police. It's my job to know everything about the famous lobster killer who then presents her victims to her customers in the form of a recipe invented by her brother the Devil."

"Well, I confess that we do murder lobsters here," she smiled.

"That does it then," René said. "We can't have the lobster population decimated without a proper investigation. We will have two orders of lobster Fra Diavolo, but only as evidence of the crimes you've committed in this place."

"Very well, Inspector," said the mistress of the house. "We will supply the proof you need to convict the criminals who routinely commit lobster murder in the first degree."

"That should solve the case, thank you," René replied gratefully, whereupon the murderess headed for the kitchen.

The inspector turned his attention back to Kate and raised his glass for a toast.

"To the best French criminal chefs in Marseilles."

"I'll drink to that," Kate said, raising her glass. "May these criminals always continue to do their dastardly culinary deeds. And on another subject, your humble informant must tell you that there's been a change to the list of shopkeepers that I gave you."

"What change?" he asked, suddenly growing serious.

"Well, a certain Mr. Shlomo Litwak has purchased the jewelry store in Cannes, which was formerly owned by a Mr. Steinmetz."

"Is that all?"

"The problem is," Kate continued thoughtfully, "Shlomo Litwak didn't seem to know that his predecessor was paying a commission on purchases made by clients brought to him by Casanova's tour guides."

"Do you suspect he'll refuse to go on paying Henri Casanova?" the inspector asked her. "If so, that could create a little stir among the Mafiosi."

"I don't know if he'll hold out or make a deal, but he did ask me to inform Casanova that he wanted to discuss the matter with him."

"And did you notify him?"

"I did," Kate replied. "But he didn't react in any way."

"Sounds as though Casanova doesn't trust you yet."

"My guess would be that he trusts nobody."

"What kind of man is Litwak?" René wanted to know.

"He seemed very reasonable to me, but I had the feeling he could be stubborn. He also seemed to have a great deal of quiet self-confidence, so he might just decide to stand up to Casanova."

"I should pay Mr. Litwak a visit and discuss his options with him," René said, as he thought about how to get him to cooperate in bringing down the Corsican Mafia, or at least the dynasty with Henri Casanova as its leader.

"I'm sorry if I injected a business topic into our time together," Kate said. "But I do believe that to a great extent we are what we do. You're a lawman, and I'm a French student. We're still young enough not to be cynical, and we each work long and hard in our disciplines, so it's only natural for us to discuss the work that occupies so much of our time. I'm not offended when you take the opportunity to discuss your work. I'm flattered, actually."

"You're wise beyond your years, Kate Evans," René smiled. "Although I know very little about your field, I'd also be flattered and interested to learn more about it, and even to help you with it, if that's possible."

"That's very generous of you, but I think in our present situation I'm the one who can help *you* with *your* work, and not the other way round."

"If you're willing to do that, and if I can keep you safe, I accept your assistance," the inspector agreed gratefully.

"You make it sound dangerous. Is it really a question of my safety?"

"You have no idea how perilous it can be," René said, reverting to his inspector's demeanor. "These Corsicans will cut a throat as easily as they light a cigarette."

"Isn't that a racially prejudiced attitude?"

"Of course I don't mean all Corsicans, only those in the Mafia," Martin added quickly. "However, I reject the idea that every time a law is broken, society is guilty rather than the lawbreaker. I believe that each individual is accountable for his own actions."

"You sound like an American libertarian."

"Justice has no nationality," René said, "but the cause of human liberty owes a debt of gratitude to America for its continued sponsorship of freedom under democratic rule."

"Idealism is often held in contempt because it's regarded as naive. We do our best to allow the wisdom of the world's philosophies to pass through our democratic filters. Anything good sticks, and the bad ideas are supposed to wash away peacefully. But lately we've been letting political correctness pass all sorts of evil through our filters, as though all the good ideas come from other parts of the world."

"The check has come," René said. "Why don't we take a stroll around to see if we can digest that wonderful meal. We can continue our conversation as we walk."

The couple walked and talked for an hour or so. From the hillside where the restaurant was located, the night view of the city lights was breathtakingly beautiful. The statue atop the basilica was lit and appeared to be guarding the city of Marseilles like a brilliant angel in flight. The busy port was active even at night, proving that the mariners of the Mediterranean were paying attention to the running lights of the vessels nearby as they followed the ancient rules of their watery road. René took Kate's hand, and she unhesitatingly gave it. They spoke in low tones, admiring the view of the primeval scene before them. They hated the thought of having to go to work the next day.

In the car on the way back to the hotel, Kate mentioned that she was scheduled to take some Russian tourists to the Casino at Monte Carlo the next night. They would have preferred to be with each other, but they had already learned that when life offers a banquet, it seldom repeats the favor. In response to her news about the upcoming gambling expedition, the ever-inquisitive inspector was prompted to ask about something that had bothered him for a long time.

"Tell me, Kate, do you get a commission for taking people to the casino?"

"Yes, depending on their losses, it can be very profitable for me," Kate replied. "Do you think it's wrong of me to profit from my clients' losses?"

"In principal I don't approve of gambling," René said. "There are just too many illegal activities connected with the gaming industry."

"Such as?"

"Well, take the fact that the odds so strongly favor the house," René began. "The players tolerate the mathematical advantage of the house, but when a gambler wins too often the house assumes he's cheating. That doesn't seem like gambling to me, and certainly not on the part of the casino.

It's a mystery to me how the casino owners manage to convince their clientele that they're always just on the verge of a lucky streak. Besides, the owners of the casinos are too frequently gangsters for it to be coincidental."

"Are you saying that the Monte Carlo Casino is fixed and operated by racketeers?"

"I believe that all casinos are operated by people with a gangster mentality. However, that casino is not in France, it's in the Kingdom of Monaco, and therefore it's out of my jurisdiction," René admitted. "Unfortunately I can't protect you there, Miss Evans."

"Well, Inspector Martin, much as I'd like to be under your protection, I'll have to look after myself tomorrow, won't I? All this talk about gangsters makes me want to ask you if you think the Bank of Monte Carlo is a royal front for white-collar criminals, too."

"I do. It's not as impossible as you may think. Over the centuries all the monarchies have borrowed large sums from sketchy money lenders in order to fund their wars and high living. That's how the Medici, Pazzi, and Rothschild families became rich. The popes at the Vatican Bank were into money lending right up to their miters too, in spite of the Bible's admonitions against usury. Why would the House of Grimaldi be any different?"

"You don't rank the banks very highly on the moral scale, do you Inspector?" Kate said. "Is everyone a felon in your estimation?"

"Everyone is a suspected felon in my eyes, until they're convicted. After that, they become *real* felons," Inspector Martin declared. "As far as I'm concerned, bankers are at the top of my list of suspected criminals. Imagine greedily causing a worldwide depression by their ridiculously careless lending practices, and then turning around and asking the government to bail them out! I have the feeling that there are many more dangerous felons working as executives for financial institutions and large corporations than there are prisoners in the jails, or mobsters in the Mafia."

"You paint a bleak picture of our society," Kate said, but she had to admit that René did make some excellent points. "What should we do, then, about all this corruption?"

"We'll have to leave the solution for another time, now that we're at your hotel."

Kate had been so involved in their conversation that she hadn't noticed that they'd arrived. She hated the evening to end, because it had been the nicest date she'd ever had. It was on the tip of her tongue to invite him up to her room, but he seemed anxious to get away, and perhaps it was better that way for now. He came around and opened the car door, giving her his hand to help her out. He had been a perfect gentleman, so she gave him a goodnight kiss. He was a bit shy because the doorman was watching them. He knew that doormen were an unending fount of gossip, and that this little piece of tittle-tattle most probably would find its way back to Henri Casanova. René had an uneasy feeling that Casanova would soon know that he and Kate were more than acquaintances, and that was not likely to be good for Kate's health.

When she arrived in her room she found the flowers and the card that René had sent. If she had any doubts about her feelings for the detective, they were gone now. His card read, "Thank you for a wonderful evening. I know in advance that it will be the best time I've ever had."

Didier Albertini was feeling bitter again. Instead of sending him to strong-arm Litwak, Henri Casanova had decided to send Pierre Mondragon to do the job. There was not much Didier could do about it. How long would he have to wait in the shadow of Mondragon's little performance in Corsica? Mondragon had seniority, yes, but was he really a Corsican? Could Mondragon shoot as accurately as *he* could? Was the few years' difference in their ages sufficient to keep Pierre perpetually ahead of him? Was Pierre as cool as *he* was in difficult situations? Like so many men working in the wake of a superior, Didier Albertini thought himself a better man than Mondragon. He couldn't understand why Casanova, with all his experience as a boss, failed to recognize that he was Pierre Mondragon's superior in every possible way.

Didier decided that he needed to do something big that would make a splash, but he didn't know what. His thoughts kept returning to the jeweler, Litwak. What a cocky little bastard! How did he have the nerve to tell Henri Casanova to come to see him? Why couldn't he just pay up when he came to collect, like old man Steinmetz? Didier was itching to kill Litwak. Still, he realized that if Litwak were dead he couldn't pay commissions to Casanova and the Mafia, and that would definitely not impress the boss.

Finally the idea came to him that if he stole Litwak's jewels he could present them to Casanova, and it would make up for a lot of missed commissions. A major robbery loss would no doubt send Litwak into bankruptcy, and it would get rid of him without Didier having to ask Casanova for permission to kill him. Once he had this idea, he began to plan the caper that was sure to elevate him in Casanova's eyes. The first step for any professional thief is to monitor the victim's activities, and stealthily reconnoiter the victim's premises. Didier Albertini jumped into his car and headed for Cannes to begin his surveillance.

CHAPTER TWELVE

Opulent was the first adjective that came into Kate's mind to describe the famous casino at Monte Carlo. The casino had survived all the various European political eruptions that had broken out in every era since its inception as the world's most famous gambling house, but it never, even for a minute, lost its patina of opulence. To Kate's American eye the building was straight out of a 007 movie, but to her Russian tourists it smacked of the Empire, St. Petersburg, and the Romanov Dynasty. They ate it up, all of it. They were like kids in a candy store. The Mantis walked tall on her spike heels, and towering over her stubby hubby, she did her best to look imperious and supercilious.

Her overdone make-up made her large eyes seem to bulge out of her triangular face. She blinked and stared at the scene in front of her, concentrating on the other women, their clothes, their hair, and especially the jewelry they wore. Kate noticed that she was wearing the new pieces they had bought at Shlomo Litwak's shop. She thought the jewelry that the Mantis was wearing looked more at home in the present venue than did its owner. The long, gangly arms and spidery hands of the Russian woman held on tightly to her gem-encrusted purse, as her overstuffed escort in his tuxedo went to the cashier to purchase some chips.

He paid with a handful of large denomination French francs, and left with a tray of multi-colored poker chips. He pompously walked ahead of his two female companions, confidently expecting that they would naturally follow him as he headed for the roulette table. Kate stood aside at a respectable distance, trying to be unobtrusive. She watched for hours as the short Russian version of a linebacker made several trips back to the cashier to buy more chips, and bit by bit lost them back to the casino. The man was absolutely fascinated by the little white ball bouncing on the spinning wheel, which never landed on the numbers he had bet on, almost as though it had a supernatural aversion to resting in places chosen by this player. The Russian placed his bets with clumsy movements of his short arms. His heavy hands and thick fingers had the dexterity of bear's claws. He tried to emulate the regally dissolute nobles he hated so much, but in his attempt to copy their actions, he only succeeded in demonstrating his envy.

Kate envisioned the panoply of Russia's history being played out in front of her. The dour faces of the oppressed peasants were reflected in the eyes of the Russian couple as they sought to redress centuries of wrongs by reversing the tables on the aristocrats. Kate saw clearly that it was a sad, pathetic exercise to gain the upper hand, only to lose it by changing the players but not the game.

When the Russians finally left the roulette table, the croupier smiled cynically at the tragicomedy. He had seen the newly rich and powerful of all nations behave in the same way before. They thought they had achieved political power by being smarter and braver that those they replaced, but the laws of mathematical probabilities had leveled the playing field, so that both were losers. All that was left for Kate to do was to take the couple back to their hotel. The smoldering Russian, smarting from his losses, would not be interested in the Mantis's ovipositor that night, she thought.

Henri Casanova had just come from a session with Tiffany Chance. He had long ago given up marital sex. His wife was too old, insufficiently attractive, and knew him too well. He turned to professionals to satisfy his needs, and except for the occasional willing woman who happened across his path, call girls were his sexual staple now. Tiffany had created a resurgence of interest in him for the opposite sex. She was so very young, and her clean, innocent-looking Scandinavian features and California surfer body were irresistible to him.

What had come as a surprise was her capability as a lover. Tiffany was far in advance of her age in bedroom science. Furthermore she seemed instinctively to know how to handle an older man's diminished capacity, and this was rare for a young woman.

Henri's mood was elevated, having just come from his latest encounter with the American girl, and he was in a rare state of cheerfulness as he greeted his reinstated henchman, Pierre Mondragon.

"Pierre, my boy, I've got a job for you," he said. "Your man Didier reported to me that old man Steinmetz sold his business in Cannes to a young Jew named Shlomo Litwak, but the old fox didn't tell his buyer about our arrangement. So when Didier tried to collect from the new guy, he resisted and demanded to speak to the boss. For obvious reasons I don't want him to be able to identify me, so I want you to pay him a visit and bring him into the fold."

"All right, Boss," Pierre replied respectfully. "And if he refuses to cooperate?"

"Find a way to make him cooperate," Casanova said. "But don't off him. At least, not yet. We don't want to kill our customers, now do we?"

"I guess not," Mondragon answered thoughtfully.

"Actually, I admire the Jew," Henri said confidentially. "He's got chutzpah. It takes either guts or stupidity to go into the jewelry business in a glitzy town like Cannes that has a Cartier branch. Find out which it is."

Pierre would have preferred to perform a straight hit. One quick surprise attack, no witnesses, and it would have been over. The way Henri wanted it, Litwak could identify him and sic the cops on him. Pierre Mondragon was already trying to decide what method he would use to accomplish his assignment as he settled into his car and drove away from Casanova's villa. He wanted to get back in Henri's good graces, so failure was not an option.

For his part, Casanova wanted the the shop's revenues to be back on his sleeve, as he called it. But he wanted to know more about Litwak first. It was possible that he was a member of the Jewish Mafia, trying to muscle in on his territory. He decided to put his G-men to work investigating his background. He wanted to find out if Litwak was an independent operator, or if he was fronting the competition's effort to oust the Corsicans. Maybe he was a plant put there by the police to see how far the Mafia would go to keep control. Knowing his enemy was like the difference between lancing a boil and starting a war. Henri went down to the underground basement computer center that operated out of his villa, and commissioned Guido and Giovanni to dig up all the dirt they could find about Shlomo Litwak.

Inspector René Martin was continuing to work on the cases of the murdered professor and the dead man in the basilica. He was almost certain that Casanova's men had committed the murders, but his success rate in solving crimes was directly linked to a prosecutor's getting a guilty verdict, and that had to be based on more than the detective's intuition. Luciani, the corpse found in the basilica, was a known associate of the Mafia.

Inspector Martin was inclined to believe that Luciani could have angered Casanova and brought retribution down upon himself. That was a plausible reason for Luciani's murder, but there was no such clear motivation in the case of Professor Jolicoeur. If he could discover a link between the two killings, perhaps he could uncover the missing motive for the professor's murder, which in turn would point to the identity of the assassin. This was on Inspector Martin's mind as he drove to Cannes to speak with the new owner of the Steinmetz jewelry shop.

At this point René Martin had no reason to suspect that Litwak was anything other than an Israeli businessman who had innocently blundered into one of the Corsican Mafia's protection rackets. If the man had spine and was willing to help him bring down Casanova's scam and also save himself the tribute payments, this was Martin's chance to enlist his help before he began paying up.

Inspector Martin entered Le Bijou Sabra jewelry store and found himself in the public showroom. He noticed a few changes that had the effect of making the shop's appearance more elegant than it was in the time of the previous owner. The enclosed glass showcases were spaced around the shop in such a way that several buyers could simultaneously have privacy in discussions with the clerks behind the counters. Martin went up to a conservatively-dressed saleslady and asked for Mr. Litwak. He was directed to the back of the store, where a man stood behind the counter watching him approach.

"Mr. Litwak?"

"Yes, I'm Litwak. How may I help you?"

"I'm Inspector René Martin," he said, showing Litwak his I.D. "I'd like to ask you a few questions. Do you have a place where we can speak in private?"

"Yes, please follow me, Inspector," Litwak said, almost as if he had expected the visitor. "There's a private room in the back."

When they had taken their seats, Martin got right to the point.

"An informant told me that you've been approached by a representative of an illegal organization that's demanding protection money from you as the new owner of this store, and that these payments are a continuation of an arrangement they had with the previous owner. Is this true?"

"Well, Inspector," Litwak began thoughtfully, "it's not exactly true. It was described as a commission to be paid in exchange for tour guides' bringing customers to my store."

"I see. But I'll bet they're expecting monthly payments whether or not they send customers."

"Perhaps, but I can't say for sure yet. I've asked to have a visit from the boss, a Mr. Casanova, to discuss the terms, and I'm waiting to hear back from him. Is there something illegal about this?"

"Maybe, maybe not," Martin replied. "It depends on whether you're paying for a legitimate service, and whether you have the option of rejecting the service without prejudice to yourself or your business."

"You're suggesting that this tour guide company is a front for a shake-down racket, is that it?"

"That's precisely it," Inspector Martin said. "I've been trying to put a stop to this kind of racketeering on the Riviera since I was first posted here a few years ago. Unfortunately, I've never found a merchant brave enough to testify in court, because they're so afraid of reprisals from the Corsican Mafia who are behind the schemes."

"First things first, Inspector," Litwak cautioned. "I must be sure who these people are and what they want."

"Fair enough," René said. "Would you be willing to wear a wire when you speak to them?"

"A person shouldn't say anything that he's not willing to have recorded, at least that's what I believe. I'll wear the wire for you, but I reserve the right to erase the interview afterwards when I've had a chance to listen to the recording, so I can decide if I want to risk the after-effects."

"That's reasonable," Martin agreed. "We don't intend to force your cooperation, but we'd appreciate it. If I may say so, it's courageous of you to go this far."

"Well, you probably realize I'm a Jew, and our people have been leaned on by the worst that society has to offer for thousands of years," Litwak said fervently. "It's only since the formation of Israel that we've managed to confront our enemies boldly. It's the only thing that has worked for us. So you see, I'm willing to stand up if it's required."

"That's very reassuring," Martin replied. "Please take this recording device. Do you know how to use it?"

"I think I can figure it out."

"Good, then. Please be sure you hide it well. I don't want you to have any unfortunate repercussions as a result of your cooperation."

* * * *

Didier Albertini was a murderer and a thief, but he wasn't any kind of criminal mastermind. He was ambitious beyond his level of competence, and was more of a snatch-and-grab opportunist than an organized planner. His approach to this unsanctioned robbery was simply to observe the habits of his victim to see if he could find a pattern of behavior that left a vulnerable opening that he could exploit. He wanted to get into the jewelry store, grab the merchandise, and take off, preferably without anyone seeing him. If he was successful he would make a big score and present the loot to Casanova, thereby proving to the boss that he was capable of more than just muscling the Jew into paying protection money.

His personal desire for recognition was uppermost in his mind. He was a soldier who couldn't be happy following orders. He had to do things his own way. Didier had no idea that he could, by being fearless and loyal to his Corsican Godfather, bring down the entire organization that Casanova commanded. As a centurion in the Mafia Legion of iniquity he was expected to do evil deeds, but he wasn't the one who was qualified to develop the strategy or plan the maneuvers. He was too unsubtle to exercise those duties. Commanding a secret army dedicated to perfidy and avarice required a general who was equally malevolent, one who could carry out a démarche as well as an execution. That is why neither Pierre Mondragon nor Didier Albertini were qualaified to succeed Henri Casanova as Mafia boss – their ambitions to the contrary. What they did do, however, was undermine his leadership by making blunders in judgment.

It turned out that Pierre, following Henri's instructions, and Didier, following his own, simultaneously descended on the Bijou Sabra. They hadn't consulted each other, but for similar reasons they both intended to time their arrivals for the moment before the close of business – Didier by the back door, and Pierre through the front door of the jewelry store. Didier's idea was to steal the displayed diamonds before

Litwak had the opportunity to put them away in the safe for the night. Pierre had selected closing time because all the customers and Litwak's sales staff could leave the shop and not be privy to their conversation, which he expected could become heated.

Occasionally Kate Evans enjoyed a day off when she had no tourist clients to chaperone anywhere. She had consulted her appointment book and saw that she was free that day. When she mentioned this to René Martin he was quick to invite her to lunch, telling her that he had some time off too, and that perhaps they could spend the afternoon and evening together. Kate jumped at the offer, and the couple agreed to meet at noon in the lobby of her hotel.

She told herself that any time she had an opportunity to walk along the old Mediterranean port in the warm sunshine, holding hands with a handsome gendarme like Inspector René Martin, she ought to take it and be grateful. That was exactly what she was doing, but somewhere beneath the pleasure of the moment, she was questioning herself about what she was getting herself into. It was clear that she was falling for him in spite of the obvious problems that came along with having a relationship with a foreigner. She could sustain an affair for a while, but eventually she had to go home to the U.S. She hadn't slept with René yet, although things were moving in that direction. She was pondering what she would do when it came to that point, but she put on the sexiest underwear that she owned before she went down to meet him so she would be prepared for any eventuality.

Experimenting with sex in her undergraduate years had left her with mostly unpleasant memories of her experiences. She didn't want to use René to expand on her earlier foibles, but she could hardly expect to receive some sort of pledge of fidelity from a man she had just met. It was a conundrum for most modern unmarried twenty-somethings. Ever since the introduction of reliable birth control methods, the reasons for practicing abstinence had suffered a fatal blow. It was no longer possible for women to demur in the granting of their sexual favors.

They had had a lovely bouillabaisse for lunch with some French bread and wine, and now it was just about a foregone conclusion that they would go somewhere private.

"Kate, perhaps you've wondered why you've never been to see my apartment," the Inspector blurted out, proving that he had been thinking along the same lines as Kate.

"I thought it was because you are a bad housekeeper," she said, with an ironic smile.

"No, it's not that," René said seriously.

"Oh? Then what is it?" Kate asked.

"I think it's because of the expectation that if we go to my apartment you'll feel obliged to have sex with me," the inspector replied.

"And you think something is wrong with that?"

"Most certainly yes, if you feel sex is obligatory."

"Are you so sure that we couldn't resist the temptation to abstain?"

"Speaking from the male point of view, and considering my feelings for you, I'm pretty sure my will power wouldn't be up to the challenge."

"Don't worry. My will power is as unassailable as the iron chastity belt I'm wearing," Kate joked. "I'd like to see your place, though, and until I do, your housekeeping will always be suspect."

"All right, but you were the one who asked," he said. "Just remember that. It's a bit of a walk from here, but it'll give you a chance to change your mind."

After about twenty minutes they arrived at an old but well built stone apartment house. He opened the downstairs front door gingerly, half expecting the concierge to pop out of her apartment that adjoined the front hall through which all tenants and their guests had to pass. He gestured for Kate to go up the stairs, and as he followed her he watched her lovely muscular young legs climb up effortlessly.

René opened the door to the apartment and stepped back to let Kate enter first. Her immediate impression was that it was just about what she expected. It was neatly furnished with contemporary Scandinavian furniture; the fabrics were masculine, and conservative in color. All in all, it was what she would have expected from a bachelor with a fair salary and reasonable male taste.

"Have a seat, Kate," he said. "Would you like a drink?"

"Thank you. Something without alcohol, please," Kate replied, as she sat on his couch. "I had enough wine with lunch to do me. You French men are always plying women with drinks, aren't you? Is it something your fathers pass on to you at puberty?"

"Yes, and because of it, the whole country is rife with half-drunk women being seduced by cleverly-trained sons. How many Frenchmen have you known in order to discover our secret? I'll make the drinks while you count them up."

Kate looked around the apartment more carefully as she waited. She stood and walked around the room, stopping to examine the books on a shelf, and feeling surprised that he had so many live plants. After her little tour she sat back down on the couch, and René handed her a glass of ice-cold lemonade. They clinked glasses as he sat down next to her. After they had each taken a sip from their glasses she put hers down on the nearest end table. He leaned across her and placed his glass on the same table. As he attempted to straighten back up, Kate intercepted his arm and put it around her shoulder. The taste of the lemonade on his lips was exactly the right combination of sweet and tart.

Just then her cell phone, which she had neglected to turn off, began to play La Marseillaise, the ring tone she had chosen as a joke when she had first landed in France. It didn't seem so funny now as she pulled away from René in order to search her purse for the cell phone so she could turn it off. Kate found the noisy instrument and looked at the screen to see who was calling.

"Oh no!" she said. "It's Casanova! I'd better answer."

"I know it's your day off," came Casanova's voice, "but I have to ask you to work tonight. Where are you?"

"I'm out," Kate replied curtly.

René could also hear the unmistakable voice from three feet away. He sadly withdrew his arm from her shoulder and remained protectively by her side. Casanova already knew where she was, but he just wanted to see if she would lie in answering the question.

"The Russian couple specifically asked for you. They want to go to the casino again tonight, and for some reason they want to make an early start. I'm sending the limo for you as usual. It will be there in one hour. Please be ready." He clicked off as usual without waiting for a response.

"I'm so sorry, René!"

"I'm not sure which of us is more sorry," René said regretfully. "But we have our whole lives to finish what we started today. If you want, I'll drive you to your hotel so you can change into your evening clothes."

"You're a good sport," Kate said. "I promise I'll make it up to you next time."

"Good. I don't want to let this particular Casanova get the better of us."

"Don't worry about that, he won't, nor will any other Casanovas. I'm not through with you yet, Mr. Detective."

Inspector Martin drove her to her hotel in plenty of time for her to get ready. As Kate was dressing, she thought how ironic it was that Henri Casanova had interfered with her love life for the third time with his intrusive phone calls. Of course, the first two were welcome calls that removed Pierre Mondragon in a very timely fashion from her presence. But this last call was an entirely different matter. Still, she thought, it was strange that it was a call from Casanova each and every time. It was almost as though he knew what was going on in her life from minute to minute.

The limo pulled up in front of the hotel exactly on time. The verbally-challenged driver said nothing as he took her to the Russians' hotel. As soon as the couple got into the limo they told Kate that they wanted to go back to Le Bijou Sabra where they had purchased the diamond jewelry the previous day, before continuing on to the casino. They informed Kate that the driver had to be told to hurry in order to get them there before the shop closed.

CHAPTER THIRTEEN

Shlomo Litwak had no way of anticipating the trouble that was heading his way, but as a veteran of the First Lebanon War, he was always leery by nature. He had served with distinction in an elite military unit of the Israel Defense Forces (IDF) during that conflict, and the lessons he learned about the value of preparedness hadn't been lost on him. Just as Israel's neighbors wanted to acquire the Jewish homeland for themselves, there were those who might also want to get their hands on his diamonds. His experience in the diamond trade had come in handy when, during several attempted robberies, he acted with foresight and courage in order to stay alive and in business. As a result of his hard-earned knowledge of the ways of the world, Shlomo Litwak had made a number of improvements to the security systems that his predecessor had overlooked.

As in all jewelry stores, there was an able safe on the premises of the Bijou Sabra. The previous owner had also installed the usual security devices, such as cameras and coded keypads at both entrances, but Litwak had judged them to be insufficient, and he had had them upgraded. Now it was impossible for anyone to enter the shop without a key, the code, and passing a newly-affixed fingerprint interpreter that permitted no one to enter except Litwak or his wife. Furthermore, he had added another level of protection, one that suited his own brave character. He had a second set of steel shutter doors installed which would, on his signal, slam closed behind any unauthorized entrant, thus locking the interloper inside the store and automatically alerting the police. Litwak hoped he would never need to use this feature because it meant he would be locked in with the unwanted guest. To handle this unlikely event, Litwak concealed two fully-loaded military issue Uzi pistols in the shop in hiding places known only to him. A truncheon used by Israeli police to break up riots was also hidden under one of the display counters in the event he needed a less lethal problem solver.

Litwak was confident that his shop and merchandise were quite secure. After all he was a Sabra, someone born in Israel and raised in the midst of almost daily conflicts. His idea of maximum security was that he be left alone to defend himself with no holds barred. His belligerent, independent nature demanded that if any thieves were foolish enough to try to rob him they would be punished severely, first by him, and then by society and its laws. He was pleased to have met Inspector Martin, who also seemed think that criminals deserved punishment more than mercy. So Litwak, with his suspicions aroused by Casanova's people but reassured by Inspector Martin, waited in his stronghold, prepared for any event that might occur.

Many years prior to this time, the power of the Corsican Mafia had been voluntarily limited by a peace arranged between competing organized crime lords operating in the nearby Mediterranean region. Henri Casanova had played a leading role in negotiating the final settlement. In fact, he was regarded by many in the Mafia as being *the* wise old man of crime. At the definitive meeting of French bosses in Marseilles, Henri had argued successfully that territorial claims be laid down permanently, and that the exigencies caused by internal Mafia growth and expansion be removed by implementing policies that were aimed at getting the syndicates their pound of flesh from foreigners.

An example of Casanova's pacification strategy was that foreign shipping and transportation interests were forced to pay higher levies to the Mafia for moving their merchandise through the ports on the Riviera. This decision increased the flow of graft money into the Mafia's coffers, while at the same time reducing prison terms for criminals arrested for participating in gang wars.

Casanova had recently called another meeting of the top Mafia leaders in order to present his latest plan for refining the criminal activities of the syndicate. He was counting on his reputation as a clever peacemaker to bring his colleagues around to his way of thinking about the future. The theme of his new program was to move the Mafia into legitimate businesses by slowly taking over companies operating within each of the areas controlled by the leaders attending the meeting. Casanova was spending most of his time gathering examples of white-collar criminality to present to the group. He hoped that by citing some of the fraudulent corporate incidents that had made it into the light of day he could, by allusion, show his confreres the lucrative possibilities that either hadn't yet come to light or, more likely, represented the crimes of freebooters that had so far gone undetected. His point was that public corporations were the theoretical master criminals because they provided an environment in which entrepreneurial criminals could enrich themselves. Casanova's position here was that the syndicate should try to organize these independent corporate criminals and bring them under the Mafia's own banner.

They had organized the petty criminals into a strong brotherhood, but now Casanova was recommending that the syndicate should be targeting and penetrating the more sophisticated and richer corporations. He was thinking of the opportunities his own G-men had uncovered in the realm of white-collar crime, and the salutary effect it had had on his unit's bottom line. He was going to ask his associates in crime what could be accomplished if the computer hackers, the identity thieves, and the gentlemen swindlers could be organized. It was undeniable that Henri Casanova was a big thinker. Under his guidance the Mafia could easily become the most powerful economic entity in the world, and do it without the costs of government or corporate infrastructures. They had managed to gain control of large organizations like the Teamster's Union, for example, by enlisting their officers in Mafia schemes. Why not recruit the equally anonymous greedy corporate officers of the nation's public companies, using the techniques that had worked so well with the labor unions?

It was to be expected that this kind of macro thinking had taken Casanova's eye off some of his micro problems. The ambitions and the various independent activities of some of his underlings were passing by relatively unnoticed. In this category was the competition between Pierre Mondragon and Didier Albertini. He should have, and were he not otherwise occupied, he would have seen in advance the coming problem that these two Cro-Magnon Corsican men would cause him in his plan to dominate corporate crime in the future. He understood that his organization occasionally needed muscle, but he had no intention of allowing the type of individuals who possessed it to set organizational policy by acting on their own. So while Casanova fiddled at home in Marseilles, his empire was being put to the torch by his lieutenants now speeding towards Cannes in their cars. A student of war and tactics, Henri Casanova was determined to win the war, not just a small battle wherein individual heroics might result in tiny victories.

Inspector Martin had been sorely disappointed, though he tried not to show it to Kate. To have been interrupted when he was so close to the pinnacle of love's bonding, only to lose the opportunity because of his nemesis Casanova's ill-timed summons, was more than another episode in his game of cops and robbers – it was an invasion of his personal privacy. After dropping Kate at her hotel he decided to go to Cannes to see how things were coming along with Shlomo Litwak. He was hoping that the tough little Israeli was going to be a key player in cracking the Corsican Mafia. Litwak could be the catalyst in his quest for revenge on Casanova. So instead of going home, he turned his vehicle and took the road to Cannes, hoping to catch Litwak before he closed his store for the day.

During the pleasant drive along the curvy road to the east, René had plenty of time to think. It was difficult for him to get his mind off Kate. He didn't know why, but he felt he didn't deserve her affection, but it was clear that she didn't feel that way. She hadn't dismissed his attentions, and that proved that she had romantic inclinations towards him. His modesty about his worth had always gotten him into trouble with women. Usually they seemed to expect men to be supremely confident of their own masculinity. It was not as though he had doubts about his ability to perform as a man. It was more a question of his having respect for the woman in question, of making sure her needs and desires were met. He needed a soul mate. His idea of a lover was someone who knew the song in his heart and could sing it back to him when he forgot the words. He had an idea that Kate could be that person. His fatal flaw as a lover, however, was that in his hierarchy of priorities, work took precedence over his personal life.

Martin was the kind of man who liked to be kept busy. He was a thinker about his personal life, but not an obsessive one. It was about his police work that he was obsessive to a rare degree. He had unsolved murders on his plate, and though he was sure he knew who had committed them, they would stay in the unsolved column until he could make a case stick against the suspects he had in mind. To a less committed person René Martin might have seemed to be an obsessive-compulsive. He had the operations of a secret crime syndicate headed up by Henri Casanova to obsess about, and he was compelled to get the proof needed to send him to prison for racketeering. In his mind the juxtaposition of his interrupted sex life and his desire to convict the master criminal, Casanova, were equal in intensity. In spite of all his mulling, Inspector Martin had nothing to show for either, and his patience was wearing thin.

He looked at his watch as he turned into the street that housed Litwak's shop. In the second that it took him to do this he missed seeing Pierre Mondragon's BMW that was parked a block away from the store. He didn't fail to notice the limousine, however, that was now parked directly in front of the jewelry store. It was Casanova's, the one that he used for squiring his wealthy tourists around the Riviera, and the one that Kate was probably using to transport her clients to the casino. He got out of his car and went toward the limo to see if Kate was in it. He expected her to be at the casino, and he intended to see if she was going to be as surprised to see him as he was to see her. He was approaching the limo from the rear, and was about to peer into the tinted windows to see who was inside when the unmistakable sound of pistol fire rang out from the direction of the jewelry store.

Just as René turned to see what was happening in the store, the plate glass shattered and Shlomo's steel protective shield slid across the window frame – a shield intended to prevent someone from throwing a brick through the window and grabbing the jewelry on display. At this point, however, it blocked his view of the interior of the shop. He ran to the front door, and found it locked. He couldn't see inside, but he had heard the crackle of gunfire. He pounded loudly on the door using the butt of his revolver which he had instinctively plucked from his shoulder holster as soon as he had heard shots being fired.

"Police, open up!" he shouted, pounding harder on the door.

It was at this unlikely moment that he realized that he loved Kate Evans. When he thought she was inside the shop, in danger and possibly hurt, his heart began pounding as it never had before. He ran around through the alley between the buildings to see if he could get into the store through the back entrance. He found the back door locked by the same type of steel security device as the front door. He rapped desperately on the door.

"Police, open up immediately!" he shouted. When nothing happened, he ran to his car and put in an emergency radio call to his headquarters.

"This is Inspector Martin, badge number 37402, on site at the Bijou Sabra jewelry store in Cannes. Shots fired. Probable robbery in progress. Perpetrators and civilians locked inside. Can't tell what's happened until I get inside. Better send the SWAT team. We may have to break down a steel door to gain entry. Send an ambulance, paramedics, and enough uniformed officers to contain a crowd. Have Assistant Inspector Benamou get here immediately. Wait. Hold up on the SWAT team. Someone inside is opening the front door to the shop now. Just send the local cops, the crime scene investigators, and the medics. I'm going in. I'll radio in later if I need more help. Out."

The inspector put down the radio, stepped out from behind his car, and ran, gun in hand, to the entrance of the shop. Just as he arrived, a disheveled Shlomo Litwak came out of the door, hands held above his head, a pistol in his right hand. The men nearly collided as Martin attempted to enter the shop as Litwak was exiting.

"Ah, Inspector, I'm very glad to see you," Litwak said, as cool as could be.

"What just happened here, Litwak?" René Martin asked, taking the gun from his raised hand and smelling the muzzle to see if it had been fired.

"Come inside and I'll tell you," Shlomo said, and they walked into the shop together. He shut the door behind them to obstruct the view of the gathering crowd on the street.

Holding two guns, his and Litwak's, the young inspector gazed at the crime scene. The store was a mess; broken glass and jewelry items of various kinds were strewn all over the floor. In the front of the store was a male body lying face down, blood puddling beneath him. In the back of the shop was the body of another man, lying on his side, his head and face covered by a ski mask. Near both bodies were pistols of the same make and caliber. Off to one side two more people were lying with their bodies – a man and a woman – next to each other. The heavy-set man's body was still, as though he were unconscious. The woman was sniveling and babbling in a profuse combination of unintelligible Russian words and incomprehensible French ones. Her streaming tears wet the heavy layer of cosmetics she wore, so her face resembled one of Picasso's frightened figures from his painting of Guernica. She seemed unhurt, so Martin went on questioning Shlomo Litwak.

"Now can you tell me what just took place here?" the inspector asked Litwak.

"It looks like a horrible mess, I know, but actually it's the best thing that could have happened," the jeweler began. "The guy in the mask broke into the store. I don't know how he got in, but he had a gun and came rushing into the store from the back room, demanding that money and jewels be put into the black leather bag he was carrying. At just about the same moment this guy," he pointed to the body lying on the floor in the front of the store, "came through the front door. When he saw the masked man, the second guy reached into his jacket for a gun so the masked guy fired several shots at him, but the shots didn't kill him outright because even though he was hit, he fell to the floor upsetting my jewelry counter on the way down. But he was still able to get off a return shot, which seems to have killed the masked thief. He fell where you see him now. While the shooting was taking place I ducked to the floor, hoping to get hold of my own gun. It was too far away for me to chance going for it, but I was able to reach my truncheon."

"What good would a club do you, if the other men had guns?" the inspector asked.

"It was not for the gunmen that I needed the club. By this time they were both wounded or dead on the floor," Litwak stated in a matter-of-fact tone.

"So who was the club for?" Martin asked patiently.

"For that guy there." Litwak pointed to the unconscious form lying near the wailing Russian woman. "As soon as the shooting started he began shoving every piece of spilled jewelry he could safely reach into his pockets. The woman saw what he was doing and followed suit. I saw what they were up to, so I crawled around behind him and cold cocked him with that truncheon," Litwak pointed to the police baton on the floor some distance away. "Then I got my gun in the event there was going to be any more violence, and that's when I came out to meet you."

"Is that everything?" Inspector Martin asked.

"That's it. You were expecting more?" Litwak smiled. "You see, that's why I said it was the best thing that could have happened under the circumstances. You checked my gun, so you know it wasn't fired. If you reach into the fat guy's pockets you'll find them full of my jewelry. And if you search the woman's purse you'll find it stuffed with diamonds also belonging to me. Furthermore, if you search the woman's panties you'll find a few other diamonds that I saw her hide there, although as you can see I don't envy the person who has to fish them out just now."

Martin walked over to the unconscious man, stuck his hand in his jacket pockets and found that Litwak had spoken the truth. He searched the woman's purse over her strident but incomprehensible objections and found jewels present as the jeweler had reported.

"Do you know any of these people?" Martin asked.

"Not really. These Russian thieves came in a day or so ago and bought several pieces. They paid cash. They came back again at closing time today, and they tried to sell them back to me. He said he'd had some temporary losses at the casino and he wanted to raise some cash so that he could win back the money he'd lost. I don't know the dead guy in front, but the masked guy could be one of Casanova's men, although I can't be sure until I've seen his face."

"If everything you've told me is true, as it appears to be, then I have to agree with you, this affair has ended much better for you than you could've expected. I just have one more question for the time being. Where is Kate Evans, the tourist guide who has been squiring these Russians around the Riviera?"

"I don't know. She didn't come into the store with them this time. You know she works for Casanova, don't you?"

"How do you know that? And what do you know about Casanova?" the young inspector asked suspiciously.

"She came with the Russians the first time. She didn't mind mentioning that she expected to receive a commission from any purchases the tourists make. She told me straight out that she worked for Henri Casanova. I told her to tell him to come see me, as I hadn't made any such deal with her boss. That's all I know about her, except that she's very attractive and seemed highly intelligent."

At this time the uniformed gendarmes arrived, along with the medics and the reporters. The area around the store was immediately cordoned off to keep the public out and the media at bay. The paramedics quickly moved from body to body, pronouncing the two shooters dead. Smelling salts partially revived the unconscious Russian. The medics told Martin that the Russian was in need of medical attention before he could be questioned.

"Benamou," Martin said to his assistant. "Search this man's pockets before they take him to the hospital. You'll find diamonds and jewelry belonging to Mr. Litwak, the owner of this store. Make an inventory of the jewels. They're evidence of attempted theft. You can check the inventory with Litwak and make him a receipt for the jewels. He'll need it in case he has to make an insurance claim. I'll question the injured man later. Take this hysterical woman into custody. Search her purse – you'll find stolen property there too. Get a female officer to take her some place and do a strip search. I'm told she hid some of the stolen jewels in her underwear. See that the man stays under guard while he's in the hospital, until we can arraign him and move him to a cell."

"Anything else, Inspector?" Benamou asked.

"Yes, I'm going to need full DNA analyses to identify these bodies. Have ballistics work on the bullets to see if they match any from prior cases."

"Anything else that you can think of?

"Yes, these weapons look like guns used by the mob. See if you can trace them. I'm also looking for an American woman named Kate Evans. She works for Casanova as a tour guide. She's the one who brought these Russian thieves here, but she's nowhere to be found now. I think you may remember her. The professor that was murdered was in her room, and I questioned her at that time. Do you remember?"

"I think I do, Inspector," Benamou replied. "Wasn't she the American girl who was tied to the bed?"

"You remember that part quite well, don't you? Then help me find her."

Martin's investigatory analyses of crime scenes always began with trying to understand the motives of the people involved. In this case he believed what Litwak had told him about what had occurred, but he wasn't sure why it had happened. Why had the masked man immediately started shooting on sight, when he saw the other fellow? Did they know each other? There was more to this apparent robbery than met the eye. And where the hell was Kate? Could she be in the limo that was out front? He walked to the front door of the store intending to search the limo, but it was no longer there.

When the shooting at the jewelry shop started, Kate had been in the back seat of Casanova's limo. The Russian couple had asked her to remain behind, because they didn't want her to know that they were on a mission to return the jewelry they bought on their first visit to Litwak's store. If Kate were to tell Casanova that his clients were short of cash he wouldn't be so anxious to give them the royal tourist treatment that they'd been enjoying. This turned out to be a good thing for Kate, because when bullets are flying it's always good to be somewhere else.

The instant the first shot rang out and the steel shutter closed over the smashed window, the limo chauffeur sprang into action. He shoved the big car into gear and took off from the curb in front of the Bijou Sabra. Kate was thrown back in her seat from the force of the scratch off, and she never saw anything that happened inside the shop. What she did know was that all the doors of the limo were locked and she was being taken away, whether she liked it or not.

She had no way of knowing that this particular limo was custom made, armored, and fitted with one-way glass. An experienced criminal get-away driver was operating the vehicle, but Kate didn't know anything about him except that he was extraordinarily close-mouthed. Evidently the vehicle was made to keep people in as well as out, for she couldn't pop the door locks. After traveling for a time without a word from the driver, Kate realized they were heading back in the direction of Marseilles. More time passed, and she became aware that they were going to Casanova's villa. She tapped on the glass partition that separated her from the chauffeur.

"I'd like to go back to my hotel please," she said, and receiving no response to her request, she tried again in a louder voice, "Take me back to my hotel!"

The glass vanity blind slid up so she could no longer see the back of the man's head, nor could he see her, and the limo proceeded on its way. She tried again to lower her window, but the button that raised and lowered the glass was locked.

Kate Evans was a prisoner, at least for the moment. She sat there boiling in silent anger, certain that when she told Henri Casanova about the man's behavior, he'd be shocked at the intransigence of his employee.

CHAPTER FOURTEEN

When the limo rolled up the driveway that led to Henri's mansion, Kate Evans was surprised that it continued on to the boathouse without stopping at the house. She tried to open the limo door but it was still locked, so she had to just sit and wait. In a few minutes Casanova's strongman, Carlo Santori, came ambling up to the vehicle and exchanged a few words with the driver. Kate couldn't make out what they were saying, but the language sounded like Corsu to her. The next thing she knew the locks popped up and the door opened. Santori beckoned to her to get out, then he gently but firmly took her by the arm and silently led her to the boathouse. They passed down a hall that led to a room that could only be described as a comfortable, windowless cell. Santori guided Kate into the center of the cell, released her arm, and quickly retreated out of the room, locking the door from the outside. She tried the door handle to make sure it was locked, and found that she was indeed a prisoner.

Hours went by. A long series of disturbing doubts and questions passed continually through her restless brain. Why had she been brought here? When would Casanova tell her why she had been spirited away from Cannes without a word of explanation? Surely he had made some horrible mistake. She had done nothing to harm him. She had even doubted René Martin when he described the avuncular Henri as a Mafia boss. She felt like crying or crying out, but did neither. Crying of either variety would have made her appear weak, and she didn't want to give anyone who might be watching the satisfaction of knowing that she was scared. Could she expect to be rescued by René? She doubted it. Even if he went to Casanova's house, he would simply deny knowing anything about her whereabouts. It was night, it was dark, and she was tired.

The dim light in the cell revealed a cot against one wall. A blanket was folded up and rested on one end of the cot. She was wearing a red cocktail dress and her highest heels, and she didn't want to mess them up. Evidently she was going to be stuck in the cell until morning, so she decided to try to get some sleep. She removed her dress and draped it over the only chair in the stark room. She used the open toilet in the corner demurely, as she was not sure if anyone was watching her movements through a peephole or a hidden TV camera, then she stretched out on the cot and pulled the blanket up over herself.

It occurred to her that this could very well be the cell where Casanova held his enemies until he fitted them with cement-block shoes before loading them aboard his yacht and dropping them into the Mediterranean. She remembered that image from gangster movies, and now here she was in the same situation herself. This was her last thought before she drifted off to sleep to the sound of water slapping against the concrete columns at the foundation of the boathouse.

Inspector René Martin was frantically trying to find Kate, while at the same time attempting to project a matter-of-fact attitude in front of his associates. He called her hotel and had the room clerk go up to her room to make certain she wasn't there. He called the Casanova residence and was told by the houseman that she wasn't in the house. Finally he called Tiffany Chance, hoping that she might have gone there, but there was no answer at her hotel or on her cell phone. He left messages for Tiffany to call him as soon as she could. In spite of all the modern technology that he had at his command, he still had no idea where Kate was.

He was sure that Casanova had something to do with Kate's disappearance. It was his limo, after all, that he had seen parked near the jewelry store, and the Russians were his clients. It never occurred to the inspector, however, that

Henri Casanova was so powerful that he was able to monitor the police department's activities to a greater extent than the gendarmes could monitor his. How was he to know that the Mafia boss was capable of maintaining a surveillance of his personal and professional movements? Martin had never met the man whom he regarded as his nemesis, but he felt he knew him even so.

Casanova was certain, from information gathered from his informants in and around the precinct, that the inspector was his sworn enemy. When his spies told him about the romantic connection that was developing between René Martin and Kate Evans, Casanova decided to intervene. He admitted to himself that his pique with Inspector Martin was partially due to his jealousy over the fact that Martin had gotten to Kate before he had had a chance to sample the merchandise himself. But that was not his main motivation for wanting to gain control over the loyal gendarme whom he hadn't been able to corrupt with bribes. The history of the Mafia was always entwined with crooked policemen who accepted payments to turn a blind eye to the syndicate's operations. Ever since Martin had been transferred to the Marseilles area, however, things had become more difficult for the Corsican mob. Casanova wanted to bring this young loose cannon under his control, and he decided he could do it by kidnapping his sweetheart, Kate Evans.

Casanova suspected that Martin had planted Kate in his employ as a police informant. He had yet to find that out for certain, but Henri had his ways, and he was sure he would discover her treachery with time. He intended to question her in his own way, and he needed to have her completely under his control in order to do it. Now that Henri was sure that Mammon, the god of money, was not Martin's Achilles heel, he needed to find another weak spot in the detective's character. The threat that harm would come to his girl might be the catalyst that Casanova could use to bring the inspector to heel. The incident at the jewelry store in Cannes had been coincidental and unpredictable, but he had planned to kidnap Kate anyway at the end of the night at the casino.

Casanova was looking forward with great relish to his interrogating sessions with the attractive American hostage. His approach would be subtle, and include aspects of both physical and psychological torture. Now that he had the woman in his private chamber, he was in total control of her destiny. In his brief relationship with Kate, she had displayed a certain amount of independence and courage. Casanova was eager to test the limits of her individualism, and it would be a great deal more fun for him if she turned out to be more than just a run-of-the mill submissive female. His first ploy would be to reduce her self-esteem, and for this he brought out Didier's photograph of her bound to the hotel bed with her tattoo clearly revealed.

Inspector René Martin had a great deal of police work to do, and he had to do it while enduring enormous angst over the whereabouts and safety of his beloved Kate. To make things worse, he'd been officially assigned the task of finding her. This mission was urgent in that it was not yet known whether she was dead or alive, or even if she had been kidnapped or not, so at that point she was presumed to be alive. Another missing person case was opened when Tiffany Chance was also nowhere to be found. Inspector Martin's close personal connection to the missing Evans woman had to be hidden from his boss lest the case be taken away from him and given to another detective so as to satisfy police regulations concerning objectivity.

Martin was also under pressure to solve the murders in the basilica and the hotel, which were now growing beards, in the words of the superintendent. The two corpses in the jewelry store still had to be identified and investigated, and attempted robbery charges also had to be laid against the Russian couple. In short, Martin's work was backed up, which meant that his long-term objective of closing down the Corsican Mafia's operations had to be put on hold for a bit longer. A break in the most recent case was about to occur, however, and it would have a deep effect on all the others.

The DNA tests had been duly expedited, and the results confirmed the identification of the dead bodies that had been visually recognized by Martin and Litwak in the jewelry store. As soon as Benamou had confirmation that the bodies belonged to Pierre Mondragon and Didier Albertini, he dug out rap sheets for them. They both had several arrests for small crimes in their youth, but neither man had had any serious recent charges brought against him. It was as though they had suddenly had a change of heart and gone straight. Or, as René told his assistant, they had come under the protective legal wing of the Mafia.

Both the dead men had cell phones that had been found on their bodies. Martin put Benamou to work investigating their cell phone records to see if there were frequent calls made to or from Henri Casanova on either of the dead men's phones. An hour later the officers had confirmation of many calls made to and received from Henri Casanova's phone. This information confirmed that when they were alive they were both working for Henri Casanova. It was no stretch, then, for Martin to conclude that they had known each other before the shooting started.

It wasn't until the police received the results from the forensic ballistic testing that they could positively confirm Litwak's story that the men had killed each other. But the reason why was not yet clear to Martin. Was there some sort of internecine war between Mafia soldiers going on? Had Casanova had any part in this gunfight that had ended in a deadly draw? Benamou told Inspector Martin that he was still waiting for the results of the ballistic tests performed on the weapons owned by the deceased and on the bullets found in their bodies. Among other things, he was eager to know if the test results could associate the victims with outstanding cases of unsolved shootings. Martin ordered his assistant to obtain these results and report them to him as soon as they were available. He also charged the junior officer with the task of having the Russians arraigned, and charges brought before the court. For his part, Inspector Martin was going to question Henri Casanova at his home.

Carlo Santori, the bodyguard of Henri Casanova, showed Inspector Martin into the large room that Casanova used as an office. Santori had a sneer on his face as he closed the door behind him. He hated cops.

"Mr. Casanova, I'm Inspector René Martin. I'd like to ask you some questions about a case we're working on."

"Oh, really? How can I be of help?" Casanova inquired innocently, as though it were impossible that a man like him could have any knowledge that was of interest to the police.

"For a start, do you have two employees by the names of Pierre Mondragon and Didier Albertini? And if you do, are you aware that they were killed in a gunfight yesterday?"

"These names are vaguely familiar to me, Inspector. I believe they're employed by one of my companies," Henri replied evasively. In actuality his G-men scanned every police radio signal, so he already knew about the death of his henchmen. "Why do you ask? Do you think *I* killed them?" Henri said incredulously.

"Not at all," the inspector replied firmly but pleasantly. "Unless you'd like to confess to the crime."

"What crime would that be? You said they killed each other," Casanova stated confidently, projecting an innocent demeanor.

"No, Mister Casanova, I only said they were killed in a gunfight, not that they killed each other," the inspector reminded him. "It's true that they killed each other, but how could you have known that if you weren't involved in some way?"

"That's a very good question," Casanova said, realizing he'd been caught in a lie. "But you see, I was contacted by someone in the media this morning, and she told me about the unfortunate incident. That's the extent of my knowledge of this unfortunate event."

"You said you only knew these men slightly, yet the cell phones that we found on their bodies showed that they had made numerous calls to your number. How do you account for that?"

"Ah, Inspector, I have a very large staff, and I receive many calls every day. Too many, in fact, if you ask me," Henri replied, in the manner of an extremely busy executive.

"Why do I get the feeling that you're fencing with me, Mr. Casanova?"

"That's because in the course of my lifetime, Inspector, policemen have never brought me good news," Casanova replied smoothly. "The police always arrive on my doorstep, usually unannounced, and like hungry mongrels they expect me to provide a meal of facts, information, and evidence. Is it any wonder that I fence with you? It's your job to dig up your own bones. When you come to me with something other than suspicions and accusations, perhaps I'll change my attitude toward the police. Tell me some good news for a change. Tell me about how you've protected me from a burglar, for instance, or how you've prevented a thief from stealing my property, and I'll listen attentively."

"So you've nothing to say about the gunfight involving two of your employees?"

"Only that I wasn't there, know nothing of the incident, and would like to get back to work, with your permission," Henri said icily.

"Very well, Mr. Casanova. But before I go, I have some questions about the whereabouts of two other employees of yours."

"You seem to think I'm the missing persons bureau, as well as the Oracle of Delphi. Who is it that's missing now?"

"You have two employees by the names of Kate Evans and Tiffany Chance, do you not?"

"I do. What of it?"

"I haven't been able to contact either of them," Martin said, staring closely at Casanova to see if he could detect any flicker of guilt. "Do you know where these women are?"

Casanova had anticipated that the police would come to him with questions about Kate Evans' disappearance. He'd ordered Tiffany to move into his villa partially for obvious reasons, but also so he could use her as a diversionary device against the gendarmes. He reasoned that if Tiffany didn't know where her American friend Kate was, and he had gone to great lengths not to let her know that Kate was being held prisoner on his estate, then how could the police expect *him* to know? Casanova knew that the police had to wait forty-eight hours before they could act on a missing person report. The fact that Inspector Martin was looking for her already proved that he was on a personal quest, not an official one.

"I don't know where Miss Evans is," Casanova lied, "but she has been completing her assignments as a tour guide right along. As far as I'm concerned she has not missed any work, so I'm not looking for her because I don't consider her to be missing. Perhaps she has a secret lover and is hiding in a love nest somewhere," he concluded, knowing that image would upset the inspector.

"And Miss Chance?" Martin asked. "Do you have any idea, romantic or otherwise, where she can be found?"

"Aha, at last, an easy question!" Henri, exclaimed. "She can be found in my bed, inspector. Would you like me to call her down? It's time she was vertical anyway."

Caught off guard, the inspector stammered, "Y-Yes, I'd like to speak to her for a minute."

Casanova nodded his head and flicked his eyes upward to indicate to Santori, who had stationed himself at the far end of the room, that he should fetch Tiffany and bring her downstairs.

"While we're waiting for Miss Chance to come and join us," Inspector Martin continued, "I want you to tell me why your limo was parked outside the jewelry store at the time of the shooting."

"It was waiting there to take two Russian clients to the casino," Casanova replied. "Would you like to question my driver about that?"

"Yes, I certainly would," the detective answered.

Just then Santori returned with Tiffany.

"Ah, perfect timing, Santori. Now you can turn right around and bring Marius here. And while you're at it, fetch a cold refreshment for Miss Chance."

The bodyguard looked daggers at the inspector as he left on his mission, as if Martin were personally to blame for this demeaning fetching and carrying that had suddenly become his unwelcome responsibility.

"Please have a seat over there, Miss Chance," Casanova said, attempting to project an attitude of avuncular concern. "I trust you've been comfortable in every respect during your visit to my villa," he added.

"Very comfortable," Tiffany assured him.

"I'm sure the inspector will be gratified to hear that."

The door opened and Santori returned with a nervous Marius in tow.

"Marius, this is Inspector..." Casanova hesitated, as if the name had escaped him.

"Martin. I'm Inspector Martin," René said, content to play along with his little game. "I'd like to know why you were waiting outside the jewelry store instead of going to the casino as scheduled."

"Why, Miss Evans asked me to stop there for a moment so the Russian couple could do an errand of some sort before continuing on to the casino."

"What happened when you got to the store?"

"They got out and went inside."

"All three of them?" the Inspector asked. "Please think very carefully before you answer."

"Yes, they all went inside," Marius repeated.

"Then what happened?"

"They were in the store for a few minutes, and then I heard some shots being fired. After that I saw some iron shutters close down over the windows."

"Then what did you do?"

"I took off as fast as I could," the chauffeur replied.

"You mean you left Miss Evans and her clients in the shop?"

"Yes, Inspector."

"So you drove off without your fellow employee after you heard shots fired in the store?" Martin asked again, to make sure he'd heard correctly.

"Yes."

"I'll ask you again. Are you sure Miss Evans went into the store with the clients? Or could she have ducked around the corner and gone somewhere else?"

"I saw her go inside the store," Marius repeated.

"I'm told that the limo you were driving is an armored vehicle. Is that true?"

"Yes."

"Well Marius, if you were in an armored vehicle, why did you leave the scene? Weren't you safe inside the limo?"

"I didn't want to take a chance. Besides, I have a police record and I didn't want to get involved in anything that could put me back in the slammer or get me fired."

"Did you return to the scene later to see what had happened?"

"No. I came back here."

"Didn't you wonder what happened? Didn't you care how your clients and Miss Evans were going to get back to Marseilles?" the Inspector asked.

"It occurred to me, but I don't get paid to get shot," the chauffer replied sullenly.

"All right, you can go now," the inspector said.

Marius looked at Casanova to see if the inspector's order complied with his wishes. Receiving a nod from his boss, he turned and left the room, exchanging winks with Santori as he passed by.

"Now, Miss Chance, would you care to join me and the inspector in a little question-and-answer session?" Casanova said in unctuous tones. "Please have a seat next to young Mr. Martin, here. He has expressed an interest in gleaning some information from you on a topic that seems to be very dear to his heart."

Martin turned to look at Tiffany, ignoring Casanova's effort to gain the upper hand. She was wearing a diaphanous dressing gown that left nothing to the imagination. It seemed to René that she was her usual carefree self. He doubted she could be harboring a great degree of derogatory information about Casanova, or hiding any knowledge of her friend's whereabouts while she had such a calm demeanor.

"It's nice to see you again, Miss Chance," the inspector began. "You're looking well."

"Thank you. It's nice to see you too."

"I'm trying to find your friend, Kate Evans. She seems to have disappeared," the inspector said. "Do you have any idea where she can be?"

"No, I have no idea at all. I haven't seen her for days," she assured him. "Actually, we seldom see each other, even though we both work for Henri as tour guides."

"So you have no idea where she could be? Was she seeing anybody? Could she have gone back to the States?"

"I'm sorry, Inspector, but I just don't know. We're on friendly terms, but we're not really friends. Kate's a very private person, and she doesn't discuss personal things. At least not with me."

"Well then, thank you for your help, Miss Chance," the inspector said.

"You can go along now, my dear," Casanova added, in a proprietory voice. "The inspector and I are just finishing our business. I'll be up to join you in a few minutes."

"What about my cold refreshment?"

"I'll have Carlo take it up to your room."

"All right, then," Tiffany said, gathering her elegant frills around her sleek body and walking away in a dignified but obedient style.

"I think that concludes our interview," Casanova said, when they had both had ample opportunity to watch the striking blonde make her exit.

"For the moment, yes," the inspector said, intimating that Henri Casanova had not seen the last of him, nor heard the last of the matter.

But Inspector Martin did feel that he had lost round one.

CHAPTER FIFTEEN

When Inspector Martin got back to headquarters, an excited Benamou greeted him with good news. The ballistics analysis report had come back, and the weapons used in the jewelry store incident had indeed been used in other unsolved crimes. Chief among them were the murders in the basilica and in Kate's hotel room. As Martin read through the information, he realized he was going to be able to close the files on four killings at one time. It was an incredible coup for his department, and it would loosen his schedule so that he could concentrate on finding Kate Evans.

The ballistic report on the gun found near Mondragon's body proved to be the same one used to kill Luciani, the corpse found in the confessional at the basilica. Martin's suspicions had been correct. Mondragon had executed the man and then sidled up to Kate, who in her innocence could not imagine that he had just killed a man a few seconds before. Kate had said that she couldn't believe that Pierre could coolly turn on the charm a moment later for the benefit of a tourist who would unknowingly help him cover his escape. Kate clearly had no knowledge of the pathological psyche of a professional killer, which was another sign to René that she had no part in the criminal activities going on around her.

The second gun, belonging to Didier Albertini, was the one that fired the bullet that had killed Professor Jolicoeur in Kate's hotel room. The killer had worn a black knitted ski mask, according to Kate's testimony. So here was the body of a dead hood wearing a mask and using the same gun found in his hand at both scenes – the basilica and the hotel. It was only circumstantial evidence, but since the suspect was now dead, Martin thought he could close the case on the Professor's murder. He had the killer, but he still lacked a motive. Later he would be able to supply that as well.

"Benamou," said Inspector Martin, "we've solved two murders simultaneously, and the murderers have killed each other too, thus saving the government the expense of a trial. Since France so generously gave up the death penalty, we've also saved the expense of keeping these killers alive during a lifetime of incarceration."

"Yes Boss, I'm sure that in the annals of criminology it will be recorded as a magnificent accomplishment."

"But the credit will go to Lady Luck, not to the hard-working detectives who solved the murders," Martin added with a sigh.

"Cheerful about the gratitude we get in our profession aren't we?" Benamou replied.

"Just being realistic," Inspector Martin said. "Now we'd better go find the missing American girl, Kate Evans. By the way, I did find the other girl, Tiffany Chance. She's living with Henri Casanova, it appears."

"Too bad for her," Banamou replied.

"Perhaps not, she seems happy to be living in the lap of luxury, but I doubt that she knows how dangerous Casanova really is. Although she's just another naïve American, she may be helpful to us later."

"Maybe she will. Now what would you like me to do?" Benamou asked.

"Let's find Kate Evans as fast as we can."

"OK, let's do that," Benamou agreed. "What specifically can I do to help?"

"Contact the Evans girl's next of kin. You can get the number from the Sorbonne," the inspector told him. "Call and ask her parents if they've heard from her at all, or if they know where she is. We don't want to go on a wild goose chase if the girl only went to a spa, or something like that."

René Martin appreciated the talents of his assistant. He wasn't creative, but if he was told what to do he would never give up trying to do it. Benamou was not only tenacious but he was also a team player, seeking results before looking for personal recognition. The differences between René Martin and Benamou lay mainly in subtleties such as intuition and erudition.

Kate was thinking carefully about her situation. She still felt that Casanova had probably made some sort of mistake, and that she would be able to convince him of this as soon as she had a chance to speak with him. Henri's distractions had so far kept him from entertaining himself at Kate's expense. She had closely inspected her environment and decided that there was no way she could escape. If she had some tools and a lot of time, maybe she could force her way out of the room, but she had nothing to work with but her bare hands and her brain. She decided that unless something happened from the outside, she was going to be stuck inside for as long as Casanova wanted it that way.

When she heard the sound of heavy footsteps outside the door of her cell, she thought her release was at hand. After a few fiddling noises, a tray slid under the door through a small opening cut just above the floor. It was a tray of food. She jumped up, ran to the door, and yelled.

"Hey, let me out!"

When she got absolutely no response she tried again. "Hey, I'm locked in here!"

How stupid, she thought. They knew she was locked in there, otherwise why would they have brought her breakfast? She thought she could hear some heavy footsteps receding. Probably Santori's, she guessed. There was nothing left to do but eat, so she sat on the little chair at the table against the wall and sniffed at the scrambled eggs. She wondered briefly if the food was drugged or poisoned, but she quickly dismissed her suspicions. Who would want to poison her? If they wanted to kill her they could have done it already, so why resort to poison? Anyway, the food tasted fine. Better

than fine, in fact. She didn't give much credence to the
drugging possibility either.

Whoever was holding her captive must have his reasons
for doing so. What could they possibly be? She wasn't
anyone special – just an ordinary American student at the
Sorbonne. If it was money they were after, she wasn't rich,
or a celebrity who might bring a large ransom. She didn't
feel she had any information that could be of use or of harm
to anyone. So what was she doing there? It had to be Henri
Casanova who was responsible for locking her up. After all,
it was his estate she was on. René Martin had tried to warn
her about Casanova, but she'd chosen to ignore his warning.
How smart was that? Maybe that was it. Perhaps Casanova
thought she was in league with the police because of her
relationship with the inspector. But how did he know that
there was a relationship between them? She had certainly
never discussed it with him. Her mind was clicking away
furiously over every motive that he might have for keeping
her locked up like this.

Could he be planning a sexual assault? That didn't seem
credible either. After all, he seemed to have lined Tiffany up
for that purpose. Why would he need her, if he had Tiffany?
Her lack of self-esteem was still working fine even though
she was a kidnap victim. It amazed her how, in spite of what
could conceivably be a life-threatening situation, she could
still summon up enough insecurity to allow her charms to be
overcome by Tiffany's Miss California beauty and sexuality.
She made a clear effort to dispel that kind of unproductive
thinking. She remembered that René appeared to find her
attractive, even when compared with the blonde bombshell
herself. That was reassuring, and she did believe that her
inspector was out there looking for her at that very moment.
Had she but known that he had failed to find her when he
was only a few yards away from her on Casanova's estate
that day, she might have worried that he would now give up
looking for her there.

The day passed painfully slowly for Kate. The night was worse – total silence except for the waves sloshing against the shore. Finally, after she had finished eating her breakfast the next morning, the door was unlocked and Casanova came in with Santori in his wake.

"I'm sorry I couldn't stop by to see you sooner, but I've been very busy," Casanova said, without the slightest hint of apology or explanation. "I hope the meals I sent you were to your liking."

"Mr. Casanova, why was I brought here? And why am I being held prisoner?" Kate asked him.

"You were brought here because this is where I want you to be. As far as why you're being held prisoner, that's exactly why you are here, to find out why."

"I don't understand, sir," Kate said politely, hoping that if she didn't get angry maybe he'd be tolerant with her.

"It has come to my attention that you've been seeing Inspector Martin socially," Casanova said, as if she should be ashamed at being caught in a compromising position.

"I don't deny that we've had several dates, but what of it?" Kate said straightforwardly.

"Well, my dear, he's a detective gendarme, and we can't have our employees consorting with undesirables. When you first came to work for me I said you were free to do anything you wished with our clients, but I didn't give you permission to date policemen."

"Why should I need your permission?" Kate objected. "Isn't this a free country?"

"My dear child, you have a lot to learn," Henri smiled. This is a free country when I say it is, but until then you must follow my instructions. Now, let's get down to business and stop arguing about your choice of boyfriends. If you answer my questions truthfully, I just might allow you to get back to the inspector's apartment so you can finish what you started the other day."

"What are your questions?" Kate asked him, ignoring the innuendo but wondering how he knew about intimate details like that.

"It's not your shame that I wish to elicit, but rather your honesty," Casanova continued. "I have a perfect right to be concerned about a female employee of mine who consorts with a police officer who wishes to put me out of business."

"But Mr. Casanova, I don't know anything about your business, so it shouldn't matter if I see a policeman socially."

"If only life were that simple, Kate," Casanova replied. "But it really isn't, you see. So I have to ask you if during your pillow talk, or at any other time, you've divulged any information about our business to your detective?"

"No, we don't talk about your business, and I wish you'd stop talking about mine," Kate said, trying to be firm with him, but realizing that she was not in a strong position.

"I see," Casanova said patiently. "So you're saying that never, even once, did the inspector ask you anything about what you were doing for me?"

"Well, I told him that I was a tour guide and that I led rich clients on exclusive private tours of the sights on the Riviera," Kate answered. "That's all I said."

"I'll test the veracity of your statements and let you know if you passed my honesty exam tomorrow. If you really are a student, as you say, you'll understand that you can't advance to the next stage until you've passed the first. Now let me have your dress and I'll have it cleaned. I know it's your best and only dressy dress. You've been wearing it day and night for several days, and it's beginning to look awful. We can't have our employees looking like that."

"I won't remove my dress," Kate objected strenuously.

"Don't be stupid, girl. I'll have it cleaned and returned to you in a day or two."

"No. I have nothing else to wear," Kate replied.

"You're not going anywhere, and there's no one here to see you. You must learn to obey me. I can have Santori take off your dress for you if you prefer, but I fear the garment may be torn or damaged if you struggle with him."

Kate stood up and walked over to the cot. She removed the blanket and wrapped herself in it to cover her body as she unzipped the red dress, stepping out of it as it fell at her feet. The dress was lined, which eliminated the need for her wearing a slip underneath, and as a result she was now left with nothing on but her bra and panties. She was feeling very vulnerable as Santori collected the dress from the floor, incidentally taking her shoes as well.

"That's better, Kate," Casanova said confidently, having had his pound of obedience. "Now I want you to spend the next twenty-four hours remembering if you told Inspector Martin anything that you shouldn't have."

Benamou had made his call to Kate Evans' parents. He informed Inspector Martin that the girl's parents had no idea where she was. They assumed she was still traveling in the South of France, gathering information for her thesis. They told the assistant inspector that they had spoken to her a couple of days before, and she had told them she was fine. They seemed to become more concerned as the conversation continued, so Benamou reported that he had reassured them by telling them his inquiry was routine, and asked them to have their daughter call him if she happened to get in touch.

"That was good," Inspector Martin told his assistant. "No sense getting the parents riled up unnecessarily."

"That's what I thought," Benamou replied. "After all, she's only been missing for a couple of days."

"Right, and we haven't received any request for ransom money, or any reports of anyone fitting her description being hospitalized," the inspector replied, as if trying to convince himself. "Still, I don't believe what the chauffeur told me about that night in Cannes. What if Kate stayed in the car, and didn't go into the jewelry store, as he claimed? In that case, if he didn't drop her at her hotel or someplace else along the way, he'd have brought her back to Casanova's villa."

"Casanova's a snake, but would he be foolish enough to keep a hostage in his house when he knows we're looking for her?" Benamou asked.

"He's a megalomaniac, and thinks he's above the law," the inspector mused aloud. "It's just possible that he has her locked up somewhere on his estate. He knows the law and therefore he knows we've got to have reasonable cause in order to get a search warrant for her. I know he disrespects the police, and he'd enjoy leading us on a wild goose chase. If I had to guess where Kate is, I'd bet anything that at a minimum he knows where she is, and most probably he's the one responsible for having had her kidnapped."

"What are you going to do about it?" Benamou asked.

"I think I've got to pay an unscheduled visit to his estate and make my own search," Martin said. "I know searching without a warrant is illegal, and it might mean my career if I'm caught, but I can't let this snake, as you call him, use the protection of the paper law to enable him to commit crimes of physical violence."

"Be careful, Inspector," Benamou warned him. "It isn't just your career at stake here. All the groundwork we've done to prepare a racketeering case against the Corsican Mafia may go down the drain if you're caught making an illegal search."

"I realize that, my friend," Martin said, "but I can't just let this snake take innocent people off the street and make them disappear."

"I can't help thinking that you have a special interest in this particular girl," Benamou suggested.

"You're right about that," Martin admitted. "And I may be responsible for her being where she is now."

"How did you reach that conclusion?"

"Well, I asked her to give me a list of the places she was told to take her tourists," Martin said. "I hoped it would help me line up the vendors that were being bled in the protection racket. If Casanova found out somehow that Kate was acting as an informant for me, he could be holding the girl as insurance so we won't come after him."

"That's one theory," Benamou said, "but why hasn't he released a ransom note, or in some way let us know that he has her?"

"He's too smart for that," the inspector theorized. "He's subtle. He's going to let this drag on. Somehow he found out that I have a special interest in Kate Evans, and he's trying to make me back off my investigation of the Corsican Mafia by using her against me."

"How did he find out about you and Kate?" Benamou asked. "Even *I* didn't know, until you told me just now."

"Please keep it to yourself," Martin said. "If you say anything, the superintendent will take me off the case, and I couldn't bear that."

"I understand," Benamou said, "but no more lone wolf stuff. You've got to tell me what you're doing and where you're going. Trust me on this. I'm done if you keep me out of the loop."

It was the first time Benamou had ever been so firm about anything since he had partnered with him, but Martin didn't think too much of it at the time.

Casanova was pleased with himself. His first interview with his prisoner had gone well, he thought. He had applied the first turn of the screw. He had emphasized the helplessness of Kate's position. He had successfully demonstrated his absolute authority over her. His ruse about having her dress cleaned for her was brilliant. Getting her to take off her dress was the first step in increasing her vulnerability. Nakedness was often a condition used to pry information from prisoners. The military interrogators at the Abu Ghraib prison in Iraq knew that, but public opinion trumped military ruthlessness. Henri Casanova, however, didn't have adverse public relations to contend with.

His next step would be similar to the first, but would heighten the fear element. She would have to be forced to turn the control over to him. If it could be done in his phony avuncular fashion so much the better, but if not, he wasn't averse to using physical means to loosen her tongue and break down her resistance. He dressed himself stylishly while he was thinking about his next visit to Kate's cell. Emphasizing the difference between his elegance and her nakedness was a subtle way of demonstrating his role as the powerful man, and her utter subjection to him. Casanova regarded this next visit as one more step along the way. The domination of his will over hers by the use of his techniques was a source of great satisfaction to him.

This time Casanova had Santori stand outside the door, but only after he'd made sure that Kate knew the strongman was there.

"Good morning, Kate," Henri said cheerfully. "I hope you slept well."

"Have you brought me my dress?" Kate said curtly.

"No, my dear, it hasn't come back from the cleaners yet," Henri lied, as he had no intention of sending anything belonging to Kate off the estate.

"I'm not going to answer any questions until you return my shoes and my dress," Kate said adamantly. "It's not fair. Look at you, all dressed up as though you were going to a party, while I'm shivering in nothing but a blanket."

"You Americans are always worrying about what's fair," he said coldly. "You should really be thinking about how your situation could worsen if you don't tell me what I want to know."

"I've already told you that I don't know anything. "And I haven't told René anything I don't know, either."

"Ah, now it's René, is it? You expect me to believe that when you were poring over the paper together in the bar at your hotel it had nothing to do with my business?"

"How do you know about that?"

Kate reddened as she realized that she had now admitted that she had conspired against him with the inspector.

"Don't you feel better now that you have admitted your guilt?" Henri asked, as he continued to question her. "Just think of me as your father confessor."

Kate was scared now. Casanova had trapped her into an admission. She had no idea what he would do now. Then it occurred to her that she had never told him what was written on the paper. He was only on a fishing trip. She resolved to be more circumspect. She would watch every word she said to him.

"I don't know what you think I confessed to," Kate said. "So you saw us talking together and going over a piece of paper, but what does that prove?"

"What was written on that paper is what concerns me," Henri said.

"It was nothing important," Kate assured him.

"I'll be the judge of that," Casanova said. "Now take off your bra and hand it to me, please."

He spoke in such a natural, soft-spoken manner that she thought she must have heard him wrong.

"What?" she said.

"I said," Casanova repeated in a pleasant but firm voice, "remove your bra and hand it to me."

"No, I certainly will not," she replied in a feisty tone.

"I'm afraid you have no choice in the matter, Kate, so don't be difficult. If you don't do as I say, the guard outside the door will remove it for you."

Casanova extended his hand as if to receive the article of clothing. Kate quickly picked up the blanket, wrapped it around herself with rebellious panache, and removed her bra without his seeing her body. Then she hung the bra from her index finger, so that he would have to come and get it. Henri snatched it from her and turned to leave.

"You needn't be shy with me, Kate. I've already seen you undressed," he said. "I'll be back tomorrow, and when I come I expect you to tell me every word that was on the paper you were so avidly studying with your sweetie pie."

"What are you talking about? You've never seen me naked!"

"Well, it's of little importance, anyway. Don't abandon hope, you who are confined here." Casanova smiled at her over his shoulder as he went out the door.

His parting words hung in the air as Kate thought about them. The tattoo! He was referring to the tattoo! How many times had she regretted acquiring that piece of indelible artwork? Only her sorority sisters knew what it said and where it was. How could Casanova possibly know about it? Perhaps it was just a coincidental farewell in the form of an adaptation of the famous quote? For that matter, how did he know about her meeting with René Martin? Did the Mafia have her inspector under surveillance? Wasn't it the police who did surveillances? Kate was beginning to believe that nothing was a coincidence when it came to Henri Casanova, and she was right.

CHAPTER SIXTEEN

The sun was at its apogée when Tiffany decided to go for a swim. Ever since she had moved to Casanova's villa, it was part of her daily routine to have a swim in the Mediterranean. She loved the sun, and she loved the fact that everyone on the Riviera swam au naturel. Back home her tan would trace the outline of her bikini. Here there were no ridiculous white patches, just a smooth tan all over, the way everyone wants their skin to look. Tiffany couldn't imagine why the people in the States made such a fuss about nude bathing. Who really cares? Probably only those whose bodies aren't in good shape and who don't look good in a bathing suit, she mused.

If Tiffany had thought about it, the hypocrisy of the European naturalists was daily being made manifest by the fact that Casanova's male staff would position themselves in hiding to watch the daily show, an event that Tiffany hadn't failed to notice. Depending on the actual degree of physical attractiveness of the peeping Toms, she would sometimes be annoyed with them and sometimes feel rather flattered.

Her routine consisted in walking from the villa to the beach, where she would disrobe and lie on a chaise longue, turning over occasionally in the sun. When she got hot she would walk into the sea and swim for a while. After that she would walk nude to a cabana that was built close to the villa for the purpose of allowing swimmers to shower off any sand that they might otherwise have tracked into the main house.

It was on this walk, and in this shower, that Santori, the gardeners, and the security guards were rewarded for their vigilance. If Casanova had known about this intramural activity on the part of his employees, he would not have been pleased. His women, for however long their tenure lasted, had to endure the European double standard, whereby they could enjoy the attentions of no other men, even though he had no reciprocal exclusivity contract. His rule was well understood by all, but Tiffany didn't think it applied to her daily swim and the ablutions that followed. She regarded it as a harmless performance that she put on for her various admirers. It was harmless enough until Casanova discovered her Susanna and the Elders routine.

Casanova was completely occupied for the moment with the speech he was going to deliver at the meeting with the other dons. He was too busy with more important matters to supervise his exhibitionist girlfriend for twenty-four hours a day. He should have remembered, however, that inattention to small details tended to lead to the creation of much larger problems. He knew this was a possibility, of course, but he couldn't resist the opportunity of enhancing his reputation as the wise man of the crime bosses of France.

He was preparing a case study to demonstrate how a few key strokes injected into an international bank's accounting system by a talented hacker could result in the transfer of more money to the Mafia than could be had by breaking the knee caps of all the recalcitrant merchants in France. He realized that his long-time crime partners had to be weaned away from their antiquated operations in gambling, money lending, drugs, prostitution, and conventional racketeering. He would point out to his colleagues how the government had inexorably moved in on the Mafia's traditional rackets, appropriating them for themselves. He was going to cite how the government had closed down the numbers racket by substituting lotteries, and how they had taken over off-track betting, displacing the mob's bookmakers.

The government, in fact, had clearly become the crime syndicate's biggest competitor. He would show the other dons how they could improve their traditional areas of doing business by streamlining them with some modern electronic management methods. Then, after they saw the advantages gained by modernizing their traditional businesses, he could move them to new fields in 21st century white-collar crime that were simply begging for organized exploitation. Once his associates were properly trained, he thought happily, the sky would be the limit.

Assistant Inspector Benamou was in a very ticklish position. He was searching the living quarters of the dead men found in Litwak's jewelry store, looking for clues that would link them to the Corsican Mafia. He feared that what he found in Didier Albertini's apartment might upset his police partner more than it would the Casanova Mafia family. Inspector René Martin had told him in confidence of his love for Kate Evans. Now this piece of evidence might very well break his friend's heart.

There it was on Didier's computer screen in the photo file, a picture of Kate Evans, tied up and bound to a bed. At first Benamou didn't absorb all the details beyond the fact that she was a lovely young woman. Then he remembered that she had been discovered that way, and had been untied by the hotel maids before he and Inspector Martin arrived on the scene. In her statement to the police, Kate had neglected to mention that someone had taken photos of her.

When he examined the photos closely, the policeman could see the name of the hotel printed on towels visible in the background. It was obvious that the man who murdered the professor also tied up the witness and took the photos.

A host of questions came flooding into the cop's brain. Why hadn't the witness also been killed? The murderer was taking a big risk by leaving a witness alive. Had she been spared because she and the killer were in this together? Did the murderer spare her life because they had some sort of an intimate relationship? If either of those possibilities were her reasons for keeping silent, it would mean she probably knew who the killer was all along, and therefore had intentionally lied when making her statement to the inspector when she had told him that she couldn't identify the killer because he was wearing a mask.

When Benamou looked even more closely at the photos he saw that Kate's wrists and ankles were not yet chafed from the ropes that bound them, which led him to conclude that the pictures were taken hours before the maids found her. He recalled that when the inspector took her statement, her wrists were red and bruised from having been tied for a long time. Was the whole crime scene a set up? Benamou was confused except for one thing, and that was that none of these possibilities enhanced the reputation of the girl whom Inspector René Martin loved.

One last thing that also offended the Muslim detective's sensibilities was the close-up of Kate's tattoo. Although his family had immigrated from North Africa two generations ago, they had nonetheless held onto their Islamic principles. So his ideas about female behavior were always were held in tension between his Muslim beliefs about female modesty and the depravity of modern French culture.

Benamou wasn't familiar with Dante's quote, so he assumed the inked printed warning on the tattoo was the mark of a whore. "Abandon hope, all ye who enter here." To Benamou this was an open invitation to every man who laid eyes on her. He was going to have to be the one who showed René these photos. Being the friend who tells a man that his intended bride is a whore was not a position the detective wanted to be in.

It got even worse when he called the phone number that was attached to the stack of Kate's bondage photos that had been left next to the computer, presumably by the killer. He immediately recognized the voice and name of a porno flick producer who had been involved off and on with the police concerning pederasty and other suspected sex crime charges.

The porn king readily admitted purchasing the photo of a new bondage girl from Didier Albertini, who had described her as an actress. He had had no reason to doubt Albertini, and paid him a fair price for the pictures. He particularly liked the close up, quirky shot of her tattoo, which was now in wide distribution. Ironically the porn producer asked Benamou if he could put him in touch with the actress, as he wanted to use her in some of his upcoming film projects.

Inspector Martin was at his desk, mentally preparing his invasion of Casanova's villa complex so he could perform a search – legal or not. If he had been able to get a search warrant he could have called upon the resources of the police department to invade Casanova's Corsican Duchy by force, but as things were, he would have to go in alone. There were some advantages, however, to a stealthy, one-man mission. The primary one was secrecy, but confidentiality was a close second. The young inspector didn't know whom to trust in his own department. Casanova's corruption of officialdom reached broadly across the gendarmerie, the judiciary, and political circles. He had made up his mind to go it alone, but he had promised Benamou not to engage in any one-man heroics.

Could he even trust Benamou? To what extent should he confide in him? They had been associated only since Martin's recent transfer to the Marseilles region, so although Benamou seemed perfectly dependable and trustworthy, he might be in Casanova's pocket along with the rest. If he told his assistant about his plan to search for Kate, and Benamou turned out to be a traitor, he would warn Casanova that he was coming. In that event he might be killed, but his career would surely be over if he were caught conducting a criminal break-and-enter without a warrant. Kate's life might lie in the balance, so his decision about whether to trust Benamou was critical. In the end he felt that the deciding factor had to be Kate's life and welfare. Martin couldn't risk it. He'd have to be a lone wolf regardless of his promise.

René Martin had reached that point in his reflections when Benamou approached his desk. He had just come from searching Didier Albertini's place, and he was gathering his nerve to show the pictures he had found there to his boss.

"Inspector, I've got something to show you, even though it distresses me to have to do it."

"What is it, my friend?" Martin asked.

"It's..." Benamou shifted his weight as he spoke. "It's these." He handed his boss a large envelope, and waited for his reaction before saying anything else.

"What are they?" the inspector asked him, hesitating to open the envelope.

"You'll see. I found those photographs in Albertini's apartment," he added, as Martin began looking at them.

"Do you think these copies are all there are?" Martin finally asked.

"I'm afraid not. The little weasel sold one to that porn producer we arrested a year ago, and he distributed them widely. I'm guessing that by now most of the creeps in France have seen them, and probably found the tattoo quite amusing."

"And what do you think about the photos and the tattoo, Benamou?" Martin asked.

"What can I think? It's pretty obvious that the girl's a little tart," he blurted out.

"That's a pretty harsh judgment, isn't it?" the inspector said indignantly. "You're jumping to conclusions. What if there's a perfectly good explanation for the tattoo? Don't you think she should be given a chance to tell you about it? Isn't it possible you're jumping the gun?"

"Perhaps I could be, but what else can a man think of a woman who has such a tattoo, especially there," Benamou said, sorry that his boss found it necessary to defend his concubine. "Are you suggesting that she was forced to get that tattoo?"

"No, not necessarily that," Martin replied, "but the tattoo could be just the result of a dare, for instance."

"If it is, it's an unfortunate one for a woman to play at," Benamou said with authority, because he firmly believed that every man seeing that tattoo was going to think the woman was a whore.

"Have you any idea how many women have gotten tattoos in recent years since the practice became popular?" René asked.

"A good many, I suppose."

"Yes, and can they all be whores?"

"Maybe not all, but a good many are, and women who get them where she got hers probably are."

"Look carefully at this photo, Benamou," the inspector said. "Look at her eyes instead of where your focus has evidently been. If you do that you'll see that she's terrified, and completely ashamed to be in the position she's in. Her facial expression, in spite of the tape over her mouth, shows a total disgust for her captor. She's an obvious victim, not a conspirator."

"Albertini said that she was an actress," Benamou said, relentlessly defending his position. "Perhaps she was just acting for the camera."

"Did you read what the tattoo said?" the inspector asked his partner.

"Of course I did."

"And what do you think it means?"

"It's clear that it means that any man having sex with her is going to hell," Benamou said, with complete self-assurance and conviction.

"What it says is a quote from Dante's *Divine Comedy*. It's a poetic allegory, and I don't interpret its meaning on Kate's body to be a warning that any man having sex with her is going to hell. My interpretation would be entirely different."

"Look, René, I didn't want to be the one who told you about this. And I didn't know it was a quote from a poem. In Islam we don't believe in porn, whether it's a poem or not. And we don't marry women unless they are virgins, but what you Christians do is up to you. Now if it's all right with you, I'm going over to Mondragon's pad and see what revelations I can find among his belongings."

"Good. You do that," Inspector Martin replied curtly. "We'll catch up later."

Both men were glad to get off the topic of Kate's virtue. It was instructive to both of them to see the basic differences in attitude that societal and religious mores had managed to produce in two modern men of approximately the same age. The Muslim was intolerant of human foibles, and demanded absolute adherence to Islamic principles. The Christian was indoctrinated with the concept of universal sin and the hope of redemption. When these principles were applied to an actual case, the differences were antithetical, and Martin didn't see any possibility of reconciliation with Benamou's attitude. He resolved, therefore, not to share with him his plan to conduct an unauthorized search for Kate on Henri Casanova's estate.

Henri had made his final preparations. He was now ready to attend the meeting of Corsican Mafia bosses at which he would present his ideas for revolutionizing the Cosa Nostra. Tradition had it that wives and mistresses were not invited to these affairs. The attitude held by the stony men of the Mafia was that business was not for women. After their business was concluded they might hold an orgiastic party, but the women present at these affairs were not wives or women with whom they had ongoing relationships.

As a result, Henri Casanova didn't plan to take Tiffany along, although he would dearly have liked to show her off to his fellow dons. For her part Tiffany had mixed feelings about being left behind. On the one hand she would have liked to meet the other men that Henri counted as colleagues so that she could strut her stuff, but pampering herself in an elegant Riviera villa was good too.

Two young hoods had been promoted from the ranks of the Mafia to come to the mainland and work for Casanova in Marseilles. Their first assignment was to act as security on the don's estate while he was attending the big meeting. They had a couple of days of orientation with him and his man, Santori. Tiffany had been introduced to them briefly. She didn't particularly like them, as she thought they were greasy, strutting dolts, at once provincial and egotistical. Although normally she enjoyed being admired for her physical characteristics, she hated being ogled by these two leering idiots who never missed a chance to watch her swimming routine. She was afraid to speak to Henri about this, as she knew his jealous reaction would be violent. She would put up with their ogling as long as they didn't try to touch her or speak to her with vulgar language. She decided to keep mum about the hoods, which only served to make them cockier.

Before Henri left for his meeting he wanted to have one more session with Kate in her prison room in the boathouse. He intended to use the electronic intelligence his G-men had assembled as an example of the way that information could be gathered about the private and public movements of the police. Then he would point out this information about the private lives of policemen could be used to bring them into the Mafia's circle of corruption. He planned to cite how finding out about the secret relationship between Kate and Inspector Martin was a way to force the inspector to cave in to the don's desire to get him on the sleeve.

Before presenting his case study, Henri Casanova had to be sure he had received all the information he could get from Kate. He donned his cream-colored jacket, straightened his flowered necktie, gathered up some photographs from his desk, and strode off to the boathouse.

"Good day Miss Evans," he said cheerily. "I trust you slept well and that the food is to your liking."

"What difference do those things make? I'm in prison!" Kate shouted. "Food and sleep don't replace freedom. Why have you taken my clothes away and kept me here against my will? You should be ashamed of yourself," she added courageously, wrapping the blanket more tightly around her body.

"My dear young woman," Henri said calmly, trying to sound as reasonable as possible. "You simply refuse to learn that things can always get worse. Your attitude forces me to demonstrate that even in the pitiful state that you claim to be in, things can still get much, much worse. Please remove your last undergarment and give it to me," he demanded, holding his hand out as before.

"Are you some kind of sex maniac? Is this some kind of a strip poker game you're playing with me? Why should I be stripped naked in order to answer your questions?"

"You're being unfair to me," Henri objected. "Have I even so much as touched you?"

"No you haven't. So then why then do you insist on my being naked?"

"To be perfectly frank," Henri said, with an ingratiating smile, "a naked young woman is innocently vulnerable and more likely to tell the truth when all her artifice is stripped away. It's one of the nicer ways to elicit information from an unwilling informant. Don't you agree?"

"Of course not! As far as I'm concerned there's nothing nice about it at all."

"Oh, so would you prefer painful torture, then?" Henri snapped, losing his patience. "Hand over those ludicrously skimpy little panties that cover barely anything, and nothing I haven't read before."

"What are you talking about?"

"Just these," he said, handing Kate the photographs that Didier had taken of her. He waited a full minute while she studied them. "Now will you remove those absurd panties? Or will Santori be given the pleasure?"

Kate returned the handful of photos to Henri. She gripped the blanket tightly around her neck with one hand while she used her other hand to help her wriggle out of her underpants. When her last article of clothing fell to her ankles, she stepped out of them with one foot, and with the other foot lifted the garment with her big toe, and presented it to her tormentor.

"Now that we've got that settled," Casanova said, "Let's return to the question of what was written on the sheet of paper that you and Inspector Martin were studying with such great interest. Are you now prepared to tell me?"

"I did tell you," Kate reminded him, flipping her hair in defiance. "I told you it was nothing of importance."

"Now, now, don't be difficult. You'll force me to take further steps."

"What else can I possibly give you?"

"The blanket, perhaps?" Casanova replied, with an evil smile.

"All right," Kate admitted, "I gave the inspector a list of the shops that you told me to take the clients to. That was all. Now will you please let me go?"

"That was your confession, but I still have to decide what your penance will be."

"Who appointed you to be my judge?" Kate said angrily. "What harm did it do to tell the inspector that little snippet of information? He could have followed me and gotten it anyway, without asking me for it."

"You miss the point, Kate," Henri said. "You betrayed me. I employed you, paid you, and you gave away pertinent business information to the cops. It was private information. You're nothing but an ambitious little police informant, and you penetrated my organization using your feminine wiles. Now I must make your punishment fit your crime."

"But you said you'd let me go if I told you what you wanted to know," Kate protested.

"There are penalties that must be levied," Casanova said angrily, looking into her eyes. He grabbed the blanket at her throat where she held it, and yanked with all his strength. It came away from a terrified Kate, who quickly crouched over to cover her nakedness.

Then Henri turned and swaggered out of the room, like a bullfighter dragging his cape after successfully impaling his foe and driving it to its knees. His plans for Kate had nothing to do with nudity, nor had they ever involved nudity. This was just a little diversionary exercise that he engaged in to teach his hostage a lesson. He knew right from the start exactly what she had told the inspector, and how little use the information would be to him.

CHAPTER SEVENTEEN

Tiffany Chance had just performed her swimming ritual to everyone's satisfaction. Casanova was away at his meeting. She stretched out on her beach chaise and did her daily homage to the sun. The cackling teen-aged guards had enjoyed their peep-show and had gone off to perform other duties. After an hour or so of lotion-enhanced sunbathing, Tiffany took it into her head to have a look at the boathouse. She had never dared to veer off the beaten path before, but since Henri was absent, she thought she'd just have a little look around. After all, wasn't she the lady of the house? Surely this gave her carte blanche to do what she wanted and to go where she pleased. Convinced, she walked in the direction of the boathouse, approaching it from the seaside beach instead of along the path from the villa.

The exterior of the boathouse had the same architectural influences as the villa. Inside, however, it was essentially a warehouse to store and launch Henri's smaller water toys. Coming inside after being out in the sunshine, Tiffany's eyes had to adjust to the shade. When her vision cleared she saw that the center of the structure was a dredged-out mini harbor that connected to the Mediterranean. It was a sort of roofed-over, open-ended swimming pool for small craft. On two sides of the concrete retaining walls were racks that held samples of the entire range of available watercraft. At the center, floating in the water and at the ready, was a thirty-five foot cigarette boat capable of rending the water at over sixty miles per hour. It reminded Tiffany of a U-Boat pen from WWII. A large, boomed lifting-crane could reach any of the stored vessels and drop them into the water or pluck them out when they returned.

Along the third side were racks and shelves containing every kind of nautical gear imaginable. A steel staircase led up to a second-story balcony that looked down on Henri's personal marina. The upper deck had three doors that could have been either shops or offices. For some inexplicable reason Tiffany decided to see what was behind those doors. She climbed up the noisy steel stairs and walked along the railed passageway.

The first door opened when she twisted the door handle. Inside was a small but well-equipped machine shop. The second door was an office suitable for a marine architect. When she reached the third door, Tiffany saw that it was locked with a padlock. She peeked inquisitively through the peephole, expecting to see some expensive electronic boat gear that was being kept under lock and key for safekeeping. But when she put her eye to the little peephole, she jumped back in astonishment when she saw a green eye peering back at her from inside.

"Tiffany?"

"Kate?"

"Yes!"

"What are you doing in there?" Tiffany asked.

"First tell me, are you alone?"

"Yes, I'm alone," Tiffany replied.

"Did anyone see you come in here?" Kate asked. "You could be in big trouble if anyone saw you."

"I don't think I was seen."

"Listen, Casanova has me locked up in here."

"He hasn't touched you, has he?"

"No."

"I thought not," Tiffany said confidently.

"What do you mean?"

"He's impotent, and I should know."

"Get me out of here, Tiffany! I need your help!"

"What can I do? There's a huge padlock on the door, and I don't see a key anywhere."

"Are there any clothes out there? If so, you could shove them through the trapdoor that they push food through. You could use that if you find anything that I can wear."

"I'll push my beach robe through. You can use that. What else can I do?"

"Call Inspector Martin and tell him where I am," Kate said urgently as she pulled Tiffany's robe through the trap door and put it on. "Don't call him from the villa, though. Henri will find out. I'm sure he'll kill him if he sets foot on the estate."

"OK. I'll go back to the villa now and see if I can figure out a safe way to get in touch with René for you."

"Thanks, Tiffany. Please hurry. And be careful!"

Inspector Martin had studied aerial surveillance photos of Casanova's villa and the surrounding grounds, and he had noticed a vulnerable spot. The pictures revealed that boats were taken into the boathouse while they were still in the water. If there was water inside the boathouse, he could enter the property unseen by swimming under water until he was inside. A plan began to gel. He carefully studied the nautical charts of the waters off the Casanova villa, then he gathered up his scuba diving equipment and put it in the trunk of his car. After that he drove to a dive shop, where he rented a suit that he hoped would fit Kate.

Before taking off for the villa, he decided to check his phone messages. There was only one, and it was from a woman who was evidently attempting to disguise her voice and speaking in American English. "Boathouse, upstairs, last door." That was it, the entire message. This four-word message must have come from Tiffany Chance. Who else would leave such an enigmatic message in English for a French policeman? He silently blessed the Californian for this tip, and raised his opinion of her accordingly.

He consulted a commercial fisherman he knew by the name of André, and outlined his plan to him. Like most of the fishermen in the area, André hated the Corsican mafiosi who had been running scams on them for years. Whether it was cheating them on the weight of the fish they caught, or overcharging them for the fuel and supplies they were forced to buy from Mafia operations, there were few fishermen who wouldn't have helped René to inflict a little reciprocal pain on the Corsican Mafia. When André heard what Inspector Martin wanted him to do, he was only too happy to oblige. They loaded the scuba gear aboard his vessel and went into the pilothouse where they pored over a chart of the area of interest to the inspector. René pointed out a channel marker buoy located about half a mile seaward of Henri Casanova's boathouse.

"I'd like you to dump me off at this buoy," the inspector said, "and then you should go somewhere as far away as you can, but still within sight of the buoy. I'm going to swim to shore. I don't know how long I'll be on shore, but I'll signal you when to come back and pick me up. If I'm successful, there'll be two of us making the return trip home with you."

"What's the signal?" André asked.

"According to the chart, this light flashes once every ten seconds. If I put a black bag over it for two minutes, will that be long enough for you to know that you can start coming back for us?"

"Yes," André replied. "I'll keep watching the light. If it goes out for two minutes, I'll certainly see that."

A half hour before darkness settled in, André turned the key and the diesel engine rumbled into life. As they left the harbor and turned down the coast in the direction of the Villa Casanova, Martin donned his scuba suit and double-checked his air tanks, valves and gauges. It was pitch black by the time they arrived at the buoy. Martin directed André to slow down and pass the buoy so the beefy forty-five foot fishing boat was between land and the buoy. In this way no one on shore could see the inspector go over the side.

As the fishing boat pulled away, Martin looked at his wrist compass and took a bearing on the boathouse. Just before he dove under the water he noticed that the boathouse had a tall mast that rose up from the roof for an estimated forty feet. It had a red light on top that was visible from a great distance. He lined himself up with the two lights and realized they formed a range light that could be used to pilot vessels into the boathouse at night in the dark if they just kept one light above the other as they ran in on the shore. René calculated that it would take him approximately fifteen minutes to swim the distance underwater. His progress was slowed by the drag of the waterproof bag tethered to him, which contained some gear and the other scuba suit that he had brought along for Kate.

When he surfaced he was inside the boathouse, and just inches away from the bow of the cigarette boat. He slid along the hull, making as little noise as possible. He looked around and couldn't see anyone, but thought he heard men talking and guffawing from higher up in the building. He moved along until he reached the stern of the speedboat, where he could see who was doing the talking. Two young guys were shoving and elbowing each other good naturedly, trying to get a view of the inside of the room through a peephole in the door. It was the last door upstairs. Martin had to use all his self-control to remain quiet as he listened to them.

"Come on little wildcat, show me what you've got," one of them said.

"Yeah kitty, show us your pussy. Meow," he laughed, scratching his nails on the door.

Eventually they got tired of their little game and came down the steel staircase, joking with each other about having to do night security duty for Casanova.

"Where the hell is he, anyway?" one of them said to the other. "He leaves these two sensational-looking American whores here, and then he takes off! Is the old man crazy?"

"Yeah, why didn't he leave them to us, since he's not using them?" the other man replied.

"That would've been nice. I sure could use a piece of one of them," the first man said.

"Which one would you choose?" the second man asked.

"Why choose? We could swap 'em and do 'em both."

The laughing and talking faded as they made their way out of the building and back toward the villa.

René pulled himself out of the water and up onto the cement apron that surrounded the seawater. He took off his flippers and tucked them under the stairs, then he went up silently in his bare feet and approached the door at the end of the corridor. He quietly peered into the room, and he saw Kate with her back to the door. She was wearing some gauzy creation that he didn't recognize. She was either asleep, or feigning sleep so that she could avoid the taunting of the guards. He decided not to try to attract her attention for fear she would think he was just another sex-starved idiot.

He reached into the bag that he had towed to shore and pulled out a pair of heavy-duty snips. He put the jaws over the loop in the padlock and squeezed with all his might. The metal made a cracking noise as the loop was severed in two. He gingerly removed the lock and opened the door wide enough for him to slip into the room.

Kate had heard the noise, but thought it had nothing to do with her. She had grown accustomed to men peeking at her through the door when they thought she wasn't looking. She kept her back to the door as much as possible to avoid the prying eyes of voyeurs.

This time it was different. She knew someone was in the room with her, and she readied herself for the assault she had been expecting for days. So as René approached her, every fiber of her body was alerted. She was coiled to fight the attacker with every ounce of strength she had.

"Kate," he said in a low voice. "It's René. I've come to take you away from here."

She flipped over to see if this was a trick that Casanova was playing on her. He was in a wet suit and it took her a second to recognize him. Her eyes welled up as she saw that it really was René. She reached out to hug him, but he raised his finger to his lips to indicate that she should be silent.

"Here, put on this diving suit," he said, as he passed his waterproof bag over to her.

"Where are the others?" she whispered.

"What others?"

"The other policemen," she replied.

"There are no others," René answered. "We've got to make it on our own. I'll explain later. Just squeeze yourself into that suit as fast as you can. Can you swim? Have you ever used scuba gear?"

"Yes, I'll be fine," Kate replied as she struggled her legs into the rubberized suit.

"I need you to follow me and do exactly what I tell you," he said in a low voice.

Kate nodded and zipped up the vest. She gave him the thumbs up sign to tell him she was ready. Once outside the room, Martin replaced the padlock to make it seem from a distance that everything was in order. Then he took her by the hand and led her stealthily down the stairs. They were just about ready to slip into the water behind the cigarette boat when they heard guffawing voices approaching from the direction of the villa. Hurriedly, the inspector untied a spring line that went from the concrete dock to the boat. He coiled the rope and he and Kate adjusted their masks and air tanks, then slipped unseen beneath the water, keeping the speedboat between them and the voices.

The voices turned out to be the same two Corsican thugs who had taunted Kate through the door of her cell. This time they had more purpose, and they headed to the speedboat and scrambled aboard. In a minute or so the throaty engine of the overpowered vessel sprang to life. The men let go of the lines that tied it to the bollards, failing to notice that one of the spring lines was missing. They steered the boat slowly out of the boathouse.

While the guards were preparing for their departure, Martin had made some preparations of his own. He reasoned that the best way to get away from the boathouse and the villa was to allow themselves to be towed out to sea by their hosts. So while the hoods above were getting ready to shove off, Martin was under their boat making his own exit plans.

He made one end of the stolen line fast to the rudderpost of the boat. He tied two loops in the other end of the line. They would each hold on to a loop, and he and Kate would be towed along below the water, like submarine water skiers. At least that was his plan. The unknown, and thus imperfect, part of the plan was the speed at which the Corsicans would travel. Martin had no idea if they would be able to hold on if the two fools at the helm decided to rev the engine up to the boat's maximum RPMs. He and Kate could always let go and swim the rest of the way to the buoy if necessary, just as he had planned to do in the first place.

Casanova's hoods did go faster than they needed to, especially since they had not turned on their running lights. But fortunately they weren't going far enough to open the engine up to full throttle, so the underwater stowaways were able to hang on. Martin, of course, couldn't see where they were going from underwater, but when he consulted his compass he was pleased and surprised to find that they were on a magnetic heading of 180 degrees, the reciprocal of the course René had taken on his way in to the boathouse. In other words, they were heading right toward the buoy where André was to pick them up.

In a couple of minutes they arrived at their destination, feeling a lot fresher than they would have if they had swum to the marker buoy. As a hedge against any unforeseen foul ups, Martin wrapped the tow rope around the oversized propeller. If the two Corsican hoods happened to spot them getting into the fishing boat, the fouled propeller would at least prevent them from giving chase.

Martin quietly surfaced on the far side of the speedboat to find out what the two thugs were up to. He needn't have worried so much about being spotted, because the two men were busily occupied with the purpose for their short boat trip. The speedboat was idling to seaward of the buoy. The mistral winds were blowing onshore and holding the boat against the French Coast Guard's aid to navigation. This aid to navigation was doing double duty as a means to assist Casanova's smuggling and drug running operations. Martin noticed that in its present position relative to the buoy, the boat was cutting off André's vision of the buoy's light. He would assume that Martin had covered the buoy's light and he would come alongside, as he had agreed to do when Martin signaled that he was ready to be picked up.

The Corsicans were busy hauling something heavy up from the ocean bottom. Whatever it was, it seemed to be tied to the buoy. Evidently the Mafia was using the buoy as a maritime mailbox. Martin knew he had to take advantage of his incredible luck. It was obviously something illegal that they were hauling up, but it didn't matter what it was, as long as he caught them red-handed. These Corsicans worked for Casanova. Perhaps, when he had them in custody, the government lawyer could get them to give evidence against Casanova in return for a plea bargain. Even if they couldn't get the old don for this crime, Martin thought, it would still cost him a lot of francs. With that satisfying thought in mind he fished his revolver out of the waterproof bag and climbed over the stern of the Corsican's boat.

Just as he expected, André had seen the flashing red light stop emitting its warning signal, and he headed back to where he had last seen the light, but he could barely make out the strange scene from such a distance. The speedboat was so close to the buoy it looked as though it had collided with it. Believing that the speedboat had crashed into the lighted bell buoy, André sped up and turned on a searchlight that he used to light the deck when he was fishing at night. He believed that he was going to the aid of possible accident victims, so he gave the fishing boat full throttle.

The Corsicans, however, thought he was a Coast Guard Cutter on patrol. They scrambled to get back amidships to the boat's controls, hoping to take off and outrun the Coast Guard vessel. One of the thugs jumped into the driver's seat, threw the engine in gear, and revved up the motor. The prop spun once, encountered the rope that Martin had wrapped around the prop, bound up, and stalled out, leaving the engine smoking and the boat unmovable.

By this time the second Corsican jumped into the other seat and reached under it for a gun, but Martin came up from behind and surprised him, cold cocking him and pointing his pistol at the man at the wheel.

"You're under arrest," the inspector shouted. "Don't move or I'll shoot."

"Is there something I can do?" Kate asked, clambering over the stern.

"Find some rope and tie these two monkeys up so they can't get out of their seats," René said. "I'll keep my gun trained on them until you're finished."

"Are you all right?" André shouted. "What can I do to help?"

"Rig this boy toy up so you can take her in tow," the inspector commanded. "Her prop is fouled so she can't move on her own. And make fast that big bundle on the foredeck. It's evidence of smuggling."

The fisherman maneuvered his able vessel into position to take the cigarette boat in tow. Using a hawser he kept for emergencies, he led the rope from a deck cleat on the bow of the yacht to a cleat on the stern of his boat. Kate managed to bind the prisoners up like a couple of mummies while the inspector searched the boat for guns, collecting a half dozen assorted illegal automatic weapons. When all of this was accomplished Kate and René stepped aboard the fishing boat in their wet suits. André slowly moved ahead, pulling his tow in a wide arc to clear it around the buoy, gaining speed gradually as he moved toward home.

"Better call the Coast Guard and tell them you have a vessel in tow and will be dropping it off at their dock," the inspector ordered. "Say nothing else. Give no details about the vessel or the prisoners. I don't want to give Casanova any warning of what's coming his way."

"You're the boss," André replied, preparing to make the call to the Coast Guard. "But can you tell me why I shouldn't explain the details to the Coast Guard?"

"I can't be sure, but it seems to me that Casanova may have some undue influence with the Coast Guard, and I don't want this arrest to get fouled up."

"Now that I think of it," André said, "when that channel marking buoy was put there by the Coast Guard, I remember thinking it was in the wrong place. The channel runs west of this location. Maybe it was put there as an accommodation to the Mafia."

"It could be," the inspector said. "Anything is possible with that guy. He's tangled up in more things than the prop on his boat."

While the fisherman guided his boat to shore, René at last had a chance to turn his full attention toward Kate. She was leaning against the stern rail watching the two tied-up miscreants facing her in the bucket seats of the racing boat that was being towed behind them. She smiled when she saw René approaching her.

"Who did you say I was when you were talking to the fisherman?" Kate asked him.

"I told him you were my girlfriend."

"How did you know how to find me?"

"My experience and my intuition told me that Casanova was the culprit, but until I got the message from Tiffany on my answering machine, I didn't know where you were."

"Oh God!" Kate exclaimed. "Tiffany!"

"What about her?"

"She's in terrible danger because of me."

"What do you mean?"

"Well, when you found me I was wearing her beach robe. She passed it through the trapdoor for me when she realized that Casanova had kidnapped me and was keeping me naked and on display in that room, like some kind of wild animal. Oh, René, I left her robe behind when you gave me this wet suit to wear! He's going to know that she had something to do with my escape when he finds that beach robe in the room."

"Casanova will torture her to get her to tell him who helped you to escape, and after he gets that information out of her, he may kill her."

"What are we going to do?" sobbed Kate. "She saved my life, and now my stupidity is going to get her killed. We've got to go back and get her."

"We can't do that, Kate."

"Why not?"

"Because there's a better way."

"What's that?"

"I'll arrest Casanova. He won't be able to do her any harm from jail. Then we'll go get her. When you testify about your kidnapping and we produce the boat and drugs as evidence, we can put him away for a long time. If I'm lucky I might be able to hang charges of racketeering on him some day. I'd love to involve all the other Mafia dons, and clean up the whole criminal syndicate all at one time."

"And why can't you do that now?"

"I don't think I have enough verification yet," René confessed. "To shut down organized crime in France I need to have bullet proof substantiation about every facet of the Mafia's cooperative operations. It's not easy to gather that kind of evidence. One man alone simply can't do it. It would take a national task force with a fearless, independent lawman as its leader."

"You could be that leader," Kate said.

"No, I'm only a detective with no political connections," René said. "No one's going to give me sweeping jurisdiction over an investigation of this scope."

As they stood at the rail with the wind in their faces, René was secretly glad that Kate believed in him. It gave him the confidence to dream about a glorious future.

CHAPTER EIGHTEEN

While Inspector René Martin was conducting his one-man rescue, his assistant, Maurice Benamou, had been quite busy on his own. He had noticed that Casanova's limo was being driven around Marseilles by Marius, a convict that he personally had arrested in the past. Interested in anything that the con might be up to on his own or on Casanova's behalf, he had decided to follow the limo. It had smoky glass windows that prevented anyone from looking inside, so the police officer couldn't tell if Casanova was inside or not. The limo stopped at a topless dancing bar that Casanova had an interest in. Benamou followed the limo and noticed a big sign in the window of the club that read, "Temporarily closed for repairs."

It was possible that Henri Casanova was supervising the repairs, but Benamou thought it more likely that he was intending to use the club location for some other purpose, and needed to keep the public away for a while. The only reasonable explanation the policeman could think of was that Casanova was going to use the bar as the venue for a mob business meeting. If that's what he was planning, Benamou would plant a bug and a camera inside to find out what was being said and who was in attendance. He waited patiently until the limo and its passenger left.

If Benamou had remained in Morocco he would have gone into the family business and become a locksmith. As it was, the skills he learned as a boy would still occasionally came in handy, and he used them to gain entrance into the empty strip club. The juxtaposition of chairs and tables reinforced his suspicion that there was soon to be a meeting held on these premises. He placed his miniature electronic equipment in the place least likely for it to be discovered, and then stealthily left the building.

Inspector Martin called Benamou shortly afterward and told him that he had rescued Kate and was en route to Marseilles via boat. He asked Benamou to inform their boss, the superintendent of police, and arrange with him to have some uniformed policemen at the Coast Guard pier to take his prisoners into custody, along with the boat and the drug haul. René wanted the superintendent to be there to resolve jurisdictional problems with the commanding officer of the Coast Guard. He realized that in making arrests out in the Mediterranean he might have exceeded his authority, and he wanted those higher up in the establishment to work out these administrative details. Inspector Martin could imagine that the two bureaucrats might spend hours negotiating the jurisdictional details of who was in charge, and who would get the credit for the drug bust. Even more important to Martin was his desire to keep the superintendent busy, for he didn't completely trust him.

He was about to hang up when Benamou, who had been waiting to get a word in, told him about the meeting that he expected would be taking place at the topless club. Martin realized immediately that he would find Casanova there. It was his one opportunity to capture all the Mafia leaders in one place at the same time. The fact that all the dons were at the same meeting and were also acquainted with one another was prima facie evidence of a conspiracy. The inspector knew that he had enough evidence to convict Casanova of several crimes, but now there was a chance to capture all the Mafia family heads simultaneously. He quickly outlined what Benamou should do to organize the largest bust the gendarmes had ever done in the south of France. He told him he should assemble the men on the pier where the fisherman moored his boat, and he'd be back in time to lead the raid.

Things went pretty much as he had foreseen at the Coast Guard station. The superintendent was waiting at the dock with several policemen. Next to him stood the Coast Guard

Commander with several of his guardsmen. The gendarmes took over the prisoners, and the guardsmen impounded the crippled cigarette boat. René introduced the superintendent to Kate Evans, and said he'd take her to the station to give her statement about the circumstances of her kidnapping. The superintendent was amenable to that, and went off into the Coast Guard building with the commander to resolve the jurisdictional problems in private. That would leave him time to be with Kate. In all the excitement he really hadn't had time to talk with her about her experiences as a kidnap victim, or to show her how glad he was that she was safe.

When everything at the Coast Guard dock was finally resolved, the inspector told André that he could take his boat, along with Kate and himself, back to his mooring place on the fishing dock. As they proceeded slowly into the busy harbor, René Martin explained to Kate that he still had to lead a team to arrest Casanova, and that he wanted her to go to his apartment and stay there until he returned. Martin gave her the keys to his place, telling her that André had agreed to drive her there. He hoped she would understand that he wanted to stay with her, but that he had to arrest Casanova before he escaped. Kate wanted to go with him, but when she saw Benamou and what looked like most of the Marseilles police force waiting on the pier for the inspector to take charge, she realized that he had to do his duty before they could be together. Martin went to his car and changed out of his wet suit and into his street clothes, whereupon he took leadership of the raiding party.

On the way to Martin's bachelor apartment, Kate and André talked and joked about their experiences as adjunct detectives. Kate liked this fishing boat captain, and she could see why René liked him too. She was surprised to learn that he was married and had six children, although he was only in his thirties. When they arrived at Martin's building, Kate squeezed his hand and thanked him for his part in rescuing her, saying she would never forget what he did.

Upstairs in René's familiar rooms, Kate felt safe for the first time in a long time. She struggled out of the wet suit and took a shower. When she had dried off she realized that she had no other clothes of her own to put on. With that as her excuse, she slid into René's bed, hoping he wouldn't think that she was too forward.

The ambitious eyes of every imperious crime boss in France had been focused on Henri Casanova when he delivered his speech recommending that the Mafia concentrate its future activities on white-collar crime. To some of the dons this revolutionary suggestion coming from a Corsican nonentity was reminiscent of General Bonaparte's tactic to gain control of the French army. Henri was regarded by most of his colleagues as a wise but small don-fish swimming in a big sea full of large don-sharks. He was going to need allies if his message of change was going to be accepted by the majority. He was planning on working the room to see what the general reaction to his speech had been, when Santori sidled up to him and whispered in his ear.

Casanova's face grew serious as he listened to what the bodyguard was saying. After receiving the entire message, Henri told him to have Marius bring the car around, as they were going to leave at once for the villa. The formal speech portion of the meeting was over for the night, so even though Henri was the host of the meeting, he told the club manager to introduce the acts and entertainers so he could leave at once. Casanova made his exit as unobtrusively as he could, and climbed into his limo with Santori. They took off with Marius at the wheel, and headed for the suburban coast to the east of Marseilles where the villa was located.

A few minutes later Inspector Martin led a parade of cruisers with their sirens and lights flashing around the parking lot of the club, trapping all the vehicles inside and blocking any cars from leaving. In a minute the swat team left their armored vehicles and approached every car, guns in hand, rousting the drivers who were waiting for their bosses, and taking them into custody.

The Mafiosi inside immediately recognized the noise and confusion outside as a police raid. Most thought it was a vice raid because of the naked women that had been dancing, but they soon realized it was more than that. One by one they were quickly loaded into the paddy wagons after they had been patted down. Inspector Martin carefully watched these proceedings.

When the last of the dons was aboard, Martin pulled Benamou aside.

"Casanova isn't here. Where the hell is he?"

"I don't know, Inspector. I only know that he was here earlier."

"Damn it, how did he manage to escape?" Martin asked. "Do you think he was forewarned? Have we got a mole in our midst? See what you can find out. I'm going to beat it back to his villa and see if I can apprehend him there. I'll take a couple of these cars with me. Now that this operation is over with, you won't be needing them."

"By the way," said Benamou, "where is the kidnapped girl?"

"She's with the fishing boat captain. He's taking her to my place."

"Kate Evans is a material witness against Casanova," Benamou reminded him. "I don't suppose I have to tell you that she should be in custody."

"No, my friend, you don't," Martin said, a little irritably. "Right now I'm more worried about the other American girl, Tiffany Chance. She's still at the villa, and Casanova may blame his problems on her. He may think she informed on him."

"Did she?"

"Yes, and I don't want any harm to come to her because of it. Now I'm going to see to it that she's okay. You can clean up the rest of this mess. Get all these hoods properly booked and put in cells. In a few hours we can expect their lawyers to descend on us, and I don't want any procedural foul-ups."

"You're right, Boss," Benamou said. "I'll take care of it, and I'll look for the mole, too."

"Good," Martin said as he ran to the waiting cruiser.

Casanova marched into the villa with Santori in his wake. He demanded to know how his hostage had escaped. He was told by one of his guards that he had been sent to take a tray to the cell in the boathouse, and when he got there he found that the lock had been cut open, and the girl was gone. Not only that, but the two new Corsicans were gone, too. They hadn't returned after they left in the cigarette boat to make a pick up. Casanova stormed off to the boathouse to see for himself what had happened.

He went inside the room that had served as a cell for Kate. In a minute he was holding the gauzy beach robe in his hand. He recognized it immediately as something he had purchased for Tiffany. How did it get there? Obviously since he had left his prisoner naked, her friend Tiffany must have found Kate and given her the robe to cover herself with. How Kate had escaped was another matter altogether. Tiffany didn't have access to the key, which was in his pocket, and she couldn't have cut the steel lock. Who did, then? Where had the Corsicans gone in the boat? They left the boathouse to do a ten-minute pick up run and hadn't come back. Did they steal the drug shipment and take off on their own, or did something happen to them? These were some of the thoughts that were running through his mind.

As a start, he decided to question Tiffany. With the beach robe in his hand, he plowed a straight furrow to her room. He entered without knocking. Tiffany was admiring her body in the full-length mirror, and searching for signs of developing cellulite.

"Henri, don't you ever knock?" she complained.

"No, in my house I never knock," he replied. "Here, put this on," he said, handing her the robe. "Now you can tell me how this robe got into a room in the boathouse."

"That's easy, I gave it to Kate. She was naked, and the gawkers that you have working for you were spying on her and taunting her. I thought it was only decent of me to give her something to wear," Tiffany answered. "Now here's a question for you. Why are you keeping her prisoner? She never did anything to you."

"I believe she's a secret informant for the police, and that she's a traitor to me," Henri replied. "I gave her a job, paid her good money, and she turns out to be the girlfriend of René Martin, the police inspector. Maybe she's innocent, but her boyfriend is not. I don't think she knows anything about my businesses, but she makes an excellent hostage to hold over the inspector to keep him out of my hair."

"So what's all the nakedness about?" Tiffany asked. "Kate is a shy, prissy, introverted girl. She isn't like me. I was raised in a nudist camp. I don't give a damn who sees me without clothes, but it makes a big difference to Kate."

"Some shy, prissy introvert – look at this photo," Henri said, offering Tiffany the picture of Kate that revealed her tattoo. "If she's so proper, how do you account for this photo, then?"

"I don't know, Henri. Why don't we go down to the boathouse and ask her?"

Henri was shocked that Tiffany didn't know that Kate was gone. Perhaps he had misjudged her too, and she had nothing to do with the disappearance of Kate Evans. But being more suspicious than trusting, he decided to continue with his questioning.

"How did you happen to find Kate Evans?" Casanova inquired.

"I had just spent a couple of hours swimming and sunbathing at the beach," Tiffany said, "and I noticed the boathouse. I decided to have a peek at your boats. When I got inside I was just poking around when I noticed some of your landscapers looking through a peephole and giggling. So I had a look myself, and there was Kate in the buff."

"Then what did you do?"

"I spoke to her, and shoved my robe through a hole in the door so she would have something to wear."

"Is that all?"

"Yes, I planned to talk to you about her when you got back, but I didn't expect you to return tonight."

"Yes, I know I told you I wouldn't be back, but I was called home because Kate has escaped," Henri told her as he watched her expression carefully to see if her reaction would reflect surprise at that news.

"You don't think I had anything to do with that, do you?"

"No, but you shouldn't have gone into the boathouse without my permission," Henri said as he withdrew from the room, but he still wasn't sure he could believe her.

He had another way to check out whether she was lying or not. He left her room and immediately headed for the basement, where the electronic surveillance equipment was housed. He would see what his G-men could tell him about the escape and how it had been pulled off.

It wasn't long before Guido and Giovanni had searched the outgoing telephone call records from the villa. His personal G-men quickly found the four-word message that Tiffany had sent to Inspector Martin. So it was true that she had betrayed him. He resolved to deal with her in his own way, but before he left the denizens of his Intel jungle, he wanted to see exactly how Kate had been rescued. They replayed the camera record that did boathouse surveillance for the previous twenty-four hours. Henri's curiosity got the better of him and he stuck around while his staff of nerds analyzed the images. He would rue the time he spent trying to pinpoint whom to blame for Kate's disappearance.

Inspector Martin's convoy of police cruisers raced away from the topless club toward Henri Casanova's personal palace of porn. There was no longer any advantage to sneaking up on the Mafia boss, as René now had all the evidence he needed to make an arrest. What was needed now was a surgical strike that contained the elements of surprise and inescapable power. He thought he had the element of surprise on his side, but he hadn't counted on the extent of the venality that had reached to the level of his superiors within the police establishment.

Officers whose personal standard of living had been improved by their connections to the Mafia still had to act on the evidence that the maverick inspector had collected or they would lose their jobs. It still didn't keep them from resenting the newcomer who was going to cost them their periodic salary subsidy payments from underworld sources, and it didn't keep the superintendent from calling Henri to warn him about the coming raid.

Santori received the message from the superintendent, but couldn't put him through to Casanova because Henri was in the middle of his speech to the Mafia dons. As soon as his boss was finished, Santori alerted him to the possibility of a major move by the police against the Mafia, and they left the club at once. Henri believed that he was in the clear, since he wasn't one of the Mafiosi arrested at the club. He didn't know at the time that Kate had escaped and was in the custody of the inspector, nor did he know that his shipment of drugs had been impounded.

The inspector intended to arrest Casanova for the crimes of kidnapping and drug running. Later he could also be charged with racketeering, along with the other dons. The evidence provided by Benamou's bugging device would link him to the syndicate in due course. Martin's desire for instant vengeance on Henri for taking his girlfriend hostage was not likely to be satisfied by a long and complex trial linking Casanova to organized criminal activity. A trial of that sort would tie up the courts of France for an eternity, but charges on one or two specific serious felony crimes could result in quick convictions and speedy incarceration. That was René Martin's immediate aim, which took precedence over his secondary goal of cleaning up the Corsican Mafia.

The arrest of a suspect in a class-one felony crime is not the same as the capture of a suspect in an organized crime investigation. In the former case hard evidence and the evidence of a witness are critical, while in the latter case the evidence is more often circumstantial, and the victim is society as a whole rather than an individual. It was the second situation that Casanova was expecting, and had prepared for, as had all the other dons. Casanova and his colleagues had reached the status in the criminal hierarchy where they no longer were arrested for committing violent crimes; they had underlings perform those types of activities for them. When it came to the charges against the Mafia for syndicate-related crimes, however, Henri Casanova and his colleagues had legions of lawyers to defend them. Over time these men had developed defensive legal protections that served their present status in the same way as bulletproof vests had served them in their earlier stages of criminal development.

So when Inspector Martin and his coterie of officers noisily arrived at Casanova's front door, they didn't have a warrant for his arrest – they were in hot pursuit mode. This was a circumstance that Casanova hadn't bargained for. He had counted on his purchased favors with the police, the judges, and the Coast Guard to protect him from being arrested like a common criminal. Over Casanova's protests and his demands for his lawyer, he was taken into custody and hauled off to the detention cell in the central police station in Marseilles. Also arrested at the same time were Santori, the G-men, and several guards who had been found in possession of unregistered firearms. The real legal work of laying charges, obtaining search warrants, and collecting physical evidence to support the charges would be carried out the following morning.

The noise and confusion of the arresting procedures prompted Tiffany to wrap herself in a towel and come out of her room to see what was going on. She was brought before the inspector for him to determine what was to be done with her.

"What's happening here, Inspector?" Tiffany asked.

"We've arrested your patron, Henri Casanova," Martin replied. "We're taking him and his associates into custody so proper charges can be laid."

"And what about me?" Tiffany asked. "Am I also a suspect?"

"No, but I'll need you to be a witness for the prosecution later," René replied. "And by the way, thank you for sending me the message about where to find Kate. It was a big help, and she's fine now."

"I was glad to be of some help," Tiffany said. "May I continue to live here?"

"That's between you and Casanova, but for a few days the place will be crawling with cops gathering evidence."

"How nice," Tiffany said suggestively, as she prepared to leave the room. "It's peculiar, isn't it, that a nice girl like Kate should have a moment of youthful brashness, get a tattoo, and have everybody think she's a slut, while another woman whose chastity is of no concern to her should be unaffected by the opinion of others."

"It certainly seems unfair to me, and I for one don't hold that opinion of Kate," René said. "People seldom think about how future opinion will regard the foibles they commit in youth. I suspect the world is full of middle-aged people who wish they'd never gotten tattoos."

"I suppose you're right," Tiffany said, "and I'm glad you aren't going to hold it against Kate."

"By the way, Tiffany, how did you happen to see the tattoo?"

"Why, Casanova showed me a photo of it. How else?"

"Did he say how he got it?" Martin asked. "Where is the photo now?"

"I suppose it's somewhere around here," Tiffany replied, "but I've no idea how he got it."

"Did you know that the photo was taken in the hotel room where Professor Jolicoeur was murdered, and that it was probably taken by the murderer?"

"Do you suspect Casanova of killing the professor?"

"No, but it was one of his men," the inspector told her. "I'd love to know if Casanova ordered the killing."

"I can't say," Tiffany said. "Henri never spoke to me about it, or anything else concerning his business."

"You did see with your own eyes that Kate was being held hostage against her will, didn't you?"

"Yes, I saw her in the boathouse. That's how I knew to call you," Tiffany replied. "I was going to speak to Henri about it as soon as he returned."

"Didn't you know where he was?"

"No. He told me he had to attend an important meeting, and that he wouldn't be home tonight," Tiffany said. "I was surprised when he came back."

"You'll have to testify at Casanova's trial about how you discovered that Kate was locked up in the boathouse," the inspector told her. "Will you be afraid that he may try to kill you if you appear in court as a hostile witness?"

"I don't think he'll do that."

"Why not?"

"I know something about him that he won't want people to know," Tiffany stated with confidence.

"And what is that?"

"Henri Casanova is impotent," Tiffany declared.

CHAPTER NINETEEN

René Martin suddenly realized that he was exhausted. While a uniformed policeman drove him home in a cruiser, he thought wearily about the duties he would have to perform the next day. He had almost forgotten about the guest who was waiting for him at home, in spite of the fact that nearly all the energies he had expended were on her behalf. He was snapped back to reality when he saw a wet suit hanging on his bathroom door. It was so quiet in the apartment that he concluded that Kate was either asleep, or had left. He hoped it was the former, so he didn't call out her name or turn on the light. His hope was realized when he heard gentle breathing coming from a familiar head accented against a white pillow.

He tiptoed around the large bed his mother had given him when he moved to Marseilles. She had explained to him that she hoped it would be his marriage bed, so it had to be large enough for two. He was glad of it now, but unsure of what to do next. Kate might have expected him to sleep in the other room on the couch. Did she want him to awaken her when he came in? Or if he touched her, would she wake up screaming with fright because of her recent ordeal? If she awoke and found him in bed with her, would she be shocked at his gall in presuming that she was inviting him to sleep with her? He decided on a compromise approach.

He took off his clothes and stealthily slipped under the covers, trying not to touch her or awaken her. In this way he hoped to convey his willingness to be intimate with her, but without being pushy about it. After all it was his bed, and she could have chosen to sleep on the sofa.

He was dead tired, but sleep didn't come. His training as a policeman kicked in and he began to worry that perhaps his relationship to Kate was untenable as long as she was a principal witness in a case in which he was the arresting officer. Martin could just imagine how Henri Casanova's pack of legal bloodhounds would treat the news that his accuser and the inspector were lovers. The prosecution's case of kidnapping against Casanova would immediately be tainted by suggestions of collusion. The jury would then be suspicious that the police had been prejudiced against the defendant and were out to get him, and the prosecution could lose its case.

His mind began to spin imagined legal scenarios as his eyes stared into the darkness. If Benamou were questioned on the stand, a clever lawyer could make much out of his close-minded moral conclusions about the photos of Kate's tattoo. In every scenario her reputation was besmirched and her morality brought into question. Martin couldn't stand that prospect. He believed that the best proof of love was trust, and although he trusted Kate completely, he knew that a talented lawyer could make a jury believe that she was a slut of major proportions. It seemed to him that no matter what happened in the trial, Kate's reputation was headed for the dumpster.

When he thought about the effect that losing the case might have on the gendarmerie and on the public's view of the effectiveness and honesty of the police force, he reached a conclusion that he hated but couldn't escape. He slipped out of the bed, dressed, and pretended he had just arrived back at the apartment. He turned on the light, rousing the sleeping Kate.

"Wake up, Kate," René said to her as she sat up and rubbed her eyes. "I'm taking you back to your hotel room."

"What? Isn't it the middle of the night?" she asked, as she looked around for a clock. "Get in bed, you silly man."

"I can't. As much as I would dearly love to accept, I have to decline that tempting offer. The welfare of the police department and the justice system of France depend on it."

"What are you talking about?"

"Listen Kate, just put on my clean jeans and my T-shirt, and while you're doing that I'll explain," René said. "Look, if we're seen to be involved with each other, the whole case against Henri Casanova could be lost. I've made a huge effort to catch him and put an end to the Corsican Mafia. I can't in conscience allow all that to be put at risk for the pleasure of two individuals who should be able to exercise self-control and wait until a more opportune moment to deal with personal matters."

"I don't think I see the connection," said Kate, trying to understand him as she put on his clothes. "What on earth has our relationship got to do with the case against the Corsican Mafia?"

"Not much," Martin admitted, "but it has everything to do with the success of the prosecution's legal case. We're dealing with a hostile group of sociopaths with financial resources sufficient to tap into the best legal firms. These lawyers will use every means at their disposal to get their clients off the hook. Their tactics will include every trick in the book to demean, diffuse, and destroy the prosecution's case. As a witness you'll be attacked in every possible way in order to bring your credibility into question, and this will include your personal life."

"Are you saying we have to break off our relationship so that you can successfully convict Henri Casanova?"

"Yes and no," René hedged. "Yes, for the time being at least, and no, not necessarily forever. It'll be better for you, though, if we part now, as the trial will proceed very slowly. Casanova's lawyers will stretch it out as long as possible. Then if he's found guilty there'll be an appeal of the court's decision. It could take years before we see Henri Casanova permanently residing in prison. Meanwhile there a chance that the Mafia will try to take revenge on you for testifying. I won't always be around to protect you, and I don't want any harm to come to you. Furthermore, the existence of the photos that Albertini took of you tied to the bed will be a constant embarrassment. It could even ruin your reputation."

"You've said that the trial may take years to conclude, and you've told me that you can't guarantee my protection and that my reputation may be ruined," Kate summarized. "But what you haven't said is that you don't love me."

"I can't say that," René admitted, "because it wouldn't be true. But everything else I've told you is true. I can't expect you to wait forever for me to be free of these Corsican bloodsuckers. You're going to have to return to the United States at some point, and I'm obligated to remain here in order to finish my work and do my duty."

"Tell me truthfully, Inspector, how much of this is due to my tattoo?"

"It's not because of the tattoo that we must leave each other."

"Oh no?" Kate said in disbelief. "How many of your colleagues have seen the photo?"

"Most of them have seen it," René answered truthfully. "Things like that get passed around, as you can imagine. I know it was only a teenage prank on your part, but really, *Abandon hope, all ye who enter here?* I know you didn't pose for those pictures, and I also know you didn't give the photographer permission to use them, but they're all over the place now, from the internet to the porn trade."

"So they do matter to you, then!"

"They matter to everyone else, so in that sense they have to matter to me, too. They could affect your whole life."

They had been walking as they talked. He had put his raincoat over her as they strode towards her hotel. The lobby was deserted because of the late hour, except for the desk clerk. René obtained her room key for her, and warned the clerk not to give out her room number to anyone without Miss Evans' permission. They took the elevator up to her floor and walked silently down the corridor to her room. At the door, Kate spoke to René.

"I think you should know that you've made a mistake."

"I probably have," he replied, thinking that he was going to get a scolding for breaking up with her.

"No, not that," Kate said, as if reading his guilty mind. "Not for breaking up with me, but in the tattoo quotation from Dante. "There's no *all* in the quote, or on the tattoo either.

"What? I thought Dante said, *Abandon hope, all ye who enter here.* Everyone who saw it thought it referred to *all* the men who were going to be with you in that way."

"Well, they were wrong," Kate said, looking hurt and disappointed. "All it says is *Abandon hope, ye who enter here.* It signifies permanence, not traffic. I was referring to my future husband. I was warning him that he'd have to abandon any hope of having affairs with other women. If you had really known me, you would have realized that."

She looked up at him and gave him a quick kiss, then she unlocked the door to her hotel room. She turned and gave him another kiss before closing the door behind her.

Years later, when Kate Evans looked back on her student years in France, she remembered how she had once believed she had met the man of her dreams. She had thought that the mundane details like careers, nationality, and citizenship would just fall naturally into place, and that after a while she and René Martin would marry.

That didn't happen, but she had to admit that her break-up with René did serve a beneficial purpose – she found it hard to get seriously involved with other men, for they never provided her with the same sense of excitement, adventure, and foreign intrigue that she had enjoyed in the company of her police inspector. So she had dedicated herself whole-heartedly to her work, and ended up getting her PhD in French Studies in record time. Her thesis was published by a highly-regarded university press, which helped to land her a position as an assistant professor of French at a reputable university in Ohio. Her hard work had paid off. She was a gifted teacher, her students loved her, and Ohio offered no distractions to prevent her from writing numerous articles that were duly published in respectable academic journals.

She was granted tenure within five years – another record for Kate.

Back then René Martin's hopes were not unlike Kate's, until he was faced with the hard choice of having to give up the culmination of his important work so he could be with her. In the end he decided that he could not in conscience allow the criminals to continue to poison his country with their illegal activities. He had one opportunity to put an end to the Corsican reign of terror, and he couldn't have faced himself if he had yielded to a personal attraction at the cost of his nation's welfare.

After a few years Henri Casanova was finally convicted, as were many of the Mafiosi who worked under him. They availed themselves of all the legal alternatives, but only succeeded in delaying the inevitable. Many of the old dons died in prison, while others tried to run their petty empires from their cells. Generally the promotional opportunities left open by the incarceration of their bosses tempted a number of young toughs to try to accede to the newly open positions. This started some internecine wars of succession which provided the gendarmes with plenty of mopping-up chores. Henri Casanova's project of focusing in on white-collar crime as an area of expansion for the Mafia was an idea whose time had come, and with or without him, organized crime moved inexorably into the electronic age.

Tiffany Chance, for her part, never looked back. She was a young woman designed for the times in which she lived. Her moral compass was boxed using the secular majority's opinion as her magnetic North. Political correctness was her Polaris, and she steered her life by it. She accepted the good things that came her way regardless of how bad they were for her soul. As long as the majority approved of her creed, she felt justified in not having an original thought. Her good looks allowed her to become arm candy for a wealthy young Wall Street hedge fund operator. His idea of the perfect life was to rake in the big bucks by managing investment risks without ever realizing that he was losing his shirt in the even more risky long-term business of life. His concern for short-term market fluctuations were for him like pennies held too close to his eyes – they blocked out the light of the sun. Tiffany and her consort were regarded by their peers as a most brilliant couple. They marched swiftly to the tune of a familiar drummer, and never noticed that the tune was flat.

Life, however, would be dull indeed if there were never any surprises at all. Even Kate Evans and René Martin ended up being surprised by the finale to their life stories

It all began when the chairperson of Kate's department asked her to take a group of students to Paris for their junior year abroad. Kate leapt at the opportunity, for she felt a profound nostalgia for her own year abroad, with its cast of characters that included an honorable police inspector, an impotent Mafia don, a brave California Valley girl, a praying Mantis and her stubby hubby – all of whom were magnets for assorted adventures that seemed much less terrifying and far more gratifying in retrospect.

After Kate got her students sorted out and settled into their "pensions" with various Parisian families, she took the week off and high-tailed it down to Marseilles for old time's sake. It was a bittersweet experience to find herself in the busy city, strolling along the waterfront without Inspector René Martin by her side. She ended up at the police station, of course, and presented herself at the front desk.

"May I help you, Madame?" a uniformed woman asked.

"I'm looking for Inspector René Martin. Is he here?"

"I'm sorry, Madame. I've never heard that name."

Outside on the street again, Kate chided herself for being so foolish as to imagine even for a minute that René would still be at his old job after all these years, working in the same capacity at the police station. She was a hopeless romantic, and she knew she was an idiot, but she couldn't resist the temptation of going back to the little restaurant where he had once taken her for lobster Fra Diavolo. Her head told her that he wouldn't be there, but her heart kept urging her on, telling her she'd find him there if it was meant to be. What could she lose, anyway?

What she lost were some hard-earned euros, wasted on a meal that was mediocre at best. The restaurant had changed owners since she and René had dined there together, and homard Fra Diavolo was no longer on the menu. She had had to make do with some uninspiring moules marinières and a small baguette, accompanied by a glass of rather raw white wine. Where was the old Marseilles that she and René had called their own?

She left the restaurant feeling like an old fool.

"There's no fool like an..."

"No, don't give me that old cliché," she said sternly to herself as she walked along the waterfront.

The magic moments of Marseilles that she yearned for had probably only existed in her over-heated imagination. But she couldn't help seeing René in all those old familiar places... (that this heart of mine embraces all day through...)

"Oh, give it a *rest!*" she said to herself in exasperation.

Kate Evans loved Paris in the springtime, and she loved it in the fall. She also loved it in the summer when it sizzled, and she even loved it in the winter when it drizzled. She loved Cole Porter, too, for filling her heart with song, and she was grateful to her students for behaving in a reasonably mature manner and sticking to their studies without giving her too much of a hard time.

Their junior year in Paris was coming to an end, and they had acquitted themselves well. So well, in fact, that they had come to the attention of some important members of the Alliance Française, who had had the good sense to give Kate some of the credit for having prepared them well for their experience in Paris. They even invited her to give a public lecture on an aspect of Balzac's novels that excited her and which her sponsors felt would create a great deal of interest among their members. Kate was deeply touched and honored by the amount of effort the organizers devoted to publicizing the event. The least she could do, she felt, was to give her audience something to remember that night.

At the end of her presentation she was very gratified to receive some honest applause from an audience of serious scholars who were not known for abandoning themselves to their enthusiasm. A number of them approached the podium and kept her busy with their questions, but eventually they took their leave and trickled out of the lecture hall while she packed up her notes and put them back into her briefcase.

"Madame Evans," came a man's voice close by.

"Just one moment," Kate said, trying to force the lid down over the unruly muddle of papers that seemed to have mysteriously multiplied since she had removed them from her briefcase at the beginning of her lecture.

"Kate," he said, and then again, "Kate!"

Her heart recognized that voice before her head could react. She couldn't bring herself to lift her eyes, in case they revealed too suddenly and too soon the secrets of her soul.

"Kate. Look at me."

She looked. She saw. She smiled.

It was René Martin, of course. An older René. A man with gray sideburns and a subdued, knowing smile, a man whose crow's feet suggested a bemused knowledge of the world and whose flared nostrils revealed the intensity of the moment.

"It's time for dinner, Kate. Come along. I've ordered lobster Fra Diavolo."

He lifted her briefcase with his left hand and gallantly offered her his right arm.

"The restaurant is just around the corner," he said. "It's a little family bistro, and I just know you're going to love it. Come. We have a lot of catching up to do."

He was perfect, Kate thought, as she took his arm and walked next to him through the empty lecture hall. They were going to begin again with their old friend Brother Devil at their side.

"I never abandoned hope, you know," he told her.

"I never did either. I looked for you in Marseilles last week, but you weren't there. How did you find me?"

"I'd like to say I was flown to your side on the wings of eagles, but the truth is, I saw the notice about your lecture advertised by the Alliance Française."

"You were always a truth teller," Kate smiled. "That's what I loved most about you."

"Loved?"

"Love," Kate said, giving his arm a squeeze.

"I like that correction. Your French is almost perfect, but once in a while a correction is needed here and there."

The two long-term lovers walked out of the building and into the bustling streets of Paris – a city that Kate would soon be calling her own.

Chick

Truman Cottrell

If you enjoyed reading *The French Correction,* you will also like *Chick* (Erser and Pond, 2009), featuring yacht delivery captain Charlotte (Chick) Chase. While delivering a 55' racing yacht from Florida to Massachusetts, she encounters a small, unmarked boat loaded with armed men heading from Cuba to the U.S. When her vessel is fired upon, she radios the new U.S. Coast Guard that now functions under the Department of Homeland Security, and teams up with an intelligent young officer who helps her deal with the challenges she faces on the high seas. Every page invites the reader to share in an exciting, plausible, swashbuckling series of events that involve elements of mature romance, sailboat racing, national security, and good old-fashioned patriotism.

Go to www.erserandpond.com or www.amazon.com, or send a check or money order for $19.95 (please add $2.16 for sales tax plus $4.00 for postage and handling) to Erser and Pond Ltd, 1096 Queen St, Suite 225, Halifax, Nova Scotia B3H 2R9, Canada.